THE RULES

BOOK 4 OF THE *JOHNSON* FAMILY SERIES

DELANEY DIAMOND

The Rules

Garden Avenue Press
Atlanta, Georgia

ISBN: 978-1-940636-21-4

PROLOGUE

Three years ago

She shouldn't have come. She should be long gone by now, on a plane to the other side of the country, but had been unable to leave Georgia without seeing the conclusion of the trial. Terri Slade sat in the back of the crowded courtroom and listened to the judge hand down the sentence.

Five years. They only gave him five years. Not nearly enough time for the havoc he wreaked on the lives of unsuspecting victims. The scams he perpetrated generated millions in a criminal enterprise, in which he was the CEO, COO, and CFO. The effects of his illegal activities would ripple through the state for years to come.

The judge pounded her gavel, finalizing the sentence for Talon Cyrenci, and then he was being led toward the exit in an orange jumpsuit in between two deputies. Terri's eyes followed him, wary tension vibrating through her body.

He's handcuffed. He can't hurt you.

Suddenly, his head turned, and those evil eyes zeroed in on her in the back row. His jaw tightened when their gazes met and the icy green stare caused her to freeze on the wooden seat. She tilted her head higher, unwilling to cow to his intimidation tactics, even as the knot in her stomach betrayed the fear his very presence evoked. At the last moment, before he stepped through the door to exit the courtroom, the expression on his face changed. His thin lips upturned into a mocking smirk and a promise entered the depths of his eyes.

She recognized the look. It was one that she'd seen directed at men who had crossed him. Oftentimes, the look had been directed at her, and the meaning made the cold sweat of fear trickle down the back of her neck.

She was going to pay for what she'd done.

CHAPTER ONE

Present day

Gavin Johnson rolled down his pants leg when the doctor finished the examination. The past couple of months he had rested in Seattle, healing from broken bones after a rock-climbing accident in the Andes mountain range of Argentina. Today the door to freedom edged open, and once the doctor confirmed his complete rehabilitation, he was going on the road again.

"So doc, what's the word? Am I a free man?" He hopped down from the exam table.

"A bit anxious to get out of here, are you?" Dr. Amee, one of the country's leading orthopedic specialists, observed Gavin over thick glasses from his position on the rolling stool. The older man's salt and pepper hair lay swept back from his broad forehead and a wrinkled face which remained in a perpetual frown, no matter his mood.

"A little bit. I need you to confirm everything is fine and I'll be on my way." Gavin rubbed his palms together, anticipating good news.

His family had made such a stink about him remaining in Seattle after the accident, he acquiesced and did as they asked—no, demanded. They insisted he stay at his mother's house, but he compromised by renting a three-story mansion not far from hers on

Lake Washington.

Dr. Amee stood. "You're fine. The broken femur repaired itself very well, your ribs are fine, your ankle—"

"Yeah, yeah. We're done, right?"

The doctor sighed. "Yes, Mr. Johnson. We're done. But are you done?"

"What do you mean?" Gavin knew exactly what the doctor meant. The question hinted at the same cautionary words he'd heard for years.

That's so dangerous.

Slow down.

Don't take so many risks.

He heard the pleas but didn't know how to do what they asked. The adrenaline rush of extreme sports and endurance-testing competitions made his heart race and mind go blank, sending him into a drug-like state where he felt suspended in the middle of time and space. Nothing else came close to giving him the same high.

"Your mother is very concerned about you." Dr. Amee watched Gavin from beneath bushy, furrowed eyebrows.

"You know how parents are. You're a parent yourself." Gavin flashed a grin, already contemplating the next adventure. He might fly to Dubai for a fortnight to spend time with his favorite Middle Eastern prince. That guy knew how to party, and Gavin was ready to get back on the party scene.

"You're free to go, Mr. Johnson." The doctor's disapproving tone mimicked the discontent of a parent rather than a doctor.

"Thanks, doc."

Gavin shook Dr. Amee's hand and bolted from the exam room, the weight of stagnation lifting from his shoulders. On the way out, he said goodbye to the receptionists and once outside, donned sunglasses and lifted his face to the sun.

****

Hours later, a driver dropped Gavin off in front of his younger brother's building, on the corner of Virginia and Fourth Avenue in the heart of Seattle. He'd called ahead to let him know he was coming by. He took the elevator to the penthouse, and when he

3

stepped into the vestibule, used the key card to let himself into the deluxe condo. Immediately, inconspicuous speakers emitted the sound of stringed instruments to greet him.

"Trent, where are you?" he called, strolling to the kitchen.

"Be right there." Trenton appeared—light-skinned with green eyes—the physical opposite of Gavin. He wore a pair of aged jeans, leaving his tatted arms and back exposed.

His girlfriend's dog, a black and brown Yorkshire Terrier, trotted out beside him.

"How're you doing, Angel?" Gavin asked the dog.

She barked and wagged her tail before plopping down next to the wall.

"What did the doctor say?" Trenton asked.

Gavin spread his arms wide and grinned. "I'm done. No more therapy or checkups necessary." He opened the refrigerator and flicked his eyes over the offerings on the shelves. "What do you have to eat in here?"

"Nothing much. Half a sandwich I picked up from Aldi's Market and leftover Thai."

Gavin glanced at his brother. "Do you eat at that place every week?"

"Almost." Trenton rested his back against the wall. "Alannah will be here any minute. You should stick around. She's cooking tonight."

"No, thanks. You and your wife together are nauseating." Trenton and Alannah weren't really married, but they might as well be.

Trenton laughed. "After all those years of teasing me about her, and now we're together, you're mad?"

"I'm not mad, but did you have to move in together? I'm still trying to figure out how you convinced sweet, nice Alannah to move into your condo to 'save money' while she goes back to school." A weak argument if he ever heard one.

Trenton's face broke into a mischievous grin. "We were together all the time anyway. It made sense."

"Uh-huh. If you say so." Gavin lifted the sandwich from the

refrigerator and peeled back the paper. Roast beef on rye. He sniffed it. "I'll take this," he announced, and took a bite.

"Throw me a beer."

Gavin tossed a can of their family's Full Moon brew to his brother and grabbed one for himself.

The music came on again, indicating someone had entered the condo. The dog jumped up and started dancing around, and Trenton's face transformed into a big grin when Alannah appeared.

Yep, nauseating.

Gavin couldn't deny Alannah was a cutie, though, with her freckles and sweet smile. But recently she'd transformed from a quiet, conservative woman into a confident hottie. Today she wore her long hair in a high ponytail, had a yoga mat tucked under an arm, and wore pale pink yoga gear that hugged her slender curves.

Right behind her, another woman, dressed similarly, followed. This woman practically burst out of her exercise clothes with a video-vixen body—a veritable gift from the gods to his eyeballs. Her breasts strained against the top, large and hefty enough to overflow in his hands if he cupped them. Her legs, which looked as sturdy as columns, were clad in black yoga pants.

Not too tall, not too short, she moved with effortless grace, hips swinging from side to side in a way that made his loins heavy and his mouth water. An eye-catching woman. Her brand of sex appeal inspired the average man to make bad decisions—like hand over his heart and empty his wallet. Fortunately, he was not average.

"Hey Gavin, how are you?"

Alannah's bright smile rivaled Trenton's as she sidled over to his brother.

"Hey, Alannah," Gavin muttered. He watched as Trenton enfolded her in his arms and they kissed, loud and long, as if no one else was in the room and they hadn't seen each other this morning. "Don't mind me. I'm just here for the food."

"Sorry." Alannah giggled, blushing. "I'm being rude. This is my friend, Terri Slade. Terri, this is—"

"Gavin Johnson." Terri extended her hand. "Nice to meet you."

A smooth, cool voice slipped into his ears, containing a hint of sultriness that sent a shiver down his neck.

"The pleasure is all mine." He took her hand. Slender fingers touched his, and a tingling sensation suffused his palm.

Terri looked him directly in the eyes, as though challenging him. She had a firm handshake, but extremely soft hands and white-tipped, manicured nails. Everything about her seemed well put together. Ebony hair pulled back into a short French braid, arched brows above dark brown eyes, full lips, and a honey-brown complexion with a fine dusting of makeup.

And her body...Gavin stifled a groan, unable to resist making another sweep of her build, and bit into the sandwich. Chewing slowly. He tried not to stare, but it was nigh on impossible when she had curves galore, just the way he liked his women, with hips, breasts, and meat on her bones.

"You staying for dinner?" he asked.

"No. Hanging out for a bit, then I'm heading home."

"Make sure you guys are out of my kitchen when I come back out so I have room to work," Alannah said, picking up her dog. "Come on, Terri." Both women headed down the hall.

Gavin watched them disappear, Terri pulling up the rear and her heart-shaped backside swinging like a clock's pendulum in the most provocative way. What a beautiful view.

Trenton chuckled. "Come on, man." He dropped onto the black sofa in the living room and propped his feet on the ottoman.

Gavin sat in the matching chair and glared at his brother. "You no good...you've been holding out on me."

"What do you mean?" Trenton asked innocently.

"Terri!" Gavin said in a fierce whisper. He took a sip of beer and then set the can on the table beside him. "What *in the hell* is wrong with you? I've been here for months and you never introduced me to all that fineness?"

Trenton shrugged. "I didn't think—"

"No, you didn't think. At all. Your head is so full of Alannah, you forgot about me."

"She doesn't run in our circles, and I already hooked you up with several women since you've been here. What happened to Sharon?"

"She's crazy." Gavin stuffed the last bite of the sandwich into his mouth and dusted crumbs from his hands. "She's ready for marriage and kept dropping hints. When a bridal magazine 'accidentally' fell out of her shoulder bag, I knew it was time to move on."

Trenton chuckled. "She always did have a thing for you."

"Lucky me."

The women came back with the Yorkie scampering behind them. The three of them entered the kitchen, and he leaned toward Trenton.

"What's the deal with Terri?"

"She and Alannah are good friends. They've known each other a couple of years."

"You ever…?"

"Hell no!"

"Don't act like you've never slept with two friends."

"*We're talking about Alannah.*"

"Right, right, Mother Theresa. I forgot." Gavin sipped his beer.

"I'm not talking about her personality. I'm saying I wouldn't sleep with one of her friends." Trenton shot him a glare like he couldn't believe Gavin suggested such a thing.

"If it's that serious, why don't you just marry her then?"

"Maybe I will."

Gavin's gaze jetted to his brother's unsmiling face. "Are you serious?" he whispered.

"Thinking about the future, that's all." Trenton shrugged and his eyes gravitated to the kitchen where Alannah was removing pots and pans in preparation to cook.

"Listen, I love Alannah, okay. She's a great woman, but don't rush into anything. You're still young, and there's plenty of ass out there."

At almost thirty-three, Gavin didn't feel anywhere near ready for marriage, and he was two years older than Trenton.

"I've had plenty of ass," Trenton said drily. He swigged his beer.

Gavin stared at his brother. "So you're saying you're done?"

"I told you that already."

"I thought you were just saying that. You know, basically she'd be your main woman, but on the side you'd still have…" His voice trailed off at Trenton's vehement head shaking.

"She's not the main one. Alannah is the *only* one."

Stunned, Gavin didn't know what to say at first. "Okay, then," he finally managed. Trenton had clearly lost his mind, but he doubted the monogamy decision would last. "So what's the deal with Terri?"

"There's no deal. She's a friend of Alannah's."

"What does she do?"

"Works at a salon doing nails or something."

"She got a man?"

"I think so."

"I sense you're holding out on me," Gavin said. "What's the problem? Is she a nice girl or something? Cause I don't like the nice—"

"No, she's not nice."

"Then what's the problem?"

Trenton sighed and rubbed a hand back and forth across his head. "She's Alannah's friend. Don't cause problems for me."

"Don't worry, little brother. I won't."

Trenton glanced at the kitchen to ensure the women weren't paying attention and they weren't, busy talking and laughing as Alannah prepared to cook. "You better not," Trenton said in a low voice. "Cause when you're gone on your next adventure, I'll be the one stuck here in the dog house."

Gavin laughed and shook his head. "Everything will be fine. I won't mess up your perfect little relationship. You and Alannah can remain blissfully living in sin, all right?"

Trenton shot him a dark look but didn't respond, and Gavin's eyes strayed to Terri, the kind of woman not easily overlooked, no matter the setting.

He had to get to know her better.

CHAPTER TWO

With Gavin right behind her, Terri stepped into the elevator, anticipating her date with a hot, fragrant shower before slipping into bed to get some rest. The work grind started again in the morning. After working a long day, the last thing she wanted to do was exercise, but Alannah convinced her to take yoga a couple times per week. Admittedly, it could be rather relaxing after a long day.

She hadn't been the least bit surprised when she said goodbye and Gavin chose the same moment to leave and offered to ride down with her. She knew he had been checking her out in the way she always knew a man was checking her out. She sensed it. The weight of a man's stare was tangible and easily recognized.

Gavin didn't hide his interest at all. He surveyed her from across the elevator, a small smirk on his lips, arms crossed, and back to the wall.

Terri met his gaze without flinching and the smirk shifted into a sexy smile. His cognac-colored eyes, startlingly light against his dark brown skin, brightened, but a subtle shrewdness in them made her very aware of her own body—in a way she never cared when other men watched her.

"I have a feeling pickup lines won't work on you," he said.

"You're right. They won't." She took a slow, easy breath to keep her pulse rate calm.

Gavin Johnson was one fine man. He stood a couple of

inches above six feet, his hair cut in a neat faux hawk that gave him a reckless, edgy vibe. A black pullover stretched across his wide torso, chest muscles outlined beneath the material, and roped forearms revealed by sleeves shoved up to his elbows.

"In that case, when can I take you out, Terri?"

"You can't."

He cupped an ear. "Excuse me, I didn't hear you."

She tilted up her chin and boldly made eye contact. "You. Can't."

No way was she getting involved with Gavin Johnson. A wealthy man like him was used to having his own way. When he said jump, people didn't ask how high—they stayed suspended in the air until he allowed them down again.

His brow furrowed, which made him look kind of cute.

"Are you actually turning me down?"

She couldn't tell if he was joking or genuinely surprised, although she didn't doubt the latter.

One hand on her hip, she said, "I know that may be hard for you to comprehend, but yes, I am." She made a show of ignoring him and glanced up at the numbers on the panel as the elevator continued its descent.

Despite her closeness to the Johnson family, Alannah never revealed much about them, which meant Terri collected information from the gossip blogs and social media like everyone else. Unlike the rest of his family, Gavin courted attention by having active social media accounts. Images from sporting events, parties, and lavish vacations around the world littered his timelines.

If there was an extreme sport, he made sure to conquer it, and often shared shots of himself training, revealing a ridiculously fit physique with grooved muscles covering every square millimeter of umber skin, and chronicling each achievement of his goals. He was an excellent surfer, having mastered the waves off the east coast of Australia. Photos of him, his team, and their guides on top of Mount Kilimanjaro showed them hugging and wearing exultant smiles. A few years ago, he completed the Tevis Cup, a 100-mile endurance ride completed on horseback, and afterward donated one hundred thousand dollars to help preserve and maintain the historic trail.

"You have a man or something?" Gavin asked the question in a way that suggested he didn't care.

"Something like that."

"That means you don't."

"I don't have to tell you my business."

He walked to the middle of the cabin and braced a hand against the back wall. Damn, he smelled good. Masculine, but not the least bit overpowering. Clean and fresh, reminding her of the ocean.

"You don't have to tell me your business, but I'd like for you to."

Terri glanced at him sideways. "Why?"

"Isn't it obvious? I like you."

"You don't know me well enough to like me."

"I like what I see," he said, the timbre of his voice dropping several octaves.

Tiny shivers danced over her skin, and the pace of her heart upticked as his gaze dragged over her shape.

"Typical male," she said.

If she had a dime for every man attracted to her body, she could stop working. Men had been ogling her curves since she hit puberty.

Gavin studied her with nerve-wracking intensity. "There's nothing typical about me."

Terri's knees turned to gelatin. His self-confidence was sexy. "You sure about that?" She arched a brow, feigning nonchalance.

"I want to get to know you."

"You want to screw me."

"True."

The blunt answer surprised her so much she didn't move when the elevator doors glided open.

"But I want to get to know you, too," Gavin added, managing to sound sincere. "I don't see why we can't be friends."

"I've seen your Instagram and Twitter accounts. You already have a lot of friends." Terri exited the elevator.

Gavin came up beside her. "No more than the usual."

"I consider millions of followers way more than the usual, and a lot of them are female."

They walked together across the marble floor of the lobby, bright lights shining down on the expensive furnishings and the residents coming and going.

Gavin chuckled, a smug sound that confirmed her assessment of his online friendships.

With such a huge following, if he tweeted about a product, sales shot up and the item could very well go out of stock. One time he posed in a black and red scarf with frayed edging. Not only had the photo received thousands of likes, but within twenty-four hours the scarf sold out of stores around the country. He could parlay his celebrity status into lucrative contracts, but she'd never heard his name linked to any endorsement deals.

"So are you saying I don't have a shot?"

"I'm afraid not."

He frowned. "Did Trenton or Alannah tell you something not-so-nice about me?"

"Nope. I just don't need a man right now."

Not now, not ever. Experiencing independence for the first time, Terri lived her own life on her own terms and loved it. No man would ever take away her freedom again.

"Because…?"

She stopped a few feet from the exit, where a doorman opened and closed the door for incoming and outgoing guests.

"Because I don't."

"So your relationship with your 'something like that' boyfriend isn't serious?"

"My relationships are never serious."

"Well, damn. You might be the woman of my dreams. Why aren't they ever serious?"

"I just like to have fun. Men are in my life for one reason only, and that's to make me feel good. Otherwise, I don't need them."

His eyebrows shot toward the ceiling, and she took pleasure in knowing she shocked him.

"What about sex?"

"I'm talking about sex." She pursed her lips a little, a trick she'd learned that gave her already full mouth a more pouty appearance.

His gaze ran over her with overt interest. "So how many of these non-boyfriends do you have?"

"Only one right now."

"What's this chump's name?"

She angled her head to the right. "Why does he have to be a chump?"

"Because he's with you and I'm not."

Terri shook her head and started walking again.

"You're not going to tell me?"

"It's none of your business, Gavin."

"Can't hurt to tell me his name. I'm not asking for his social security number and address."

She sighed heavily. What difference did it make? They'd never meet each other anyway. "His name is Douglas."

She walked out into the cool night air and headed to the waiting car. Trenton thought the location of the yoga classes was questionable and always made sure she and Alannah had a driver at their disposal to drop them off and pick them up from class. The minute the tall, brawny man saw Terri, he exited the vehicle and opened the back door.

"Yep, that definitely sounds like a chump name," Gavin drawled.

"It does not." Despite herself, Terri giggled. He was incorrigible. "It's a perfectly fine name for a strong man."

"What does Dagwood do?"

"Douglas," she corrected, though she knew he'd intentionally screwed up the name. "He's a bank manager."

They arrived at the car, and Gavin waved away the driver. With a brief nod, the man went to sit in the front seat.

"I hope he's strong."

"Why does he have to be strong?" Terri asked.

Gavin rested an arm on the open door. "Because." His voice

dropped low, and looking up into those hypnotizing light brown eyes, she felt dangerously close to swooning. "He's going to have to be a soldier to deal with me."

"Are you saying you want to be one of my non-boyfriends?" Terri asked in a syrupy voice, equally low.

"Sure do. And I want all the benefits that come with the title."

She pursed her lips again and watched his gaze drift down to her mouth. "I don't know. I'm not the kind to jump when you say jump because you're rich. You might want to stick to those high society girls you're used to. You can't handle a woman like me."

He chuckled, and his entire body shook. He had the most delicious smile. All white teeth and mahogany lips that hinted at untold pleasures. He was definitely a pretty man. Pretty eyes. Pretty teeth. And last but not least, pretty lips. So full and pretty they made her want to sit on his face.

"You're something else, you know that? You talk a lot of shit."

"I can back it up, too." She rubbed her bare arms against the chilled air.

"Oh yeah?"

"Mhmm. Ask any of my previous lovers. But like I said, you might not be the right man for the job." She took unprecedented pleasure in needling him.

Gavin narrowed his eyes as he watched her. "You're wrong."

"I doubt it."

"I'll win you over eventually."

"You're so sure?"

He shrugged, smiling a little. "What can I say? I'm rich and I'm spoiled, and I never take no for an answer."

"Are you saying you always get what you want?" she asked.

This time, the smile was an all-teeth, *hell yeah* smile. "Always."

"Hmm. Nice meeting you, Gavin." Terri slid into the car and reached for the door, but Gavin held it open.

He ducked his head to look in at her, his face holding a seriousness that hadn't been there before. "What can I do to become a non-boyfriend?"

"Nothing." She grasped the door handle and tugged, but he didn't release it.

"I don't like that answer."

"It's the only answer you're going to get."

"What's wrong with me?"

"Nothing. I'm sure there's a nice debutante out there who would love to hook up with you."

"So getting your number is out of the question?"

"That's correct. Were you listening?"

He was quiet for a while, and they both stared at each other, neither willing to break eye contact. "I have to tell you, I don't usually find it this difficult to get a woman's number."

"I'm sure you don't find it this difficult to get anything you want. After all, you're rich and spoiled and don't take no for an answer."

He flashed milky white teeth in another one of his captivating smiles. "I can see I'm going to have my hands full with you."

"You're assuming you can get me," Terri tossed back.

"Oh, I can get you."

"You think so? You don't have much time. Alannah said you're leaving soon. Isn't that right?"

"Nah."

"Nah?" She tilted her head at the unexpected answer.

"I'm in no rush to leave Seattle." His gaze swept her body again, and when his eyes came back to hers, her breath suspended at the heat in their depths. By the determined set to his mouth and intensity in his eyes, she knew without a doubt she had become a goal he intended to accomplish—like climbing Mount Kilimanjaro or successfully surfing dangerous waves. "I think I'll stick around for a while."

He straightened and half-closed the door before swinging it wide again. "Oh, and do me a favor, would you?"

"What's that?"

He leaned in closer, as if what he had to say was of utmost importance. Every part of her tensed under his stare.

"Tell Derwin his days are numbered."

With one last self-confident smile, he shut the door and strutted off.

CHAPTER THREE

Thank goodness, the night was almost over.

The elevator doors opened and Gavin stepped out with his date, Blake McConnell. As her escort for the evening, he felt obligated to see her to the penthouse apartment, but dreaded the stop at the door. They had parted ways a long time ago and he shouldn't even have escorted her to the benefit tonight, but their mothers were friends from college back in Texas and his mother, Constance Johnson, had approached him with that sweet-as-honey Texas twang and more or less insisted he attend the event as Blake's date.

They stopped at the door and Blake looked over her shoulder at him, smiling a secret smile and lowering her lashes in the way she did when she thought she'd get what she wanted. Gavin groaned inwardly but didn't betray any emotion on the outside.

Blake was a stunning woman. Great figure, long deep-gold hair worn in an intricate upswept style, and near flawless alabaster skin. Tonight she wore a sleeveless black Michael Kors dress with a dramatic white taffeta train. Problem was, all that beauty, style, and charm disguised a whole lot of crazy. After only a few months of dating, he saw the writing on the wall and stopped seeing her.

Considering they hadn't been exclusive, her behavior had been exceedingly worrisome. She followed his social media accounts and used them to track him across the globe, showing up in random locations and screaming, "Surprise! I was just in the neighborhood." She mean-mugged any woman who approached him, even if she was only a friend, and went through his phone—an absolute no-no.

Blake opened the door and turned with a flourish, keeping one hand on the knob and placing the other on her hip. Her blue eyes held an invitation no man could resist—if he didn't know any better.

"Are you coming in?" she asked in a sex-kitten voice.

Now the awkward part.

Gavin stuffed his hands in the pockets of his black tuxedo pants. "Not tonight," he said, inflecting the right amount of regret into his voice. "It's been a long week and I'm bushed. I'm going to head home and get some rest." He covered a fake yawn with his hand.

She didn't blink, looking at him as if she knew better, which she probably thought she did. Despite ending their hookups over a year ago, she held onto the mistaken belief that he had feelings for her and found her irresistible.

Locking eyes with him, she reached back and unzipped her dress, letting it slide to the floor in a puddle of silk and taffeta around her ankles. "Are you sure?" she asked, raising an eyebrow in what she must consider to be a seductive look.

Gavin's eyes wandered from the rosy nipples to the itty-bitty string thong barely covering her shaved privates. Considering all the wild, crazy sex they'd had, his soldier didn't have much of a reaction, hardly noticing an almost naked, willing woman stood within reach. She turned so he could see her bare bottom and the tattoo etched in cursive right above the waistband of the thong: *Property of Gavin Johnson.*

He cringed. The tattoo shocked him when she texted him a picture, and the bold declaration against the flawless skin shocked him even more in person. He couldn't figure out why she thought marking her body with his name would convince him to get back involved with her. If anything, the desperate act convinced him he'd made the right decision in the first place.

"I'm really, really tired, Blake," he said, for lack of anything better to say.

He should be able to come up with a better response, but he was simply at a loss and wished he hadn't been coerced into this date in the first place. He needed to get better at resisting his mother's overtures, but who was he kidding? No one in his family dared say no to Constance Johnson.

The sultry smile wavered on Blake's face. Facing him squarely, she placed both hands on her hips, shoulders back and head held high. "You're kidding, right? You're not going to leave all this"—she swept a hand down the length of her lithe body—"are you?"

Nothing. Nada. His top head definitely ruled tonight.

"Blake, you know as well as I do we're no good together." *Because one of us is sane and the other is in*sane.

"Gavin," she cooed, voice dripping with sugar as she tried another tactic. "I'm not looking for anything more than you want to give. Come in and let's have a little fun. We can use the paddle tonight, because I need a good spanking, Big Daddy." She pouted prettily and shook her tush at him.

Gavin rubbed a hand down the back of his head. "You need to find another daddy, Blake. Move on. You're a beautiful woman and there's a man out there waiting for someone special like you." He hoped he sounded sincere. He felt sorry for the next fool caught in her web.

A tint of rose bloomed in her cheeks, and Blake's face contorted into an ugly image of anger and embarrassment. "Last chance," she bit out.

He refrained from sighing at the ridiculousness of her comment. That would only inflame her more. "I'm going to have to pass."

With the angry mutter of a four-letter word he distinctly remembered her using in a more appealing, sexual connotation during times past, Blake slammed the door, leaving him staring at her apartment number inches from his face. This time he did sigh and proceeded down the hallway.

On the way to the elevator, the phone in his pocket rang. He fished it out and Trenton's face filled the screen. Gavin almost didn't answer but gritted his teeth in anticipation of the forthcoming conversation.

"What?" He stabbed the down button.

Trenton chuckled. "How'd it go?"

"I'm not in the mood for your jokes, Trent."

"Jokes? What jokes? I called to see how the benefit went and if you and *your property* had a good time."

"That's why I don't like to tell you anything. You're trifling." Gavin stepped onto the elevator.

"Come on, who else are you going to tell? And you have to admit that's funny. I'm surprised you agreed to escort her."

"If you were me, could you have said no to Mother?"

The other end went silent for several seconds. "No, I guess you're right, but I hated it for you." He chuckled again. Apparently his sympathy was no match for the desire to laugh at Gavin's awkward predicament. "Did you ever tell Mother why you broke up with her?"

"No, but after tonight, I really should. I know Mother will be mortified by her behavior and no way am I being talked into escorting her anywhere again."

The elevator doors opened and Gavin walked out.

"Hey, Lana and I are going to The Underground tonight. You coming?"

The Underground was a club known for its hip-hop and indie rock music. Up and coming artists used it as a testing ground and launch pad for their music careers.

"You kids go ahead. I'm done for the night." He strolled out of the building to the valet, who handed him the key to his vehicle. "By the way, I need a manicure. Where did you say Alannah's friend…ah, what's her name…Terri, worked again?"

The halting question had been completely phony. He remembered her first and last name, the exact shade of her dark brown eyes, the shape of her soft-looking lips, and from visual inspection alone had a pretty good idea of her measurements.

"I didn't."

Gavin handed the young man another fifty. When he'd arrived at the building with Blake, he'd handed him fifty dollars and whispered the request to leave the car parked nearby. "Just tell me where she works."

"You can have a manicurist go out to your house."

"I want to try someone new." Gavin slid into the interior of the black Porsche Spyder, a two-seater convertible with black interior and one of only five models available in the world.

"You need to talk to Lana on this one. Hold on."

Gavin waited, tapping his thumb on the steering wheel and watching a drunk couple lean on each other, staggering toward the entrance of the building where the doorman swung open the door and let them in.

"Hi, Gavin."

"Hi, beautiful."

"You're not going to hurt my friend, are you?"

"What? I'm wounded right down to my soul. You've known me for over twenty years."

"That's why I'm asking."

Gavin shook his head and laughed. "You might have a point. I promise not to hurt your friend. Does that satisfy you?"

"I guess it'll have to do. Terri didn't say anything to me, but I have the impression she *might* be interested in you. She works at Beauty Studio Salon & Spa."

"That wasn't so hard, was it?" Gavin started the car and connected the Bluetooth. "Thank you, beautiful. Is your husband going to be up for squash tomorrow morning after the two of you get through partying tonight?"

Alannah repeated the question and Trenton came back on the phone.

"I'll be there and ready to beat your ass."

"*I'm* tired of beating *your* ass." Gavin pulled into the Seattle nighttime traffic.

"You want to put some money on it?" Trenton asked.

"You already owe me twenty grand that I have a sneaking suspicion I'll never see."

"How about we put up another twenty thousand, winner takes all?"

He shook his head, laughing at the challenge. "I would say I hate taking your money, except you don't pay your debts."

"You scared now that we're talking about real money? Is that it?"

"All right, I'll be there. Winner takes all, which means you'll owe me forty thousand dollars when you lose."

"I don't plan to lose, so you'll owe *me* forty thousand. Cash only, no checks. I'll see you at seven."

Gavin hung up and turned on the radio, letting the smooth jazz notes of a saxophone fill the interior as the city lights whizzed by outside the window. He hadn't been able to stop thinking about Terri Slade since he met her last weekend. Now that he knew where she worked, he had every intention of seeing her again.

CHAPTER FOUR

Terri tossed off her black smock and rolled her neck and shoulders to loosen the knots of fatigue embedded in the muscles. The manager, Susan, came in, a perky blonde whose fiery personality surprised anyone foolish enough to think they could run all over her because of her diminutive size.

"Don't leave yet."

Terri moaned. "No, don't say that. I need a break." After a ten-hour shift, she looked forward to falling into bed and sleeping the night away, after she tore through a large pizza and a two-liter bottle of Pepsi.

Susan placed one hand on her hip. "You can leave after this last customer. He asked for you."

Terri didn't have many male customers, so a man asking for her came as a surprise. "What does he need?"

"A basic manicure."

That she could handle, and male clients tipped very well. "All right." She looped the apron over her head and tied the strings in the back. "Who is it?"

"He's not a regular, but he said he was referred to you." Susan smiled oddly, as if bursting to spill some information but thought it would be better to wait.

Too tired to care, Terri said, "I'll be out in a minute."

As Susan walked out, Terri went over to the mirror on the

wall and checked her makeup. She dug a tube of mauve lipstick from her pocket and retouched the color. With a quick fluff of her dark hair, she took a deep breath and fixed a smile on her face, tricking her body into thinking she was no longer tired, and ensuring she'd receive a nice tip from her male customer.

She exited the back, and when her eyes landed on the sole male in the waiting area standing at the counter, she pulled up short. Gavin stood there, head bent over his phone and wearing a black long-sleeved Ed Hardy T-shirt and faded jeans.

With his fine ass.

He looked up, and she had a full view of his face and those oh-so-dreamy eyes. Her tummy did an odd little tumble, and she walked over, taking a quiet, deep breath to calm her nerves.

"Hello, Mr. Johnson."

He glanced over his shoulder, pretending to search for someone. "You talking to me? I'm Gavin."

Terri resisted smiling and basking in the warmth of that seductive smile. "Okay, Gavin."

"That's better." He held up his hands, fingers spread wide. "Can you do anything to fix these?"

She couldn't see a thing wrong with his hands. "I'll see what I can do," she said, playing along. "Follow me, please."

She led him back to her station and instructed him to sit on the opposite side of the table. A few people looked their way. An older male stylist whispered to a younger female stylist with cherry-colored hair, and a customer seated diagonally across the room from them stared. No doubt they recognized him as Gavin Johnson, an heir to Johnson Enterprises, a multibillion-dollar beer and restaurant empire.

"A basic manicure, correct?" Terri asked.

"Correct."

"No color?" She couldn't resist teasing.

"No color." The corner of his mouth twitched.

Terri held up the price sheet. "Do you need a scrub, or…"

"Whatever you think."

"I think you don't need a manicure."

Gavin shrugged. "No one *needs* a manicure, but that doesn't mean regular maintenance isn't a good idea. You're doing a terrible job at selling your services, by the way."

"Maybe because I doubt you're really here for service."

"And why would I be here?"

"You tell me."

"This is a spa, and I heard it's a great one. I personally like to take care of myself—keep my hands nice and soft. So I came to the best."

"Is that right? I'm surprised you manage to take such good care of yourself with all the crazy shit you do." She froze. "Pardon my French." She had gotten way too comfortable with him.

He wore an amused smile. "You're right. I do a lot of crazy shit."

Terri relaxed and placed a jar of scrub on top of the table. "Why is that?"

"Why do you think?"

"That's for you to say. I have no idea."

He paused, as if really considering the question. "It's the adrenalin rush. Pushing my body to the limit is exciting."

"And of course, you get a lot of attention from the media." Terri set a sponge and other materials on the table.

"I don't do any stunts for the attention." His voice sounded a little harsh, but almost immediately, his somber expression shifted and the smile reappeared. "Tempting fate is fun. Exciting. Whenever something excites me, I want to do it again…and again."

His gaze held hers and heat spanned the length of her neck. The innuendo in his words conjured thoughts of dark, sweat-slick bodies wrapped around each other.

"Real subtle," Terri said.

She took one hand in hers. It was surprisingly soft, which meant he took good care of his hands. She rubbed the scrub into his skin.

"You have plans tonight?" he asked.

"Yes."

"With Dereon?"

"Careful now. You keep screwing up his name, and I'll think you're jealous."

"Maybe I am."

Terri scooped more scrub into her palm and ignored the comment.

"Don't you feel sorry for me?" A smile played at the corners of his mouth.

"No."

She worked quietly for a few minutes. His eyes followed the movements of her fingers massaging the granules into his skin, circling his palm, and easing up to his wrist.

"You have a bed in the back?" Gavin asked, throatily.

"A what? No. Why?"

"You keep touching me like that and we're going to need one."

Terri's hands stilled. "I like to be thorough."

"Me, too," he said, holding her gaze.

Terri's heart skipped a beat, certain the level of Gavin's *thoroughness* exceeded the average lover. From what she knew of him, he did nothing halfway, and the sexual performance promised in his eyes shortened her breath with anticipation.

She picked up a flat, damp sponge and began cleansing his hands. "I'm not going to do it," she finally said.

"Do what?"

"Give you my number."

"I'm not leaving without it."

Again, she paused. Confidence in a man was her ultimate weakness, and Gavin possessed enough for ten men.

Using the sponge, she dragged the last bit of product from his fingers and then started pushing back the cuticle. As she finished up the manicure, he shared a little about himself. Not surprisingly, he'd visited every continent in the world, including going on a private expedition to Antarctica that he funded himself. There didn't seem to be anything this man couldn't do.

They wrapped up the session and both stood.

"Great job." Gavin looked at his hands. "They're baby soft."

"You're welcome." Terri untied her apron.

"You're leaving now?" Gavin asked.

"That's the plan."

"I'll walk you out." Without waiting for an answer, he left her station and Terri watched his broad back move toward the front of the spa. She went to the back and tossed her apron in the hamper with the others. She found Gavin in the waiting area, and when she approached, he extended a hand to her.

"A little something for you," he said, handing her a folded bill.

Terri took it and raised her eyebrows when she saw the one-hundred-dollar bill, the most generous tip she'd ever received. She glanced at a customer who quickly averted her eyes to the magazine in her lap.

Stepping closer to whisper, Terri caught a good whiff of him. She resisted the urge to lean in close and press her nose to the strong chord of his neck.

"This is way too much," she said in a low voice. "The manicure didn't even cost this much."

"I appreciate good service," he said, equally low. His gaze dipped to her mouth, and Terri's lips tingled with awareness at the intense focus of his stare. Did he conduct every act with such intensity, she wondered. The swooning sensation overcame her again, and she took several steps back into safer territory.

Breathing easier, she clutched the bill and watched Gavin's mouth turn up into a smile, one that hinted at his awareness of her strong attraction to him. Without saying a word, he walked toward the door and opened it, waiting for her to pass through, which she did when her feet started working again.

They crossed the parking lot and came to a standstill at her black Jimmy SUV.

"You definitely don't have a man," Gavin remarked. He swiped a finger through the dirt on the car.

Terri slapped away his hand. "Do you mind? And how does having a dirty car prove that I don't have a man, anyway?"

"Because no self-respecting man would let his woman drive

around in a vehicle that looks like this. It's just not done. Not even by a guy named Dagwood."

"His name is—you know what, never mind." She turned the key in the lock and popped the locks.

"What are you about to do?" Gavin asked.

"Leave."

"After you leave."

"Why do you care?"

"You hungry?"

"No." Her stomach growled, putting her on blast.

One of Gavin's eyebrows shot up.

"Maybe a little bit," Terri confessed. "I was going to grab a pizza on the way home."

"So you don't really have plans after all."

Caught in a lie, Terri remained quiet.

Gavin stuffed his hands in his pockets and rolled onto the balls of his feet, taking a good look at the vehicle. "Tell you what, let's get this car cleaned and we'll grab a couple slices at the pizza joint across the street from the detail shop."

"Did I ask for your help?"

"No, but I'm giving it to you." He pulled a phone from his pocket and punched in a number, then lifted it to his ear. "Faison, buddy. How are you?"

His profile lit up with a bright smile. Goodness, he was gorgeous. Disgustingly attractive.

"What are you doing?" Terri whispered.

Gavin lifted a finger to silence her. "I have a situation here." He wrinkled his nose at the car.

She pursed her lips and tapped her foot. She'd had just about enough of him dissing her car. "If you don't mind, I need to leave and—"

He lifted a finger again, silencing her. "I need you to take care of a vehicle for me. An SUV. Full detail. I'm talking the works." He opened the driver door and peeked in at the dusty floor mat and scraped a ketchup stain on the seat. "Inside and out. Can you fit me in right now?" He listened and then nodded. "It belongs to friend.

Yeah. Uh-huh….okay. We'll be there in ten."

He replaced the phone in his pocket and held out his hand. "Keys."

Fisting both hands on her hips, Terri angled her head toward him. "Now you want to drive my car?"

"What are you worried about?"

"I don't like people taking over my life."

"I'm not taking over your life. I'm taking your car to be cleaned and buying you a couple slices of pizza. You don't like clean cars and free food?"

Her mouth clamped shut.

"Keys." Gavin held out his hand again.

"Why do you have to drive?"

"Because I know where I'm going and it's easier. You going to keep playing twenty questions?"

"Are you always this pushy?"

"If you're going to hang with me, you need to go with the flow."

"Who says I want to hang with you?" Terri demanded.

"Of course you do. Why wouldn't you want to hang with me?" His brow furrowed in puzzlement. He had such a high opinion of himself.

His railroading actions felt all too familiar, and her instinctive response was to push back because she didn't before. She lost herself, but this time was different. Pizza and a car wash did not mean he was taking over her life. Calmed and viewing the situation clearly, she could admit that he was only being nice.

Sighing, Terri slapped the keys into his hand. "You really do always get what you want, don't you?"

A cocky smile came on his face. "I'm a Johnson. I don't know any other way."

Terri huffed and walked around to the passenger side. She put her hand to open the door, but was practically shoved out of the way by Gavin, who opened it for her.

"What the hell?"

"What are you doing?" he demanded.

"I'm trying to get in the car."

"And I'm opening the door for you." He swung it wide.

"Why?"

He shot her an odd look, as if he couldn't believe she'd asked such a thing. "Because you're a lady."

The surprising answer pricked her heart. He hadn't opened the door because he was a gentleman. He opened it because *she* was a lady.

A small lump suddenly appeared in her throat. "Thank you," she mumbled, eyes darting away from his.

She settled in the seat and watched him go around to the driver's side and then climb in.

A little shell-shocked by his words, she still couldn't speak. No one had ever called her a lady, and she certainly couldn't recall being treated like one on too many occasions.

Gavin started the Jimmy and pulled out of the parking lot.

On the road, he turned to her and smiled, continuing to chip away at the barrier of cool she had erected to protect against the charms of men like him.

"So tell me, what kind of pizza do you like?"

CHAPTER FIVE

The pizza joint turned out to be a high-end restaurant that served hand-tossed pizza created from fresh dough made in-house daily. Terri and Gavin sat at the counter where they could watch the pizza makers in the open kitchen. They entertained the patrons by tossing the dough high in the air and then shoving the finished product into the wood fire oven to cook.

Terri devoured two large slices of the best cheesiest mushroom pizza she had ever eaten and washed down the calories with a cream soda. While Gavin spoke to the owner and waitress, she watched him, observing the way his relaxed body bent over the counter while engaging in friendly banter. Nothing pretentious about him at all, intriguing her all the more. He seemed to be a multi-layered individual, pushy and arrogant on the one hand, yet friendly, down-to-earth, and considerate on the other.

They left the restaurant after Faison called and told Gavin the Jimmy was ready, and Terri gasped when she saw the transformation. Instead of a dull, hideous gray color from dirt, the new wax job gave the exterior the reflective surface of a shiny black pearl. In all honesty, it looked like a brand new car, and the insides doused with the pineapple-scented freshener she requested made for a satisfying olfactory experience when Gavin opened the door for her.

Ten minutes later, they returned to the spa's parking lot, and Gavin eased into a space and turned off the engine.

Terri turned to him and asked, "So what now?"

"You thank me."

She stiffened, the sting of disappointment in her shoulders. The smile on Gavin's face came off as lascivious, filled with presumption that a reward was forthcoming. He temporarily fooled her by opening doors and calling her a lady, but as she suspected from the beginning, he was like every other man—a typical male.

"You give me a fat tip, detail my car, buy me two slices of pizza, and all of a sudden I owe you?" Terri asked, balling her hands into fists.

Gavin reared back. "Excuse me?"

"What should I do? Straddle you? Or would you prefer a blow job? Your wish is my command."

"Whoa, whoa." His eyes widened and hands came up defensively. "What are you talking about?"

"You wanted me to 'thank you,' right?" Her fingers made angry air quotes.

How could he be such an insensitive brute? He *offered* to take care of her car and buy her dinner.

"Usually, when someone says thank me, the other person just says 'thank you.'" He spoke in a quietly reasonable voice, like someone trying to calm a hysterical person.

Some of Terri's indignant anger abated. "You meant it literally?"

Gavin cocked his head at her. "I really need to know the kind of men you're used to dealing with." He ran a hand back and forth over his head. "I want to get to know you."

"Why me? You can have any woman you want."

"Obviously not. I can't have you. I can't even get you to give me your phone number."

"Why are you trying so hard?" Terri asked.

"Why do you keep resisting?" he countered, resting an arm on the steering wheel and turning in her direction.

Terri gnawed the side of her lip. "Look, I haven't been serious with anyone in a long time. I'm not looking for anything serious."

"Neither am I." His voice remained calm and even-toned.

Terri cast an eye around the parking lot at a few people leaving the restaurant a couple of doors down and then crossed her arms over her chest.

"If I go out with you one time, will you leave me alone?"

"Question is, will you want to be left alone?"

Terri lifted an eyebrow at him, and Gavin rubbed a hand across his forehead. "Fine. If you don't have an incredible time on our date, I'll leave you alone. Deal?"

"There are no stipulations. One time, that's it. Take it or leave it."

Gavin frowned at her. Then a slow, triumphant smile came over his face, and Terri shifted uneasily in the seat, wondering if she should retract her offer. "Where do you want to go?" he asked.

She hadn't thought that far in advance and couldn't think of any place at the moment. "Um…a nice restaurant. You pick."

He stared out the window and tapped his fingers on the steering wheel. After some thought, he said, "Let me think about it and I'll get back to you. Are you working tomorrow night?"

"Yes, but I'm free next Saturday." Now that she'd agreed to go out with him, a tiny part of her already looked forward to the evening out.

"No plans with Drake?"

"Seriously?"

"All right, all right, Dagwood."

Terri rolled her eyes.

"I'll pick you up next week." Gavin opened his door and then looked over his shoulder at her. "Don't move."

Remaining in place, Terri's eyes followed him as he walked around the SUV to her side. She knew the routine now and appreciated this treatment. It made her feel special.

Like a lady.

Gavin opened the passenger door and she hopped onto the asphalt. He didn't step back, standing very, very close. Her skin reacted to the close proximity of his—tightening, tingling. A glimmer of heat entered his eyes and she waited, breath suspended.

Gavin handed her the keys and walked away. Disappointed, Terri stood in place for a minute. She didn't know what to expect, but she hadn't expected him to simply walk away.

She trailed him around to the driver's side. "Thank you…for everything," she said.

"My pleasure." A lazy smile crossed his lips and filtered into his honey-colored eyes.

"I guess you'll need my number," she said slowly.

"I would love to have it."

She gave him the digits. "You're not going to write it down?"

Gavin tapped the side of his head. "I have a great memory," he said, and recited it back to her. "So you're really going out with me next week?"

"I said I would."

The corners of his mouth turned upward, a sign of genuine pleasure. He opened the driver door and she climbed into the seat.

"Good night, Terri Slade."

"Good night, Gavin Johnson."

He shut the door, patted the hood, and sauntered off.

As she watched Gavin wind his way between the cars to his own vehicle, Terri recalled the promise he'd made in the salon when she told him she wouldn't give him her number.

I'm not leaving without it.

Sure enough, he hadn't.

CHAPTER SIX

Terri exited her clean vehicle and closed the door. The Jimmy glowed under the lights of the parking lot at Stack Home Apartments, where most of the windows of the ten buildings were illuminated. The three-story brick building where she lived contained only efficiency apartments and she knew a few of her neighbors, but for the most part, everyone kept to themselves and it was fairly quiet.

Trudging up the walkway, she yawned and rolled her shoulders. She entered the building and saw Mr. Raymond, a white-haired old man who moved in six months ago with a little Chihuahua named Max. Every evening before the sun went down, no matter the temperature, he and Max went for a walk around the complex. Mr. Raymond explained to her once that the exercise was good for his stiff joints.

He pulled mail from his box and one of the envelopes fluttered to the ground.

"I've got it." Terri hurried over, swooped up the envelope, and handed it to him.

"Thank you, Terri." His face beamed with a friendly smile.

"You're welcome. How are you doing tonight, Mr. Raymond?"

"Good, good. My grandson's coming to visit me next weekend. Got himself a new girlfriend he wants to introduce me to." He winked.

"Uh-oh, must be serious."

"I think so."

"How's Max? Still ruling the roost as if he's the one paying the rent?"

"Afraid so. One of these days, I'm going to show him who's boss."

Terri laughed. "G'night."

"Good night."

Mr. Raymond shuffled off toward his apartment, and Terri climbed two flights of stairs to the third floor. Walking down the hall, rock music from the apartment across the corridor blared so loud it rattled the door.

"He must be deaf," she muttered, sympathizing with the renter next to him.

The noisy neighbor was a weird little guy with shaggy hair and beady eyes who never looked her in the face when they passed each other in the hall, always directing his gaze at the floor.

She opened the door to her efficiency and flicked on the light in the tiny space, and the scent of tropical fruit air freshener greeted her nose. Inhaling deeply, she smiled.

Closing the door, she shut out the neighbor's noise. She pulled across the chain, flipped the two deadbolts—one of which she had installed when she moved in—and turned the lock in the door. Home sweet home.

For the first time in her life, she had her own place. It wasn't much—hardly more than four hundred square feet—but her name was on the lease. Quite a step down from the life she used to live in an upscale condo in the middle of Buckhead, an affluent district in metro Atlanta.

Brunch at the Four Seasons on Fourteenth Street with the girlfriends of wealthy businessmen—a makeshift social club among a small group—and shopping at Lenox Square or specialty stores for the finest clothing and home furnishings had been the norm. Although she had moments when she missed that lifestyle, she didn't miss the high cost that came with it. She lost herself, basically giving up her independence and self-esteem for a life that not only didn't last, but made her very unhappy and ultimately hurt a lot of people.

She was infinitely happier in her little efficiency. She paid the rent and bills here, and it felt damn good. White walls and white appliances helped to keep the small space from feeling too cramped. The off-white sofa, purchased at a second-hand furniture store, contained a punch of color from blue, striped, and red pillows. Opening the ivory curtain that separated the bedroom from the rest of the apartment, she took a few steps and dropped her Gucci knock-off on the bed, which sat directly in front of a large window facing the street. The other window looked down into the parking lot.

A five-drawer bureau took up part of the wall next to the door that led to the bathroom. On top was a collection of snow globes—six from the states she traveled through on her four-day drive from Atlanta to Washington; one from Arizona, gifted to her by Alannah; the other three came from visits to New York, Hawaii, and Los Angeles. One day she hoped to expand her collection to include globes from every state. Maybe even every country in the world.

She turned on the lamp beside the bed and lifted the mattress to remove the white envelope stuffed with cash. She added the C-note from Gavin and wrote the date and amount on the outside of the envelope like always.

"Six thousand, one hundred, fifty dollars."

She did a happy dance and shoved the money back under the mattress and dropped onto the bed. When she retrieved her phone from her purse, she flopped onto her back and dialed a number in Georgia. On the third ring, a female voice answered, and she prepared for the difficult conversation with her brother's fiancée, Shanae.

"Hey, it's me," Terri said in a deadpan voice, because being polite and friendly hadn't worked in a long time.

"What do you want?" Her future sister-in-law sounded annoyed, her usual tone of voice.

"To talk to my brother," Terri said between her teeth. "Is he in?"

"No."

Terri bit back a curse at the short answer. Shanae's attitude was a constant source of exasperation. Getting information from her always meant going through a game of verbally pulling teeth.

She could hear Shanae popping her gum. The annoying habit sounded even more annoying over the phone. If she wasn't her brother's fiancée and the mother of his child, Terri would have cursed her out a long time ago, but she had made a promise to her brother that she would make an effort to be nice to her. Shanae, however, didn't have the same desire to be cordial except when Damian was within earshot. Then she turned on the charm, voice dripping with sugar as she *hey girl*-ed Terri and spouted lies like *It's so good to hear from you.*

"Where is he?" Terri asked.

"He at work."

In addition to operating a crane during the day—a job that paid very well, Damian worked most nights at a warehouse to put away extra money. Not only to take care of his family, but also because with his wedding to Shanae coming up next year, he wanted to give his fiancée the wedding of her dreams. Something he could have done if not for Terri.

Shanae blamed her for the financial crisis created when Damian's investments—investments he'd entered at Terri's urging—bottomed out. At the time, Terri assumed they were all legitimate, but later learned her boyfriend, Talon Cyrenci, had set up shell corporations and laundered money through established businesses—car washes, nightclubs, and flipping real estate.

A lot of people lost money, including Shanae's parents and friends Terri could no longer face.

"Anything else?" Shanae asked, not bothering to keep the impatience out of her voice.

"Is Little Bit up?" Terri asked, referring to her two-year-old niece, LaShay.

"She sleep."

"Oh." Of course Little Bit would be asleep. Atlanta was three hours ahead, which meant it was almost midnight there. "Well, give her a kiss for me and tell Damian I called."

"Yeah."

Terri didn't even know why she bothered. Half the time, Shanae didn't pass on the messages. If Damian didn't get a cell phone soon, she was going to get one for him.

"Bye, Shanae." Before the other woman could respond, Terri hung up the phone.

She reclined against the pillows and stared at the white curtain cutting her apartment in two, recalling fond memories of growing up in the little yellow house with the green shutters on Washington Avenue. The year her parents passed away—her father from a heart attack and her mother from complications after surgery—she and her brother moved in with her mother's mother, Grandma Elisabeth. Her grandmother kept them until they entered high school, when a stroke forced her into a wheelchair. Although still lucid, she was unable to care for them any longer.

Terri and Damian were shuffled among family members for months, including an elderly aunt whose younger boyfriend used her financially—something all the family could see except her. When he emptied her bank account and ran off, she couldn't recover. She ignored the eviction notices, and one day, they came home to find their belongings being picked apart in the street by neighbors. They scattered like vultures chased away from a carcass when she and her family pulled up in the old station wagon. Even worse, what was left had been soaked through from a brief rainstorm that flashed through the city hours before.

They salvaged what they could—a few clothes, a couple of pots and pans so damaged no one wanted them. They lost most everything, but Terri hadn't cried until the shocking sight of her prized *Charlotte's Web*—an old, rare copy given to her by her grandmother—destroyed by rain and torn apart by trampling feet. At that young age—no more than fourteen years old—she vowed to never be a victim again.

After her first love failed, she saw Talon as a prince, with his cool green eyes, thick black curls swooping down over his forehead, and charming wit. But she learned the hard way that he was not royalty.

So she decided to stop wishing for a man to save her, and resolved that she would save herself.

****

Gavin strolled into breakfast at his mother's home. The formal dining room contained a long table that seated ten and could be expanded for extra seating. Two chandeliers hung overhead and offered additional elegance in the ornately decorated room.

Although he had rented his own place, he sometimes drove over to eat breakfast with his mother. Considering his wild night in Las Vegas, which took an interesting turn when a member of his party showed up at the suite with five strippers and enough vodka to kill a horse, he should be tired. Yet, he felt buoyed and refreshed.

Constance Johnson sat at the head of the table with a half-eaten plate of eggs benedict, grilled asparagus, and pieces of thinly sliced berries fanned out on one side of the plate.

"Morning." Gavin kissed his mother's cheek. Her face, a deep color that reminded him of rich chocolate, was surprisingly free of wrinkles for a woman her age.

She stopped in the middle of her conversation with his brother, Xavier, who was already dressed for work in a crisp navy suit and tie, his long dreadlocks pulled back in a low-hanging ponytail.

"Good morning, dear." Constance sipped her tea. "I'm surprised to see you this morning. I understand you and your friends took one of the planes to Las Vegas and did quite a bit of partying this weekend."

His mother had a way of sliding in comments without directly stating disapproval. Unlike his deceased father, who had been direct in all his conversations—at times, brutally so.

Gavin held his response as a member of the household staff, a young woman named Alicia with golden brown skin and a calm demeanor, filled his cup with coffee and placed two sugar cubes on the saucer beside him.

"I didn't want to miss breakfast with my favorite lady." He flashed one of his grins and Constance shook her head, a smile of pleasure on her lips.

He had taken his friends—rather, his entourage—to Las Vegas with him. Wherever he went, they went, and once he'd recovered enough to walk again, they started hitting all the hot spots in Seattle, taking short trips to California to dine at celebrity hangouts like Nobu and Tavern, and occasionally flying to Vegas or New York to party.

Compared to some, he had a small group. A male assistant answered his phone and maintained his schedule. He'd had a female assistant at one time, but after sleeping with her, their work relationship got messy and ever since, he only hired men. His two trainers were working with other clients at the moment, but whenever he was ready to start training for another sport, he could call them. They prepared him for any extreme activity he chose to tackle and brought in consultants as needed.

A personal chef traveled with him at all times, and even when Gavin wasn't around, made sure his friends ate hearty meals from the freshest ingredients and drank the finest wines available. Then there was what his family called his "hype team," three guys who didn't really have a job, so he called them assistants. One he'd met in college, the other two surfing in Hawaii. Their job was usually to get in touch with women on his behalf, run errands, and in general co-sign any behavior he chose to indulge in. His family really, really didn't like the hype team.

Constance cut into a piece of asparagus and ate it before speaking again. "I have a busy day today. All week, to be honest. I don't know how I'll fit everything in. I have to find something to wear to the Farnsworth wedding this weekend. I can't believe I let the time creep up on me like this. Then I have to look at more fabric swatches for the house in Nice."

"You're still working on that?" Gavin asked, placing a white napkin across his thighs.

"Unfortunately." Constance shook her head sadly. "I fired the last decorator because he simply didn't understand the look I wanted, and I was getting tired. I found someone new, recommended by Blake's mother. By the way, how was your date?"

"Fine," Gavin said shortly, noting Xavier's smile across the table. He was going to kill Trenton.

"Well, Celeste is back from vacation, so I'm going into the spa to get a facial. This winter weather makes my skin so dry. I think it gets worse every year." She touched a hand to her cheek.

"You look fine, Mother."

Xavier nodded in agreement. "He's right. You don't look a day over thirty-five."

Constance laughed. "*That* I know is an untruth, but I appreciate it." She turned to Gavin. "When will you be leaving? Of course I don't want you to go, but I expected you would be gone by now. You mentioned you would leave after the specialist said you no longer needed therapy."

"I did, but I think I'll stick around a little bit longer."

Xavier held out his cup, signaling Alicia for a refill of coffee. "Really? What prompted that change?"

Gavin shrugged as another servant came in and set a plate of the same breakfast in front of him. "Nothing, really. It's no big deal." An image of Terri entered his mind. Her pouty lips, her flirty smile.

"So you're enjoying your stay?" His mother smiled.

A boulder of guilt settled in Gavin's chest. She probably thought he intended to stay indefinitely, but in all honesty, he wasn't sure how much longer he'd stick around. He had barely made it through the Christmas holidays, the time of year when other people were celebrating and festive, but not him.

His mother, as she always did, flew back to Texas to spend the holidays with her parents. Unable to tolerate remaining in town because he remembered the accident that took his father's life during the same time of year, Gavin went to the family's property in Hawaii with his entourage and a few young women who wanted to party as much as they did. Under the warmth of the Maui sun, he shut out the bad memories between the legs of a set of nubile twins and drank to the bottom of a thousand dollar bottle of limited edition Absolut vodka.

"I'm enjoying my stay," Gavin confirmed to his mother.

"What are you going to do to stay busy?" Constance asked. "You can't play all day now that you're back to one hundred percent."

"I'll find something to get into." There was plenty to keep him busy—his friends, keeping track of his investments…Terri. A little smile touched his lips when he thought of her voluptuous body and sexy little smile.

"Why don't you come into the office?" Xavier suggested.

"Oh, that's a wonderful idea." Constance clasped her hands together and looked from Xavier to Gavin.

"I don't know if—"

"It'll be good for you," Xavier said, a twinkle in his eye.

His brother knew that he didn't want to work at Johnson Enterprises. According to the terms of their father's will, Gavin received a handsome monthly allowance, which allowed him to travel and fund his escapades around the world. Coupled with his own investments, a traditional job was completely unnecessary.

His siblings worked at the company to continue the family legacy and collected multi-million dollar salaries and bonuses for their efforts. At the helm, Cyrus Junior efficiently ran the entire conglomerate as the CEO. Xavier worked directly under him as the COO, a new position he was still learning. Ivy controlled the restaurant group operations as the COO, and Trenton oversaw a large department in his role as senior vice president of sales and marketing.

After avoiding the same fate for years, Gavin was now being railroaded right in front of their mother. All because Xavier knew that if Constance wanted him to spend time at the company, it was going to happen.

"I'll consider it," Gavin said, hoping his smile appeared more genuine than it felt.

"You've been sitting around doing nothing for the past few months. Might as well come in and learn something."

"This is your inheritance," Constance added.

"There's nothing for me to learn," Gavin said. "I don't have the brains for the work they do."

Xavier set his napkin on the table and immediately Alicia came by and swept it up along with his empty plate. "You have a brain and a degree in chemistry."

At one time, Gavin considered becoming a brewmaster and heading up quality control for the company's beer products.

"I think you should do it. You need to learn more about the business, even if you're not going to work at the company." His mother's gaze rested on him as she waited for a response.

Gavin swallowed the tightness in his throat. He didn't want to have anything to do with the company his father had turned into a multi-billion dollar conglomerate. It was simply too painful.

"You'll love it," Xavier said.

Gavin couldn't tell if his enthusiasm was genuine or manufactured, but it was definitely annoying. Xavier himself had been working at the company for only a short time, after abandoning his work in Africa to fall prey to the corporate grind.

"What would I do there? I have no skills."

"You don't have to do anything, dear. You simply have to go in and learn." Constance patted his hand.

"I can learn about the company from home," Gavin said.

Constance dabbed her mouth with a napkin. "I would like you to try."

The words came out quietly but firmly, which meant he didn't have a choice. Accepting directives from her had been instilled in them from the time they were young. He still remembered the first time he understood the severity of disobeying his mother—or disrespecting his mother, as his father called it.

He was eleven, and his father had been furious. While Cyrus Senior didn't often smile, a non-smiling father was a thousand times better than a furious one. Nothing made him more furious than his wife getting upset. He often thought of his father as a raging sea and his mother as a placid lake. Cyrus Senior called her his angel, his sweetheart, his better half.

"I'm the king of this castle and your mother's the queen. If I ever hear you back talk her again, you'll need a whole new set of front teeth. Have I made myself clear?"

"Yes, sir."

"I can't hear you."

"Yes, sir!" Gavin's insides quivered. He'd never seen his father so furious.

"She tells you to do something, you do it. Not later. Not soon. Right then. Now go upstairs and apologize to your mother and then you get that homework done or you can forget about spending time with your friends this weekend—or any other weekend for the rest of the school year. Understand?"

"Yes, sir!"

"All right, I'll try," Gavin said. Not that he had a choice.

He stood, food untouched, appetite gone. "I know I need to look presentable when I go into headquarters, so I'll go home and change. Excuse me."

He didn't wait for a response from either his mother or Xavier, in too much of a hurry to escape.

CHAPTER SEVEN

Gavin pulled the gold sports car into a parking space in front of Terri's building. All week he had looked forward to this evening, but when he called, he didn't tell her where they were going. She tried to pry it out of him, but he only told her to wear a nice dress and heels. His attire for the evening consisted of a black suit jacket and white shirt, no tie, and a black pair of shoes from Italian luxury brand Bruno Magli.

Upon arrival, he planned to go up to her apartment, but she made him wait downstairs for ten minutes—perhaps to make an entrance. If that was the case, she did a fantastic job, exiting the building with her head held high and neck-length hair swept back from her face in a sleek style. Black pumps were on her feet, and she wore a gray, long-sleeved cotton dress that molded to her hourglass figure. The top fit snug over her bosom, the v-neckline dipping low to reveal ample cleavage. As she approached, his eyes had no choice but to idle at the round tops of her breasts.

Terri stopped in front of him, hands on her hips, and cleared her throat. "Ready?" she asked, cocking a brow.

By the confident smile on her face, he suspected that she was not only accustomed to being stared at by men, she enjoyed it. He definitely liked this woman. Maybe a little too much.

"Ready."

She sashayed toward the passenger side of the car. "Are you

looking at my ass?" she asked.

"What do you think?" What a nice ass it was.

His answer made her switch even harder.

This time she stood beside the car and waited for him to open the door. She smelled good. So good he wanted to press his face into her cleavage and lick her skin. It took a monumental effort to resist the urge.

"You doing all right tonight?" Gavin asked as he settled into the driver's seat.

"I'm fine."

"Yes, you are."

Terri wrinkled her nose. "Ew. That was terrible."

"Yeah, it was. And not even original."

"You're better than that."

Gavin started the car but rested an arm on the steering wheel instead of driving off. "You know, the women I usually meet would have giggled and blushed at that comment."

"No way. That was whack."

"You say whatever you're thinking, don't you?"

"Pretty much."

He tossed his head back and laughed. "Terri Slade, you're all right by me." He backed out of the parking space. "Where have you been hiding?"

Crossing her legs in his direction, Terri tilted her body toward him. "I've been right here. You're the one who's been flying around the world, risking life and limb."

"It's not that bad, and hey, you only live once." He swung a right out of the complex and shifted gears so the engine revved on the almost empty roadway.

"What kind of car is this?" She trailed her fingers over the flat screen surface of the lit dashboard.

"A Belleza, a concept car created by a new manufacturer out of Italy."

"Must have cost a fortune."

"Didn't cost me a dime, actually. They shipped it to me this week to try." The computerized vehicle had been programmed to only recognize his fingerprints and voice commands. He requested the gold paint job and black interior be installed before shipping.

"Why would they give you a car? You can afford to buy it."

"You'd be surprised how much free stuff people like me get. Companies give away products for the publicity, and in this case, I got a new toy that no one else has." He glanced at her frowning face. "It's not fair, is it?"

"No, it's not." The white tip of her forefinger lightly scraped the length of the beige scar on the back of his right hand. She only touched that one spot, but every particle of his body vibrated from the sensation, and he tightened his hand on the wheel to contain his reaction.

"What happened there?" she asked.

Gavin slowed to a halt at a traffic light and ran a finger over the same spot. "Stupid accident free soloing up El Sendero Luminoso."

Terri stared at him blankly. "I don't remember you tweeting about that. You're going to have to tell me what free soloing is, because I have no clue."

"That trip happened a while back. El Sendero Luminoso is a rock climb in Mexico. Basically, I climbed it without ropes or safety gear."

"Um, that sounds ridiculously dangerous. Why would anyone do that?"

"The rush." Just the thought sent a tiny blast of adrenaline speeding through his veins. He turned in time to see her forehead bunch into a knot.

"And extremely dangerous," she said. "I don't understand why you do that to yourself."

"Don't get me wrong. Most of the time, I use equipment, but every now and again…" He shrugged, and when the traffic light changed, they started moving.

"Every now and again, you want to tempt fate? Clearly you're not afraid of dying."

"No point in living your life in fear. We could die in this car on the way to dinner."

"Seems like you're more likely to get hurt your way, though. If you slip or a bird flies in your face or something, that's it." She snapped her fingers.

"Death is always unpredictable."

"What's the most dangerous thing you've ever done?" Terri asked.

"That's like asking a parent to name their favorite child."

She laughed, a throaty, delicious sound that pulled his eyes from the road to examine her features. Bright eyes. Upturned, sensual mouth. Before the night ended, he intended to kiss her.

"Okay, Mr. Difficult, what's *one* of the most dangerous things you've ever done?"

"Let's see..." Gavin rubbed a hand across his chin. "Aside from solo climbing, maybe free diving." She frowned and he went on to explain. "Basically, you take a deep breath, dive hundreds of feet underwater, and hold your breath until you get back to the surface. You lower your heart rate and push your body to the limit. Scientists used to think the deepest we could dive and survive was about a hundred feet or so, otherwise our lungs would collapse. Today, people dive three hundred, four hundred, five hundred feet, without oxygen. It's really incredible."

She stared at him. "You weren't kidding when you said dangerous activities excite you. It's obvious in your face, and I can hear the excitement in your voice."

"Free diving is like no other feeling. The biggest danger is blacking out."

"Oh, is that all? Maybe you're a little brain dead from doing something so dangerous."

Gavin laughed at the no-holds-barred commentary. Terri spoke with no filter—genuine and refreshingly candid.

"It's hard to explain. I'm not saying you should try free diving, but there's something to be said for having that type of control over your body. And below the surface of the ocean, the silence, the beauty…" He shook his head. "It's amazing."

Even talking about free-diving relaxed him. Few activities brought him that kind of peace, allowing him to escape the stress and expectations of being Gavin Johnson.

They continued the conversation until he pulled the car to a halt in the parking lot of the Seattle Space Needle. Terri turned sharply in his direction. "You didn't tell me we were coming *here*. I've lived in Seattle for three years and never visited."

"We're going to rectify that tonight."

Her eyes narrowed. "You knew, didn't you? How?"

"Alannah," Gavin answered.

They exited the vehicle into the frosty air and walked toward a back entrance to avoid the general public. The door opened as they approached, and Gavin took Terri's hand. He didn't usually hold hands, but it seemed like the right thing to do. Her skin was soft and warm, and he liked the texture of her smaller hand. She didn't appear to mind, looking up at him sideways and giving one of her saucy smiles.

"Are we going up to the observation deck?" she asked, breathless with excitement.

Gavin nodded. "After dinner."

The elevator took them five hundred feet in the air to the SkyCity Restaurant, where a slow tune tapped out on piano keys welcomed them. The hostess, a young woman with brunette hair and sparkling brown eyes, met them at the entrance.

"Hello, Mr. Johnson, Ms. Slade. Welcome to SkyCity Restaurant. Your table is ready. This way, please."

Terri's mouth fell open when she saw all the empty tables. "Don't tell me you rented out the entire place?"

"I wanted complete privacy." The shock in her face was the exact expression he'd hoped to see.

"Are you trying to impress me?" she whispered, pressing closer to his side.

He looked down into her soft brown eyes, his heart thudding a little faster at the warmth evident there. Again, he ached to kiss her—the smooth full lips, the pert nose—but not yet.

"Is it working?" he asked.

There was that flirty smile again. "Yes, it's working."

CHAPTER EIGHT

Terri deferred to Gavin for dinner and he chose their meals. For appetizers, he ordered crab cakes with avocado cream and mango relish, as well as a stonefruit gazpacho with jalapeño honey. He insisted she try the seafood and asked for the wild King Salmon for her with a mushroom cream sauce and ahi tuna for himself. They took their time eating and lingering over each bite, and the hours slipped by unnoticed. The meal came to a close with two cups of coffee, crème brûlée for him, chocolate pots de crème for her, and vibrant conversation.

"Bullshit," Gavin said, in the midst of a debate about men and women. He pointed his spoon at her. "Deny it all you want, but women use sex as a weapon, and the silent treatment is the precursor to no sex."

"I won't deny that some—"

"All."

"—*some* women use sex as a weapon. But did it ever occur to you that we don't want to have sex if we're mad?"

"At least tell us why you're mad," Gavin shot back.

Terri sighed, the smile on her face a clear indication she was amused at his vehemence. "Why do we have to spoon-feed you everything when we give you so many hints?"

"That's the problem right there. Men don't like hints. Tell us directly what we've done wrong."

"You know when you've done something wrong. You're just being dickheads."

"I'm telling you, we really don't know. And that figure-it-out-guessing-game is bullshit."

Terri rolled her eyes. "Yeah, right."

"You know what I do when a woman gives me the silent treatment?"

"What?"

Terri spooned chocolate into her mouth, and Gavin lost his train of thought, stomach muscles tense as he watched her slowly drag the spoon between her full lips. All night he watched her eat with the innate sensuality she exhibited in everything she did—her laugh, her walk, the way she slid her gaze to him across the table and looked at him from beneath long lashes.

He cleared his throat and straightened his jacket, suddenly hot under the collar. "I leave when I get the silent treatment."

"You do not."

"Sure do. Exit stage left and keep it moving."

"You've actually done that?" She raised a skeptical eyebrow.

"Did it last summer. I was in Acapulco with friends, and a woman hanging out with us—fun, pretty—started acting funky one night. Gave me the silent treatment. I left her there."

Her eyes widened. "No, you didn't."

"I did. I left a plane ticket for her at the front desk and took off. I don't put up with that nonsense from the women I date, I'm sure as hell not going to put up with it from a woman I'm just fu—er, having fun with."

"Mhmm."

Terri's mouth fixed into a provocative moue, causing an immediate nudge in his trousers. No doubt about it, he had to find out if her mouth tasted as delicious as it looked.

She placed a finger between her teeth and narrowed her eyes. "You've never been in love."

Gavin sat back in the chair. "What makes you say that?"

"Because a man who's in love is in tune with his woman's needs and feelings. He knows when his woman is upset, no matter what she says, and tries to fix the problem."

"Women are too difficult." He scraped the last of the crème brûlée from the bowl.

Leaning across the table, Terri gave him a stunning view of her delectable bosom. "Have you ever been in love?"

Gavin dragged his eyes from her chest with difficulty. "Is this a trick question?"

"It's a simple question. Have you?"

He slid the spoon and empty bowl to the side. "Once, a long time ago."

"Oh, do tell." Terri rested her chin on her hand.

Gavin sipped his coffee. "You really want to hear this?"

"Yes."

Blowing out a deep breath, he folded his arms on the table and prepared to tell a story he hadn't shared in a long time. "We met at Stanford. Her name was Serwa, and she was a year ahead of me, the daughter of a high-ranking official in the Ghanaian government. We had a lot of fun, but her life was already mapped out. Her family arranged for her to marry a man back home—someone in politics. My money and family name didn't matter. She knew what was expected of her and was too afraid to go against her family's wishes. When she graduated, she went home and married him."

Terri's eyes softened on him. "What did you do after she left?"

Thinking back, the pain of rejection crushed him. "I just said, screw it. I didn't go back to school."

Terri's mouth fell open. "You left school? Just like that?"

"Just like that."

"What did your parents say?"

"My mother tried to be understanding, my siblings thought I was crazy, and my father was livid."

Cyrus Senior used to drive him nuts, constantly on his case about finishing school and demanding to know what he wanted to do with his life. Gavin used to wish he would leave him alone, but he'd give anything to hear his father's booming voice. Even if it were filled with disappointment. Just one more time.

"Did you ever see her again?"

Terri's voice interrupted his thoughts and forced him back to the present.

"One year I, uh…heard she was in Mozambique the same time I was, so I pulled a few strings and got myself invited to the same political function. She looked beautiful, just like I remembered." Absentmindedly, he dragged his forefinger back and forth across the tablecloth. "By then, I had finished my degree and we discussed our experience at Stanford and the jobs some of our old friends had landed after graduation. She introduced me to her husband and shared pictures of their son. To be honest, she looked and sounded happy, and I realized she'd moved on, and so should I."

Serwa had been his first love and the only woman he ever said "I love you" to. Even though losing her pained him, he had fond memories of their time together.

Terri's hand crept across the white table cloth and her finger touched his, the same one moving back and forth in agitation. The sensation of her finger was surprisingly soothing. He playfully tugged her fingertip and she smiled.

"If it was meant to be, it would have happened," she said.

"Yeah." Gavin nodded. They were quiet for a while, then he said, "Your turn. You've had me talking way more than my normal. Have you ever been in love?"

She pulled back her hand, and right away, he missed the contact.

"Huh?"

"You heard me."

"I plead the fifth." She avoided his eyes, looking out at the nighttime view.

"Come on, Miss it's-never-serious. There's a story there somewhere."

Terri covered her face. "Ugh. I do not like to share."

"I know, but all that changes tonight. Come on, spill the details."

"Fine." She took an exaggerated deep breath and rolled her eyes. "I've been in love twice."

"Had your heart broken twice?" Gavin asked.

She stared down into her coffee and didn't answer right away. "Something like that."

"What happened?" Gavin prodded.

She met his gaze. "The first time, I was young and he was a lot older."

"How young and how much older?" Gavin pressed.

She bit the corner of her lip, hesitating.

"No judgment," he promised.

"I was sixteen and he was twenty-five."

"*Okay*. What did your parents do?"

"My parents were dead by then."

"I'm so sorry."

Terri brushed away the comment. "My brother and I ended up with a very strict uncle and his family. He didn't say much when I decided to leave and move in with my boyfriend. I think by then they were tired of my acting out."

"What about school?"

"I finished. He was a truck driver and gone a lot, so I drove his car to school most days. When he was in town, he dropped me off and picked me up. My friends thought I was so cool and grown. Hell, I thought I was cool and grown. We were together for six years, if you could believe it. For the most part, we had a great relationship. Our biggest bone of contention was that he never introduced me to his parents."

"*In six years?*"

"What can I say, I was young and stupid. Oh, we actually did have another problem. I wanted to get married. I tried not to pressure him, but I didn't want to be his live-in forever. Anyway, he kept coming up with excuses for why we couldn't get married." She took a deep breath. "Then I found out he was legally married to another woman in Alabama."

"Ah, man."

"Yep." Black lashes lowered to her round cheeks, temporarily hiding her thoughts from his probing gaze. She swallowed hard. "I made some mistakes over the years."

It was Gavin's turn to reach for her hand, gently grasping her fingers. "What happened with the other guy?"

"He was a *big* mistake. One that I don't even want to get into." She waved away the question, laughing shakily, eyes dodging his. "Anyway, that's it."

"Tell me about the second guy."

Terri shook her head vehemently. "No way. I've told you enough." She still didn't look at him, and he squeezed her fingers, forcing her gaze upward.

"I thought we were sharing. You're keeping secrets."

"If I tell you everything, you won't find me interesting." She tossed a saucy grin his way, but her eyes betrayed an abundance of pain before she looked away.

A compelling story existed behind the downcast eyes, and Gavin sensed the difficulty to share didn't only stem from a broken heart. There was much more involved, and an unexpected need to protect her burned inside him.

"I think I'll always find you interesting."

He threaded his fingers through hers and stared down at their intertwined digits—his long and blunt, hers short and slender. His skin a chocolate color, hers a lighter caramel.

"It's beautiful up here," Terri murmured, staring out the window.

"Let's go up to the observation deck," Gavin suggested, going along with the abrupt change of topic.

If she didn't want to talk about her past anymore, he wouldn't push. He promised her a good time tonight, and if she enjoyed herself, maybe he could see her again. And he really wanted to see her again. He was drawn to her. Not only her physical features but her vivacious personality.

Terri bit the corner of her bottom lip. "I have a confession to make. I'm a little afraid of heights."

"Not tonight, you're not." Gavin stood and pulled her along with him.

Because of the lateness of the hour, only a few people strolled the deck. A family of six went by and a couple, arm-in-arm, stood at the railing overlooking the city. Before they stepped outside, Terri squeezed her eyes shut and stood ramrod straight, refusing to budge. Gavin stood behind her, his pelvis pressed against her bottom and one arm around her midsection. He eased forward and nudged her along with him, out onto the observation deck where cold air greeted them.

"You're perfectly safe," he murmured in her ear.

Her breathing kicked up and she let out a low whimper, but they continued the march forward.

"This is crazy," she said, a little breathless, eyes still closed.

"It'll be worth it. You'll love the view from here."

"I saw it perfectly fine inside," she retorted.

They arrived at the edge and Gavin placed each of her hands on the cold steel that ran the periphery of the Space Needle. Her fingers immediately curled around the railing.

"Open," he instructed.

Terri peeked through the slits of her eyes and then promptly shut them again.

"Come on, you're safe. You're on solid ground, and I have my arm around you. Nothing will happen to you while you're with me."

She let out a little whimper as she looked at the scenery and leaned back against him. The hand around her waist tightened. "Nothing to be afraid of," he murmured. She smelled so good, he ran his nose along her hairline.

Terri gripped the railing so tight, he thought she might be able to snap the steel. "It's...nice." Her eyes spanned the nightscape of the Emerald City.

"Real nice, isn't it?"

"Yes." She laughed, a hesitant sound, but a laugh nonetheless. A wave of cool air brushed over them and she shivered slightly. Gavin removed his jacket and draped it over her shoulders, and she turned to look at him, brown eyes sparkling. "Thank you."

"My pleasure." His thumb brushed the hair at her temple. "Absolutely beautiful."

A sultry expression came into her eyes. "Are you talking

about the view or me?"

"Definitely you," Gavin replied, without a hint of hesitation. The arm circling her waist pulled her tighter against him, compelling her to press into his heated groin. Bringing his mouth closer to hers, Gavin said, "I probably shouldn't tell you this, but I looked forward to tonight with a ridiculous amount of anticipation, and I haven't been able to stop looking at you all night."

"What are you going to do about it?" she whispered, tilting her head back.

The invitation was unmistakable, and Gavin dipped his head to taste her mouth. Finally. Her soft lips yielded to him right away, and the arm circling her waist tightened, pressing her more firmly against him. Gavin deepened the kiss, dragging sweetness from her soft lips, the honeyed caress of mouth to mouth causing desire to swell in his groin.

Without thought to the environment or the public spectacle they might make, he marched her backward into the wall—keeping their lips sealed together. Terri kissed him back as if she couldn't get enough—her mouth pliable and intoxicating, generously giving as much as she took.

Gavin grabbed a handful of hair and forced her mouth wide, overwhelmed by the need to claim her, to seize every ounce of pleasure offered by the soft curves pressed into his hardening body. He thrust his tongue between her lips, imagining another part of his anatomy sliding into the moist opening.

The kiss ended when she tore her mouth from his. Wide-eyed, she stared up at him, breasts heaving in a captivating display of arousal. She must feel it too—the out-of-control desire that overtook his brain and made him want to lift her against the wall to feed the hunger she unleashed with only a kiss.

The tip of her tongue dragged across her swollen lips, and Gavin's eyes followed the movement. He groaned inwardly at the tempting moisture left behind.

"I want to spend the night with you," he rasped.

A knowing smile slid across her mouth. A more in-control Terri dragged a finger down his chest to his waist, leaving a line of heat in the wake of her caress. A come-hither look invaded her eyes, and she teased him with a flirty glance from beneath her lashes. "I want to spend the night with you, too."

His heart almost came through his chest, but Gavin tamped down the jubilation and kept a cool head. "I hear a 'but' in that sentence."

Terri tilted her face up to his, eyes soft and inviting under the lights of the deck. "What are your expectations?"

He braced his hands on the wall and barricaded her in. "I don't expect anything. We're both just looking for a good time, right?"

"And if I say no?" she asked, keeping her voice soft.

Gavin swallowed, shunning the ugly face of disappointment that crept into the conversation. "I'd be lying if I said I wouldn't be disappointed." He wanted to get closer. He wanted to get *in* her.

"I wouldn't want you to be disappointed," she cooed.

"I wouldn't want to be disappointed."

Gavin waited for her response. Seconds dragged by, slower than molasses on an upward sloping gradient.

Finally, Terri brought her face very close to his, and the teasing light disappeared from her eyes. "Then let's go." Her breath brushed his lips, and the muscles in his arms tightened to rigid bands.

She took his hand and they walked away from the wall, toward the interior of the building. But despite the anticipation of finally getting between those thick thighs, and the thought that he'd get to fill his hands with her lush breasts, Gavin hesitated, standing just inside the doorway.

Terri twisted around, eyes questioning.

For the first time in his life, Gavin considered turning down a woman who agreed to have sex. He felt uncertainty despite the familiar scenario. Not because he didn't want Terri, but rather because an unfamiliar emotion coiled through his gut that he couldn't yet identify.

"Are you sure? We don't have to do this," he said.

"Are you turning me down, Mr. Johnson?" Her eyes smiled into his.

His gaze ran over her voluptuous figure, clearly outlined in the gray dress beneath the jacket thrown over her shoulders. He didn't think there was a man alive who could turn her down. "Not at all. I just want you to be sure."

"I'm positive. Don't you want me?" Terri placed a hand on her hip, the pose showing off the lines of her body and lifting her hard-to-miss breasts to advantage.

"Sweetheart, I've been wanting you since the night I saw you at Trent's."

"Then tonight, I'm all yours, but tonight only. I just want to have a good time. Can you give me a good time?"

The teasing light disappeared from her eyes, and the vulnerability in her face cut through him. He wanted to delve deeper and examine the reasons why such a beautiful woman would place such restrictions on her relationships. But he didn't.

"I can do that," Gavin promised.

The overt sensuality he had come to expect from Terri reappeared. With her voice low, husky, and inviting, she said, "Let's go to your place."

"Too crowded. Let's go to yours." He wanted her all to himself, with no distractions.

"I have a teeny-tiny apartment," she warned.

He stepped closer, rubbing his thumb over the skin of her hand and wondering if her entire body felt this silky. "You have a bed?"

"Of course."

"That's all we need."

CHAPTER NINE

Terri mercilessly teased Gavin on the ride to her apartment, running her hand up and down his leg and massaging his inner thigh. She took delight in driving him crazy and edged her hand higher and higher until she eventually brushed his crotch and the bulge nestled there.

The car swerved to the left and Gavin grabbed her hand. "Behave yourself if you don't want me to wreck this car."

Pouting but quietly amused, Terri withdrew her hand and crossed her legs. Gavin turned an eye to the length of thigh revealed when the hem of the dress hoisted higher, but he didn't say a word, and she behaved herself the rest of the ride. Once they reached her apartment, however, she stepped out of the vehicle and grabbed the waistband of his trousers. Pulling him closer, she pressed the entire length of her body against him.

He was hard as a rock. Her skin flushed with excitement, hot for him, craving him.

Gavin grabbed her ass and forced her against the cool metal. Dropping his lips to the curve of her neck, he licked a delightfully moist path from her collarbone up to her ear. "You're gonna make me fuck you right here."

His warm breath fanned her skin, and she shivered despite the cool weather. "It would add an element of excitement," she whispered.

Terri tugged the skin of his jaw between her teeth and sucked. Tasty. She smoothed the bite with a flick of her tongue, trembling when his thumb skimmed the underside of her breasts. Her nipples pouted, hard and straining against her bra.

Long fingers climbed into her hair and his mouth seized hers. Moist and commanding. His tongue invaded her mouth, marking the interior with bold strokes that had her clinging to his strong neck. Goodness, he was a great kisser. With lips like his, it was impossible not to be. His mouth demanded her submission and she gave in, melting against him.

Hands on her hips, Gavin dragged her against his body until his erection nestled tight against her belly. An answering throb in her loins, Terri rubbed against him, the intense ache making her weak, turning her limbs to liquid, and her thoughts to mush.

Gavin pulled back and Terri lifted onto the tips of her shoes and kept his lips trapped against hers, a fierce wave of hunger chasing away restraint. His firm hands on her upper arms finally penetrated the fog her brain had become, and she reluctantly released his mouth with a moist pop.

Head spinning, she took an unsteady step back. It was only a kiss—a disorienting, breath-stealing kiss. One that left her out of her depth and, like the kiss atop the Space Needle, knocked her sideways and clouded her brain.

Sex should be nothing more than a biological release. At worst, a way to pass the time and eliminate boredom. But the way Gavin touched her, the strong feelings he evoked, Terri knew neither of those ideologies applied in this instance.

He grasped the back of her neck and used his thumb to rub the underside of her jaw. The gentle back and forth strokes provoked a quivering sensation in her skin, and the heat in his eyes all but forced her to melt into a pool at his feet.

"Let's go," he said, and he took her hand.

Terri followed on shaky knees, up the walk to the front of her building.

Maintain control.

The reminder barely registered in the cells of her brain. She tried to remember the dire consequences that resulted when she didn't have control, when she allowed emotion to rule her actions. But coherent thought had long since evaporated and her only choice was to follow where he led.

Mumbling a greeting as they passed one of her neighbors on the climb up the stairs, Terri and Gavin made it to the third floor and seconds later were inside her tiny apartment. She walked into the bedroom with Gavin close behind her and tossed his jacket on the five-drawer bureau against the wall.

The lamp beside the bed cast a warm glow in the room, and he loomed above her in the near darkness. Under the white dress shirt, his chest moved up and down with each labored breath.

Gavin removed the gray dress, dragging it up and over her body and tossing it to the carpet. When he finished, Terri stood in the middle of the floor as he walked a circle around her and stopped behind her back. A kiss on the side of her neck followed, and she inhaled deeply, leaning into him, relishing the moist pressure of his mouth.

Another kiss followed to her right shoulder blade, where a red heart with the word *Love* and an arrow through it was tattooed onto her skin.

Terri curled her toes and leaned back for more.

"You are so damn sexy," Gavin whispered. "I can't even express to you just how sexy you really are."

Two fingers traced the edge of the lacy black cheeky that left half her bottom exposed. Terri arched her back and moaned, despising the way he teased her with such a lightweight touch. The mere brush of his hand made her skin come alive. No one had ever made her feel this way before. *No one.*

Gavin unhooked her bra and let it slide down her arms to the floor. Then he peeled the panty down her hips. But instead of letting it fall, he followed it down, easing it past her thighs, then her knees to her ankles.

Terri looked over her shoulder to find him crouched behind her. She couldn't even move to step out of the underwear. She was so frozen in place, watching as he dipped his tongue in the dimple at the bottom of her spine and traced the line of red and yellow roses on a vine etched into her skin.

He rose to his full height and Terri turned to face him. "Your turn," she whispered.

He removed his shirt while she undid his belt and dragged down the zipper of his pants. In no time at all, he was naked, and it was Terri's turn to stare. He stood in place and let her smooth her palms over his dark skin, impressed at the power of the rigid pecs and the coiled strength of his abs. His body was amazing. Tight legs dusted with curly hairs down to his calves. Firm muscular thighs held inches apart with his hard shaft standing straight up and nestled in a thatch of thick black hair.

"Like what you see?" Gavin asked.

"Yes." Terri breathed the answer and stepped closer, folding her arms around his neck and dragging his head down to hers.

Gavin lowered onto his butt to the bed and pulled her down to straddle his thighs. The kiss started slow but soon transformed into a tangle of tongues. Intertwining, they greedily lapped at each other's mouth. All the while, he caressed her hips, dragged his hands along her thighs, and trailed his fingers up her back. As if he couldn't stop touching her.

His mouth dropped to her neck and Terri's head fell back, giving him the access he needed to offer her more pleasure. Breathlessly, she clung to him as his mouth traveled lower until he licked her erect nipples. He showered her breasts with attention. Kissing. Nipping the hard peaks with his teeth and forcing her breaths to stumble as they left her throat.

She moaned and held onto him tighter, forcing his face deeper into her breasts.

"Gavin," she whispered in his ear. His mouth felt so good, and he was just getting started.

His hand slid south between them and found the swollen evidence of her desire.

"How do you want it tonight, Terri? You want to make love or you want to be fucked?"

He looked into her eyes and she could barely hold eye

contact because he continued to stroke between her legs. His fingers dipped into the slick wetness and his nostrils flared. Terri's hips bucked against his hand, anxious for him to fully possess her.

"Fuck me, Gavin. Please."

His jaw hardened with resolve and he lifted off the bed with her in his arms.

He flipped her onto her stomach and as she watched, sheathed himself in a condom.

"Your wish is my command," he said in a rough voice, forcing her legs wide.

She didn't have time to settle before he was inside of her. Terri gasped at the initial thrust—the power in it, the way he filled her up and slid deep. With firm hands on her thighs, Gavin kept her spread out before him and started to pump his hips.

"Harder. Fuck me harder," Terri begged, her voice shaking, her fingers clawing the bedding.

She buried her face in the rumpled sheets and arched her back, reveling in the bounce of his hips, each punishing thrust against her ass shaking the bed and making it squeak. Every time he withdrew, her body begged for his, forcing contact with the upward tilt of her hips.

Gavin's tongue explored the damp skin of her back as he drilled into her. And she edged toward an orgasm, beads of sweat pearling on her forehead as the climax came within reach.

Then he pulled out.

The shock of it was so jarring—like someone yanking the chair out from under her when she went to sit down—that she cried out in dismay.

Angry, Terri turned on him. "What the—"

"Not yet," Gavin said, cocky in his sexual prowess. "I want to watch you come. I want to see those beautiful eyes roll back."

He pushed her onto her back and fell between her legs again, sliding in with ease. Terri bit her bottom lip and whimpered as he filled her up, stretching her sex with the width of his length.

His hips started moving again and Terri cupped her breasts, big and overflowing in her own hands. She squeezed them together and pinched the nipples. As Gavin watched, his movements became irregular and accelerated. His eyes darkened to almost copper. Clenching his teeth, he thrust even harder.

He propped one of her legs onto his shoulder and she lifted the ankle of the other foot to rest on his firm behind. Clenching his teeth, Gavin pumped harder and faster, strain around his neck and shoulders.

Squeezing her butt cheeks, Terri rocked her hips in a display of wild need and placed her hands on his sturdy shoulders to let him have his way. Gavin crushed his face into her bouncing breasts, his tongue and teeth fastening onto one and sucking with delicious consistency. He tormented her sensitive flesh, plucking at the pebbled peaks.

"Look at me," he rasped.

At first, she didn't. She simply couldn't. It was too intimate.

"Look at me!" he demanded, dragging her hips high with one hand and forcing her gaze to his. They locked eyes as their bodies moved together. In sync, as one.

Something inside her shifted as she stared into his eyes. Her throat tightened from a block of emotion that seized her. Weak and helpless, she writhed beneath him as she chased an orgasm.

Before she could think about what was happening to her, a shattering climax claimed all thought, seized her muscles, and sent her spiraling into ecstasy.

****

Terri stretched and lifted her head to see Gavin sprawled beside her on the bed on his stomach. Her gaze traveled over the slope of his back to his ridiculously tight behind, which came as no surprise since the rest of his body was just as muscular. She wanted to reach out and touch him again, perhaps rouse him for another round. But after two rounds, she figured he was probably done for the night. Any more than that was asking for a lot, even from a man in such peak physical condition.

She slipped from the bed.

"Where are you going?" Gavin asked. He'd lifted his head to watch her. His gaze roamed over her body in such a way that she almost felt it as a caress.

Terri reached for the door to the bathroom. "To take a shower. I guess you'll be leaving soon?"

"Why do you say that?" He seemed genuinely confused.

"Because we're done for the night."

"Done for the night." Gavin sat up and swung his legs over the side of the bed. "Because...?"

"This isn't serious. No expectations," she reminded him.

"I see."

His eyes traveled over her again, and Terri's grip, which she had maintained on the doorknob as a sort of anchor, tightened.

"Is that the way it usually works for you?" Gavin asked.

Terri shrugged. "More or less. I prefer to sleep alone, so..."

"You prefer once a man does his business, he leaves."

"It's not personal, but I thought we were on the same page."

"Oh, we are."

Relieved, Terri relaxed. "Good. I'm glad we understand each other."

"Absolutely." His mouth said the right words, but his body appeared tense.

He was probably accustomed to women hanging all over him and begging for his time, but that wasn't her style.

She cleared her throat. "So...thanks. I had a good time." That was an honest statement. With delicious food, great conversation, and even better sex, tonight marked the best night she'd had in a long time.

"I had a good time, too." Gavin didn't move or make the slightest motion to get up.

With nothing more to say, Terri entered the small bathroom. She stood over the pedestal sink and tamed her rumpled hair by smoothing her fingers over the strands. Gavin would be gone when she came out of the shower. The way she preferred.

She strained her ear, listening for movement but couldn't hear any. Deciding he probably just moved quietly, Terri donned a shower cap and climbed into the tub. She pulled across the colorful paisley shower curtain and turned on the water. The massaging showerhead—a splurge she added a month after moving in—pelted her body with a lukewarm spray. The mild scent of oatmeal and almond filled the bathroom as she rubbed the bath bar into a washcloth.

All of a sudden, the shower curtain was yanked aside. She jumped back in shock and watched as Gavin climbed into the tub with her.

"What are you doing?" she demanded, clutching the washcloth to her chest.

Water bounced off his back and spattered around them. "You really think I'm a chump, don't you?"

"No, I don't."

He yanked the curtain closed. "Like I told you before, I'd really like to know what kind of men you're used to. From what I can tell, they A, don't know how to treat a lady. B, expect you to put out every time they do you a favor. And C, obviously let you do whatever you want. That's not going to work with me."

Sex, then kick them out. Her system had worked fine the past few years, and that's how she maintained control—the first rule of surviving on her own.

"You know what, you need to leave. We are done for the night."

The flash of anger in his eyes and rigid set to his sensual mouth suggested otherwise. "We're done for the night?"

"Yes."

He stepped closer in the already tiny space. "After all that mind-blowing sex?"

Terri swallowed at the thought of him hitting it from the back the first time around, so good and hard she saw stars. Then there was the second time, when he licked her sex and sucked her clit with such dedication that she almost passed out.

"Yes, we're done," she croaked. She did not sound convincing at all.

"So I should just leave?" Water dribbled down his dark skin in an enticing display.

"That would be best."

Gavin yanked away the washcloth she'd been clutching like a shield. He rubbed more soap into it, the circular movement of his hand oddly erotic. "I need to wash up first."

"You need to go home and wash up in your own bathroom."

"Matter of fact, I think I'll help you," he said, ignoring her order.

"I don't need—" Terri gasped as he twisted her around to face away from him. "I don't need any help," she insisted.

"Don't move." Gavin massaged her back and shoulders with the soapy washcloth. Not missing an inch of skin, reaching around to push the rag over her breasts and engorged nipples.

"Gavin," she gasped, hands splayed out on the cold tile as she strived to stay upright.

"I'm helping you." His voice vibrated close to her ear and contained a thickness that betrayed his burgeoning need.

He tended to her entire body, rubbing between her legs and over her engorged lower lips. She widened her legs to accommodate his movements, grinding against the pressure of his hand until she neared the brink. Cruelly, he abandoned the apex of her thighs and dragged his hand over her hips. She expelled a wail of frustration and closed her hands into tight fists against the wall.

Terri no longer cared that she expected him to leave. She no longer cared that she should have kicked him out of the bathroom. All she cared about was getting the orgasm he had viciously snatched from her loins.

"You're sure we're done?" he asked huskily.

She couldn't reply, feeling extremely vulnerable as he ran the cloth between her ass cheeks. She inhaled deeply and, unable to help herself, stretched onto her toes and bowed her back into the drag of the rough cloth.

"You sure, baby? You're sure we're done?" he asked again. Now he was just mocking her.

Gavin slipped his bare hand around to the front again and stroked the slick folds of her sex. The length of his thick erection pressed into her backside and the friction from the front and the pressure from the back created an erotic combination that brought her dangerously close to the edge. Gavin squeezed her clit between his finger and thumb and she free-fell. Legs shaking, she cried out his name. Gasping. If not for the cold tile at her cheek and being wedged between Gavin's pelvis and hand, she would have collapsed.

His hands cupped her raw, aching breasts from behind and he lowered his lips to her ear.

"We're not done yet."

CHAPTER TEN

He couldn't stop thinking about her.

Gavin tossed the blue Mont Blanc pen onto the cherry wood desk filled with files and reports and stood abruptly from the chair. How was he supposed to cram information into his brain about the company when all he could think about was honey-dark skin, husky cries of completion, and quite frankly, the best sex he'd ever had? And he'd had a *lot* of sex over the years.

He paced in front of the wall-length window in the temporary office at Johnson Enterprises, offered to visiting executives from other corporations or one of the company's other locations. Though basic, he had everything he needed—a large desk, guest chairs, currently empty file cabinets, a credenza, and a small sitting area complete with a low-to-the-floor glass table flanked by two solid brown sofas.

Rubbing a hand across his jaw as he stared over the tops of commercial buildings to the Space Needle in the distance, Gavin contemplated the untenable situation with Terri. The date went well, they both succumbed to mind-blowing orgasms all night, but the next morning, she stuck to her decision of one night only and practically kicked him from the apartment with the heel of her shoe.

He was Gavin Goddamn Johnson. Rich beyond belief and not bad-looking, even if he did say so himself. So why the hell couldn't he convince Terri to see him again? Twice, he called and left a message, but she didn't acknowledge his calls. Not even to send a text to demand he stop ringing her phone.

Was it because of her not-serious relationship with Dumbo?

Why him and not me? Gavin thought irritably.

At a knock on his door, he swung around. "Come in."

Trenton strolled in. "How's it going?"

"Good." Gavin went over to the desk and picked up a bound report, an encyclopedia of facts and figures that summarized everything about the family businesses. Pages and pages of data on how many liters of beer each brewery produced, the various brews now in production, and the ones that failed. Information on their restaurants, headed up by his twin sister, Ivy, included menus and details about the casual dining chain and the higher-end restaurant. "Fascinating reading." He dropped the thick document onto the desk.

"Hey, you're the one who wanted to learn about the company. That gives you the best overview."

"Actually, I didn't want to learn about the company. Xavier railroaded me into this, and I still have to get him back for it." Gavin frowned and fell onto the chair and crossed his ankle over his knee.

"You seem extra cranky. What's the problem?" Trenton crossed the room and stood behind the chairs.

"No problem. Everything's great." Gavin repositioned a paperweight on a blue dossier. "Have you talked to Terri lately?"

"Er, no. And I never talk to Terri unless Alannah's around. Why?"

"Nothing." Gavin lifted the glass weight and dropped it with unnecessary force onto the file.

Trenton braced his hands on the back of a guest chair. "I already know things didn't go well."

Gavin sat up. "How do you know that? Did Alannah tell you something?"

Trenton chuckled. "Nothing like that. I just know because this is the second time this week you've randomly asked me about Terri."

Gavin relaxed and tilted back the chair. "Yeah, all right.

Whatever."

"Are you going to tell me what happened between the two of you?"

"We went out."

"And you haven't heard from her since? She's not taking your calls?"

Disliking the line of questioning, Gavin shifted in the chair. "It's not a big deal. She's just another woman."

Trenton straightened and rubbed his chin. "You trying to convince me or yourself?"

"I'm not trying to convince you or myself of anything."

"Oh my, my," Trenton said, laughing. He folded his arms across his chest.

"What's so funny?" Gavin demanded.

"You. She's doing to you what you do to women all the time."

"Don't you mean *we*?"

"I'm a changed man." Trenton stuffed his hands into his pockets. "Look, Terri's Alannah's friend, and I'm not going to pretend I know her well enough to have a good gauge of her personality, but I've seen enough to know she keeps men eating out of her hand and discards them when she's done. There are very few women who treat men the way she does."

"Stop talking in parables. What's your point?"

"My point is, she's not like Sharon or Blake or probably any other woman you've ever met. She's the fuck 'em and leave 'em type. She's not the kind looking for love. If you want my advice—"

"I don't recall asking for it."

"She's the female version of you. Have your fun and move on. If you're looking for anything deeper, you're barking up the wrong tree."

"Thank you, Confucius, but I'm not looking to marry her. We barely know each other. We went on one date." Two, if he counted the night he had her SUV detailed and bought her two slices of pizza. "As you pointed out, I'm the fuck 'em and leave 'em type, too. Just because I asked about the woman doesn't mean I'm in love with her."

Trenton threw up his hands. "My mistake." He strolled across the room but paused at the door. "Oh, I came by to tell you there's a special set at The Underground on Sunday night. A group of female musicians by the name of Played Out. You probably remember them from your Stanford days."

"I do. Five women, if I'm not mistaken."

"That's them. Seems they decided to abandon their careers and revive the band to see how far they can take it. They're on a west coast tour, hitting clubs like The Underground. Alannah and I are going to hear them. You interested in coming out?"

Gavin twisted the paperweight around and around on the file. "No, thanks. I might fly down to LA for the weekend and hit a club or two with the guys."

"All right, then." Trenton opened the door and then snapped his fingers. "I almost forgot. Terri's going to be there."

Gavin straightened in the chair.

"Yeah, that's what I thought," Trenton said, smug grin in place. "See you Sunday," he tossed over his shoulder on the way out.

"Asshole," Gavin said to himself, smiling.

****

"Hi, honey!" Terri hopped into Alannah's black Lexus LS. "Sorry I'm late."

"I'm used to it," Alannah said, drily. She wore a cute, long-sleeved navy dress with burgundy polka dots, tights, and her hair pulled into a neat doughnut at the back of her head. "What kept you this time?"

"I couldn't decide what to wear." She settled on dark jeans, boots, a denim jacket, and a purple blouse. She wore her hair in a neat topknot, her go-to style the past few days, and gold earrings the size of round coasters.

Alannah rolled her eyes.

Terri shoved her. "Stop. You know you love me." She sighed. "Can't wait to see Dorothy Koomson."

Seattle was a book lover's paradise. In addition to the ubiquitous coffee shops on every street, the Emerald City claimed the title of having the most book stores per capita of any city in the country. One of Terri's favorite things to do was attend author readings and literary events at the iconic Elliott Bay Book Company. And few pastimes delivered the same giddy excitement as browsing the shelves of a small bookstore, packed to capacity and filled with the distinctive, musky odor of aged books. In a place like that, she became lost, disappearing between the pages of tales spun for people who liked to escape the drudgery of life for several hours and live vicariously through characters within the pages turned sepia with age.

Lucky for her, Alannah enjoyed reading, too, and occasionally accompanied her to events. Terri had a copy of Koomson's *The Woman He Loved Before* and *Ice Cream Girls* for the author to sign, and she intended to purchase and get her autograph on the new release she would be reading from at the bookstore.

"Is Douglas still going to meet us there?" Alannah asked once they merged into traffic.

"No, I ended it with him."

"Already? What happened?" Alannah shot a glance her way.

"Nothing happened. It was just time to move on."

"You really don't waste any time, do you? By the way, what happened between you and Gavin? You missed yoga and we haven't talked since your date last week."

"We had a good time." She told Alannah about dinner at SkyCity Restaurant, the conversation over dinner, and hinted at the sexual gymnastics they indulged in back at her place.

"Soooo, are you going to see him again?" Alannah smiled from ear to ear.

"No, my little matchmaker friend. Thank you for telling him where I work, and although he was…amazing, that night was just a one-time thing. He's a great guy, but I won't be seeing him again."

The two times he called, she had been sorely tempted to answer or call back, but chickened out. She liked Gavin a little too much.

"Why won't you see him again if he's a great guy?" Alannah asked, a bemused expression on her face.

"He reminds me too much of my ex."

"The one you never talk about?"

"That's the one."

Alannah didn't know the whole story about Talon Cyrenci and the life she led as his live-in girlfriend. She shared the bare minimum, not even mentioning his name, but provided enough information to let her friend know that being with him had been a traumatic time she preferred to forget. Talon had been charming and rich, like Gavin, and she saw the danger of falling for a man just like her ex. He could easily take over her life.

Terri threw herself into every relationship, which was why she enjoyed her freedom so much now. She dated how and when she wanted and intended to keep it that way. She was in a good place. A happy place. She didn't want to threaten the equilibrium she had attained. Not even for Gavin and his devilish grin, succulent lips, and warm caresses.

Recalling all the ways he used his hands and mouth, leading her down the path to leg-shaking orgasms, Terri pressed a hand to her forehead, momentarily closed her eyes, and sighed softly. She should forget him. There were plenty of other fish in the sea.

"You shouldn't let what happened in the past define your future," Alannah said. She glanced over at Terri, eyes filled with sympathy. Her friend was such a sweetheart.

"I'm not," Terri promised. "Right now, I'm doing me. Terri Slade is dating and having fun. I don't want any one man monopolizing my time, and I don't want to get serious with anyone right now. Besides, guess how much money I have saved?"

"How much?"

"Six thousand, one hundred, and fifty dollars!"

Alannah squealed and Terri threw up her hands and danced in the seat. Not bad for a woman who, at twenty-seven years old, drove cross country in an old SUV with only a few hundred dollars to her name.

"In no time you'll have the ten thousand dollars you want in place before you start looking for a condo," Alannah said.

"Yes. Homeownership, and all without a man. No offense," Terri added hastily.

"No offense taken," Alannah said, laughing. "I like living with Trent."

"I can't believe he convinced you to move in with him."

"He didn't."

Terri glanced at her. "Um, yes he did. You're living with him."

A mischievous smile crossed Alannah's lips. "He *thinks* he talked me into it, but I wanted to move in with him all along."

Terri's mouth fell open. "You sneaky little bitch."

Giggling, Alannah blushed. "Shh. I let him think it was his idea."

"Oh my, you're not so sweet after all, are you?"

They both had a good laugh, and when the giggling died down, Terri turned on the radio to an R&B station playing mellow tunes.

Her thoughts drifted to Gavin again. She saw him—hands on her hips, eyes squinting, concentrating, teeth sunk into his bottom lip as she rode him in the middle of the bed. Although she knew she'd made the right decision regarding their hookup, in the back of her mind, a niggling doubt took root.

Rule number one, maintain control. She'd done her best to keep control of the relationship by kicking him out the next morning—the first rule of keeping her head on straight.

But the more she thought about Gavin, his smile, and the way he made her feel, the more she wanted to break the rule.

CHAPTER ELEVEN

Gavin walked into The Underground and scanned the dark room, checking out the crowd. Being a Sunday night, a third of the tables remained empty and only a few patrons idled at the two bars positioned on either side of the venue.

Played Out grooved onstage, strumming guitars, pounding drums, and dancing back and forth. All of the women—three black, one white, and a Filipino—wore Afro wigs and seventies-style clothing that included a mix of tie-dye blouses, bell bottoms, or mini-dresses. They played seventies funk, and most everyone present bounced their heads and shimmied in the seats.

Trenton's frat brother and owner of the venue, Devin, approached with his hand outstretched. "Gavin, long time no see."

"Good to see you." Gavin slapped his hand against Devin's and pumped hard. "Is my brother here?"

"He and Alannah are at their reserved table," Devin answered, pointing with his chin.

"Thanks. We'll have to catch up later."

"Sure thing."

On the way to the table, Gavin paused once to chat with a familiar face, a young woman by the name of Carrie Ann, with whom he had a brief fling a few years ago. She was with her man but still flirted with Gavin by batting her lashes and dragging her finger down the middle of his chest. Before she pulled back from their brief hug goodbye, she slipped something into his pocket.

Striding toward Trenton and his girlfriend, Gavin extracted the business card. The front proclaimed her position as a real estate agent in embossed black and gold letters, but she must have seen him as soon as he entered the building, because the back contained the handwritten words *Call me* and a number, which he guessed must be her mobile. Under other circumstances, he would have been tempted to follow up, but his mind was elsewhere. Occupied by Terri.

Gavin sat down across from Trenton, who had his arm resting on the back of Alannah's chair. She was engaged in a conversation on the phone and had one finger plugging her ear to hear over the noise of the band.

Trenton smiled smugly and Gavin shot him the finger.

"Where is she?" he asked.

Trenton leaned forward. "She ran to the restroom. She'll be back in a few minutes."

Tapping his finger on the surface of the wooden table, Gavin looked around for a waitress. The minute he saw Terri, he planned to drag her off to a private area so they could talk. He understood the game of playing hard to get, but this was ridiculous.

Alannah hung up the phone and handed it back to Trenton. "Gavin, I didn't know you were coming tonight." She sipped her Coke through a straw.

"Your husband mentioned the Played Out performance and I wanted to see them. I went to school with those ladies."

"He's not my husband," Alannah said, although she smiled. For his part, Trenton reached up and brushed her neck with the back of his hand.

He will be soon, Gavin guessed. It was only a matter of time.

"Terri's here." Alannah glanced between him and Trenton, and a light of understanding filled her eyes. "But you knew that, didn't you?"

Before he could answer, he looked up and saw Terri coming their way. Immediately, his gut contracted as his eyes followed the way she sashayed past the tables, hair pulled into a topknot, and wearing a black long-sleeved dress whose neckline dipped all the way to her waist, exposing her silky flesh to the casual observer.

A bunch of long necklaces lay nestled between her full breasts and sparkled against her brown skin. The rounded front hem of the dress draped to mid thigh and the back hem fell to the back of her knees. His eyes were drawn to where the material pulled a little at her broad hips, giving more emphasis to the left-right motion they made as she moved across the floor in a pair of black pumps.

When a man sitting at a table with two other men grabbed her hand and drew her into conversation, Gavin shot to his feet and curled his hands into fists at his sides. Trenton and Alannah looked behind them to see what caused him to leap from the chair. If the guy didn't let her go by the count of three, he was going over there.

By the count of two, Terri was headed in their direction with the same eye-catching strut, but came to an abrupt halt when she saw him. Her eyes stretched wide. They both stared at each other from only a few feet away. Everyone and everything in the entire building receded from Gavin's consciousness while he focused on the vision before him.

Straightening her shoulders, Terri marched forward and came to stand at the table. "Hi, Gavin."

"Terri."

One would think much longer than a week and two days had passed since he last saw her—the reaction to her presence was so visceral. His heart thumped in his chest. His loins ached with the memory of her touch. And his hands itched with the need to touch her.

"We need to talk," Gavin said.

"Maybe we can talk after—"

"Nah, we need to talk now."

He grabbed her by the wrist and pulled her away.

"What do you think you're doing?" Terri demanded.

Gavin surveyed the audience and the two bars, searching for Devin. When he spotted his friend near the door, he headed in that direction, pulling Terri with him.

"Do you mind telling me what this is about?" she hissed between her teeth.

Gavin didn't bother answering the question. She knew exactly what 'this' was about.

"Devin, mind if I use your office for a minute?"

Devin glanced at Terri, who glared at Gavin, her lips compressed into a flat line. "Sure, no problem." He held up a key on the chain. "This one."

"Thanks."

Gavin took the keys and they walked to the back of the club, down a dimly lit hallway where the sound of the music had diminished considerably. He shoved the key inside the lock and let Terri precede him inside the small office. The décor comprised of wood panel walls, a messy desk and leather chair, two old file cabinets, and a navy futon against the wall.

Terri swung around, anger flashing in her eyes. "Why did you have to bring me back here, Gavin?"

"I want an explanation."

"For what?"

"For why you won't accept my calls." He tossed the keys onto the futon.

"Do you understand the concept of one night?" Terri asked sardonically.

Gavin gritted his teeth through a chuckle and shook his head. "You get a kick out of making men grovel for your attention, don't you?"

"That is untrue. I'm not some heartless bitch," Terri spat back. "I made it very clear to you from the beginning that there was not going to be anything else between us after the date. But for some reason, you can't get that through your head. The problem for you, Gavin, is that you think you're so damn irresistible. Even though I told you the parameters of our night together, you can't accept them. Whose fault is that? Yours or mine?"

"So I'm in this alone, is that it? Whatever I feel is completely on my end and you don't think about me or want me, correct?"

Hesitation. Her eyes flickered with uncertainty. "Correct."

"Bull." Sensing weakness, Gavin closed in, and Terri backed up toward the desk. "You expect me to believe that you don't think about me? After I fucked you so good you not only screamed my name, you had tears in your eyes?"

"That doesn't change—"

"Tell me something, Terri." He continued to back her up until she hit the edge of the desk and grasped onto it. He stood over her, not touching but so close he heard the sharp inhale and exhale of her breaths. He saw the rapid rise and fall of her breasts and smelled the fragrance of roses and lavender that stayed in his skin after their night together, intermingled with her own personal scent that was one hundred percent Terri and two hundred percent aphrodisiac. "Are you wet right now? Because I'm so hard I could jackhammer through concrete. And that's your fault."

Gavin waited, never losing eye contact. Terri's throat worked a hard swallow and when she parted her lips, he knew the answer before she gave it. He knew because of the unmasked desire in her eyes.

"Yes. I'm wet."

They lunged at each other.

Gavin devoured her. That was the only way to describe the out of control way he fastened his mouth over hers in a hot demanding kiss. His groin felt heavy and weighted with need. He dragged his hands up and down her back, shaping the curve of her spine, and shoved a hand under the dress to squeeze her bare bottom and anchor her to him by the hips. The jut of his arousal pressed against his zipper, eager and anxious to have her again. Opening her moist mouth under his, she allowed him to drink the nectar of her sweet sensuality like a thirsty, dying man would.

Desire pumped strong in his blood as the fire between them raged out of control. He shoved papers out of the way and several fluttered to the floor as he lifted her onto the desk. He tasted the flavor of her skin, pressing his mouth to the little crater in the middle of her neck where her rapid pulse steadily hammered a beat.

Gavin dragged the edges of the loose bodice aside to get at her breasts. The beautiful caramel mounds sat perfectly in his hands, overflowing from his palms while he showered them with kisses. Each dark nipple pouted so prettily in anticipation of his mouth that he spent a little extra time caressing them, licking them, sucking them. All the while, Terri moaned her pleasure and bent backwards, encouraging the workings of his mouth.

Gavin unhooked his belt. He hadn't planned on sex tonight, but moved quickly, unable and unwilling to stop the mad rush to ecstasy needed to satisfy the hard throb of his erection.

Terri tugged at her thong with her thumbs, wiggling on the desk until it dropped to the floor. Right after he put on the condom, she lifted her legs around his waist without prompting. Then he was inside of her. Knees weakening at the warm wet texture surrounding him. He cursed violently, taut fingers gripping the tender flesh of her thighs. She felt too good. He didn't think he could last very long.

She balanced on the edge of the desk, one arm around his neck, the other firmly planted on the wooden surface. Each thrust took an inordinate amount of effort to control his natural inclination to explode in her slick channel. Over and over, his hard flesh sank into her wet sex. He made her groan. He made her gasp. And when the orgasm hit, she tossed back her head and let loose a keening cry—a high-pitched scream that could easily be heard by anyone loitering in the hallway.

Gavin, at almost the exact moment her muscles spasmed around him, unleashed his come in a violent shudder that forced a burst of air from his lungs and a low, long grunt of satisfaction from his throat.

Clinging to each other in the aftermath, several long minutes passed before they each caught their breath and slowly pulled apart. Gavin took a good hard look at Terri. She leaned back on both hands, legs still spread apart, the hem of her dress pushed up around her hips. Her large caramel breasts were exposed—their dusky tips still hard—with the necklaces settled between them. She looked like every man's wet dream.

He picked up her thong, nothing more than two pieces of string and a thatch of cloth. Terri extended her hand to accept it, but Gavin shook his head. Lifting it to his nose, he inhaled the heady scent of her feminine musk.

Terri's eyes darkened. "Can I have my underwear, please?"

Stuffing the lingerie in his pocket, he said, "You'll get it the next time I see you."

"Which is when?" she demanded.

His mouth lifted into a sideways smile. "Tomorrow."

CHAPTER TWELVE

Gavin crossed the mahogany floors of his rented house and stepped onto the balcony to escape the raucous party inside for a few minutes. He rubbed a hand across his throbbing head. His friends had invited a bunch of women and other hangers-on over for a party. Loud talking, laughter, and alcohol filled almost every room on the second floor. He'd been there all of thirty minutes and couldn't summon the energy to engage in the revelry, which used to be easy to do.

When he saw the house months ago, the petite real estate agent droned on and on about the lakeside view, heated floors and driveway, massive master suite that occupied half of the top floor, and the chef's kitchen with the latest appliances. At the time, Gavin hadn't cared. He only needed a place for he and his friends to stay while temporarily in town, but he grew to like the tri-level house immensely and idly considered buying it as a permanent residence.

The door slid open behind him and deafening rap music poured out before dulling to a faint thump when the door closed again.

"Hey, bro, what's wrong?"

Rob, the typical surfer dude with sun-bleached hair and blue eyes, joined him at the railing. He and Rob had surfed dangerous waves in Australia and Hawaii, along with their partner in surfing crime, a native Hawaiian who was just as fearless.

Rob handed him an open bottle of beer. "You seem distracted tonight."

"I think it's all the work at the office," Gavin joked.

The real reason he hadn't been himself was the fault of a voluptuous female about five foot six with ass and hips for days. She had him by the balls. That was the only way to describe the Terri effect. The few times they'd hooked up since The Underground simply weren't enough.

Rob nodded. "Work will suck the life out of you. That's why you need to relax, man. Indulge in the ladies."

"Nah, you go ahead. Have fun."

It was quiet out here. Exactly what he needed, with only the distant sound of a car breaking the silence.

"You sure, man?" Rob leaned close, as if anyone could hear them. "The one with the green eyes won't even look at the rest of us. She only has eyes for you."

Gavin had seen her, and she was gorgeous—a different kind of gorgeous than Terri. Tall, leggy, light-skinned, she had a mane of long tresses swept over one shoulder, with a man-eating look on her face that used to turn him on. Yet he was completely uninterested. None of the eight women entertaining his friends piqued his interest.

I'm getting too old for this shit.

"I'm sure." Gavin held up the bottle. "Thanks for the brew. I'm going to stay out here for a bit."

Rob shook his head. "All right, man."

He opened the door and for several seconds the music and laughter disturbed the quiet. Then Gavin savored the silence, alone again with his thoughts. He rested his forearms on the wood railing and gazed out into the shadowy night. Large trees loomed around the perimeter of the property, and in the distance the moonlight reflected off the surface of Lake Washington.

Before he changed his mind, he pulled out his phone and dialed Terri's number.

She answered on the second ring. "Hello, Gavin," she said in a cheerful voice.

Gavin rested on his elbows, face creasing into a smile at the sound of her voice, his body already relaxing. "What are you doing?"

"Cooking dinner."

"What's on the menu?"

"Breakfast for dinner—shrimp and grits with bacon and scrambled eggs with cheese."

Gavin straightened. He never figured Terri for the cooking type, much less something like shrimp and grits, one of his comfort foods. "That's one of my favorite dishes. What do you know about cooking shrimp and grits?"

"Plenty."

"Oh yeah? Any chance I could have a taste?"

"Hmm...I don't know. Didn't I just see you two days ago?"

"You're overdue for another visit, wouldn't you say?"

"Maybe," Terri said, dragging out the word.

In his mind's eye, he saw her cute little pout and eyes narrowing into a seductive smile.

"Save me some of those grits. I'm coming over."

"I didn't say you could."

"You didn't have to, but you want me to. I can hear it in your voice." Gavin swiped the bottle of beer from the railing and turned toward the door. "I'll be there in twenty."

****

Terri opened the door to find Gavin leaning a shoulder against the wall in a maroon long-sleeved Henley and dark jeans.

"Hello," he said, eyes dropping to her chest in the tight white T-shirt before flicking back up again. He produced a bottle of wine from behind his back.

"Chardonnay. You came prepared."

"Always."

He entered the apartment, and with one arm around her waist, he drew her into a kiss. Gavin only had to touch her and she complied to his wishes. Heat radiated against her skin everywhere their bodies touched. Terri smoothed both hands over his hard pectorals and then higher up to grip his shoulders. As she arched into him, her nipples pebbled against his chest and that quickly, Gavin turned her body to warm liquid. His hand came up to the back of her neck and deepened the intensity of their erotic mouth to mouth. Just when she felt ready to forego eating and invite him back to the bedroom for a quick session before dinner, he withdrew his lips and left her panting for more.

"Those grits ready?" he asked.

"Almost," Terri replied, a little breathless. "Whew, that was a nice greeting."

Gavin chuckled behind her as she walked over to the stove.

"Glad you liked it," he said.

While he poured the wine, she spooned grits into the bowls and then added the red shrimp stew on top. Then she bent over to get the bacon from the oven. The black leggings showed the curves of her body to advantage, and she stuck out her behind way more than necessary, smiling to herself at the sound of Gavin's soft groan when she did. She removed a sheet of bacon from the oven and set the strips to drain, then broke them up, sprinkling the pieces on top of each serving of grits.

"So do you do this for all your non-boyfriends?" Gavin asked, watching her work.

"Nope. But don't tell me you never had a woman cook for you and serve you before."

"It's a rare treat, believe me."

"What kind of women are you used to?" she teased.

"Touché."

With no dining area, Terri set the bowls on the green coffee table in front of the sofa. As she gathered silverware and napkins, Gavin went to her five-shelf bookcase, stuffed with so many books she'd shoved two shelves of novels as far back as possible and placed another row horizontally in front of them. A tablet sat charging on the second shelf from the top.

"You read a lot," he commented.

"Mostly thrillers. Nice escape, you know?" She fixed her gaze on his broad back as he lifted a book from the shelf and leafed through the pages.

"I can't remember the last time I read a book." Gavin set the glass of wine in front of four Lee Child books and pulled out a James

Patterson novel. He flipped through the pages. "My father collected books. Rare ones."

"When I lived in Atlanta, I used to visit the Decatur Book Festival's rare books display." Terri lifted her glass and took a sip of the wine, recalling the walk through the climate controlled rooms where she oohed and aahed over rare finds. "Some of those books cost a fortune."

Gavin stopped flipping through the pages of the novel and gave her his undivided attention, appearing genuinely interested in the conversation about rare books. "You ever bought any?"

"No." Terri shook her head. Her ex didn't allow her to spend that kind of money on books. Cars, jewelry, and clothes were another matter altogether.

Behind her, Gavin had gone quiet, probably browsing the pages of the novel as he waited for her to finish.

She set the scrambled eggs on the table with the grits. Then they sat down to eat. After a mouthful, Gavin turned to her with admiration in his eyes.

"This. Is. Delicious."

"Told you," Terri said, doing a confident little wiggle. "Breakfast food is my specialty."

While they ate, they talked about all kinds of topics, mostly the latest celebrity gossip. Gavin knew everyone, it seemed. From singers to actors to reality stars, and offered insight into their real personalities versus the personas presented in the media.

After they ate, he washed the dishes, insisting she'd done enough. A surprise for her. Gavin lowered himself to washing dishes and wiped down the counters while she put her feet up on the table and pretended to read a novel on the tablet. Instead, she secretly watched him. The muscles under the close-fitting Henley moved as he worked, and she had to admit that watching him wash utensils and tidy the kitchenette was almost as sexy as his seductive moves in the bedroom.

Suddenly he turned and she dipped her gaze back to the electronic device in her hands and the story she hadn't read a word of.

"Dinner was great. Thank you." Gavin sat beside her and flung an arm along the back of the sofa. "You have any plans for the night?"

"No, I'm staying in."

"Mind if I hang out here?"

Her eyes slid over to him. "You want to hang out. Here."

"Sure, why not?" He patted his abs. "I have a full belly and I'm feeling kind of good. Or do you have something else you'd rather be doing?"

"I don't have any plans at all."

"Perfect. You can tell me about some of the books you like."

"You're serious?" Surely there were other things he'd rather be doing?

He laughed. "Yes, I'm serious." He eyed the device in her hand. "What are you reading?"

The screen had gone dark, and Terri woke it up by running her hand over the surface. "He's a new author."

Gavin edged closer and peered at the words. "What's his name?"

She relaxed into the crook of his arm, resting the back of her head on his bicep. He smelled earthy and manly, and warmth from his torso seeped through the material of his shirt to her arm wedged between them.

She tilted the screen toward him so he could see better. "His name is Dane Stewart. This is the only book he's published so far. It's a legal thriller and really good. I'm only on chapter three but I'm already hooked."

"Lemme see." Gavin swiped backward to get to chapter one and read the first few paragraphs. "You're right, this is good. Caught my attention right away," he murmured, eyes glued to the screen.

Terri watched his profile—the faux hawk haircut, the downcast eyes, the barely-there stubble on his jaw. She felt rather relaxed with him. "We can start over if you want."

"But you've already read this part." His eyes shot to hers.

"It's okay. I'm only a few chapters in."

"Are you sure?" He frowned.

Rich. Handsome. Considerate. Gavin Johnson wasn't so spoiled after all.

"I'm sure," she replied.

He pulled her closer. "You comfortable?" His fingers played with the shell of her ear.

"Yes. You?" Heat seeped into her limbs, but not the heat of desire. The heat of comfort, relaxation, and contentment.

"Yeah." Their eyes lingered on each other. "More comfortable than I've been in a while."

His fingers delved into her hair and the tips massaged her scalp, and a random, crazy thought entered her head. She never wanted him to stop touching her. Temporary panic seized her heart, forcing it to thump a fierce beat against her ribs.

"Are you sure this is what you want to do tonight?" she asked quietly.

"I said it is, didn't I?"

"Yes you did, smart ass."

"Perfect example of the pot calling the kettle black if I ever heard one."

She jabbed him in the ribs with her elbow and he bit the corner of her neck in retaliation.

Leaning away, she shoved his face. "Behave."

He grinned, a smile so bright it stole her breath. Terri quickly looked away and stared down at the electronic device in her hand, mildly worried about the state of her emotions. She couldn't afford to get emotional.

"You mind reading out loud?" Gavin asked.

"No."

Taking a few seconds to regroup, Terri emptied her mind of hope and joy and accepted the moment for what it was—an isolated incident. A segment of time that may or may not be repeated.

"The building loomed overhead, casting long shadows across the street. The sound of a gun popped off down the alley and broke the morning silence…"

Resting against Gavin's side, she read chapter after chapter, and he listened. Once he got up to get a drink of water, but he told her to keep reading. Every now and again they discussed the events in the book, whether or not the characters were making mistakes, and tried to guess the resolution to the story.

Men didn't look at Terri and see art and culture, and she didn't have a lot of girlfriends. Except for Alannah, women didn't like having her around because they viewed her as a threat.

So to spend this time with Gavin, chilling at home and reading, was simultaneously relaxing and worrisome. She could easily lose her heart to him, and based on experience, losing her heart to a man was a very bad idea that resulted in foolish mistakes and agonizingly painful consequences.

CHAPTER THIRTEEN

Three weeks had flown by in a glorious haze of lovemaking, late night talks, and teasing conversation.

"You promised to be good," Terri said as Gavin's hand found its way between her legs.

The tight-fitting shorts presented the bottom curve of her butt and he couldn't resist touching every time she wore them. The cotton shorts were so tiny initially he mistook them for a pair of panties. She only wore them in the apartment, and only for him.

"You know I can't be good with you lying on top of me like this."

He squeezed one thigh. "Open your legs."

She remained still, playfully refusing to budge.

"I said, open your legs." Lifting his knees, Gavin forced her legs apart. One hand slid down the curve of her bottom and nestled in the gap between her thighs. Gently, he rubbed until she moaned his name, so indecently wet that moisture soaked the shorts. His hand sought and found her breast under the camisole top and squeezed, dragging his thumb across her nipple. The additional stimulation left her gasping and grinding against him.

He started breathing hard and let out a shaky laugh. "You're gonna make me come in my pants."

Terri ignored his comment, rubbing against his hand until he twisted her onto her back. Panting, she arched her body against his busy hands and then came hard, her hands fisted behind his neck.

Gavin panted hot breaths beside her ear and fumbled for a condom. Abruptly, he yanked off her shorts and turned her onto her stomach. With her face in the pillow, she lifted her hips into the slide of his finger between her legs. She gasped at the slow caress, her body aching for a repeat of orgasmic bliss.

"You're so wet," he said in a hoarse voice behind her. She heard the zipper, and then he pried her legs open and penetrated her from behind. After two pumps, he groaned, his hands curling into fists beside her head. "I could stay up in you all damn day."

The rough denim of his jeans scraped her inner thigh as the strength of his thrusts pushed her into the soft mattress. They came fast, climaxing simultaneously, and Gavin released into the condom with a trembling groan before slumping across her back.

With a soft curse, he kissed the heart tattoo on her shoulder blade and then let out a short laugh. Terri did, too, an exhausted, breathless, tired laugh.

"Quiet evening at home, you said?" she teased.

"We were pretty quiet, don't you think?" He kissed the back of her neck.

She wiggled from under him and he rolled onto his back.

"Where are you going?" he asked when she slid off the bed.

"I gotta go pee. You were pushing all up on my bladder." She dragged the camisole top over her head, brazenly unfettering her breasts and letting them swing free in all their lushness.

"You love blowing up my head, don't you? Hurry back."

"I'll take this." Terri slid off the condom and Gavin groaned as his penis jumped.

"You're gonna be the death of me."

"But you'll die happy," she quipped, before sauntering off. Naked and comfortable in her own skin.

He rented hotel suites with bathrooms bigger than her entire apartment, yet the efficiency appealed to him. Or maybe it was the company. They usually slept here instead of his place, which crawled with party-goers all hours of the day and night—something he used to enjoy, but now found to be a nuisance.

"Have you thought about what we discussed last night?" he called out.

"You're back on that again? It's the worst idea you've ever had. Seriously," Terri called back.

"Come on, it's not that bad. You'll love it." Gavin folded his arms behind his head, enjoying himself. He always enjoyed himself with Terri.

Lounging around on Saturday morning had become his new favorite pastime. Who knew he could get such satisfaction from spending so much time with the same person—eating with her, sleeping wrapped around her, and then waking up and making sweet love in the morning. He'd been so accustomed to going, going, going, he never paused long enough to enjoy a slower pace, but now he saw what he'd been missing.

Yeah, he could get used to this.

"Please, you're only saying that because you're the giver and I'm the taker," Terri said.

She appeared in the doorway, still naked. And this was another reason he was enjoying himself. Terri walked around naked, draped in more confidence than most women did fully clothed. And he loved it, because he was the lucky recipient of all that beautiful brown skin on display. She was so damn sexy—with heavy breasts capped by chocolate areolas, bow-shaped hips, thick thighs, and an ass he hadn't been able to convince her to let him penetrate. But he was working on it, hence their current conversation.

"I think the reason you're hesitant is because you had a bad experience. Some men go too hard and too fast. We'll take it slow and easy. You'll love it."

"Just because I'm a little freaky doesn't mean I'll let you stick your dick anywhere you want."

"No?"

"No."

"Come here."

She walked over to the bed, feigning reluctance, and sat down.

"It'll be the best orgasm you've ever had," Gavin said.

"I already have the best orgasms I've ever had," she said. "Get it through that thick skull of yours. I'm not doing it."

"I don't understand. What does that even mean?" Gavin asked.

She laughed. "It means exactly what I told you when we started this conversation yesterday. I don't do anal."

Gavin scratched his head. "Sorry, I'm really confused. What language are you speaking?"

Terri ran her tongue between her teeth and lip. She leaned forward and cupped a hand around his ear. "This. Is. English. I. Don't. Do. Anal." She sat up.

"With an ass like that?" Gavin sat up and shook his head. "We're gonna have to change that. That ass was made for fucking."

Terri rolled her eyes and popped up from the bed.

"Where are you going now?" Selfishly, he wanted her close at all times.

"I'll be right back." She pushed aside the ivory curtain and left him in the bedroom. She came back almost right away and stood in the doorway. "If anal is so great, why don't you try it?"

"Er, that's not the way this works, baby."

Terri strolled toward the bed and pulled a cucumber from behind her back. "You sure you don't want to try it and prove to me how enjoyable it will be?" She slid her fingers along the length of the fruit.

"It's all about your enjoyment, not mine."

"Oh, I don't know." The tip of one slender finger traced the length. "What was it you said to me? 'A little lubricant will fix you right up. You'll barely feel a thing.' Wasn't it something like that?"

"I might have possibly said something like that," Gavin admitted, getting disturbingly turned on by her fingers caressing the green fruit.

One of her eyebrows shot toward the ceiling. She used her eyebrows a lot. To challenge him, to express sarcasm or disbelief. "That's exactly what you said. So why don't you turn over on your stomach and I'll test your theory."

"I have a better idea."

"What's that?"

"Let's test it on you."

Her eyes widened, and she only made it as far as the coffee table before he grabbed her around the waist and lifted her from the floor.

She screamed. "No! I was just playing."

"I got you now." He yanked away the cucumber and wrestled her to the bed, face down, bottom up. "Let's see if it fits." He placed the cucumber at the crease of her ass. "What do you have to say for yourself now? Not so cocky anymore, are we?"

She wiggled to get up, but he held her down. "Gavin, quit."

"I think you really want it."

"*No.*"

"You sure? I promise you'll like it. It's smaller than me, but it'll be a good way to prep you," he said wickedly, pressing the fruit a little between her butt cheeks.

"I said, no!" she shrieked, raw panic in her voice.

Gavin stopped right away. "I was just kidding, baby."

"Stop. Get up. *Get up.*"

He lifted off of her. She was shaking. Gavin tossed aside the cucumber. "Hey, I was just kidding, okay?"

She stood up and away from him and folded her arms over her mid-section.

"It's not funny," she said.

"I'm sorry. I took it too far." He held up his hands and remained seated so as not to crowd her or make her feel intimidated.

Terri frowned at the floor, and Gavin had the distinct impression that this wasn't really about him—but about something else. Perhaps someone else, who had hurt her.

"Hey." He extended his hand and she stared at it. She didn't move, but he didn't drop his hand. He held it out until she took it and he pulled her onto his lap.

"I'm sorry," he said to her neck. "Forgive me?"

She dipped her head. "You didn't do anything wrong. I shouldn't have started the game. I just got...weird, that's all."

"I would never do anything you didn't want me to. I hope

you know that."

"I do."

He tilted her chin up. "Do you?"

She nodded.

"And I would never hurt you, Terri. *Never*. That's not my style."

"I know." She offered him a trembling smile. "You're not one of those freaky crazy rich men."

"I'm freaky, not crazy." He grinned.

She laughed, and he dragged a finger down her soft cheek.

"Want to talk about it?" he asked. Anger burned in his belly at the thought of someone hurting her.

Tears sprang to her eyes and she looked down. "Not today. Maybe another time," she said huskily.

Beneath the sensual bravado she exuded, he often sensed a vulnerability, but never more than now. As if her behavior was simply a cover. In some ways, she reminded him of himself.

"Okay." He pulled her close. "So, what's on the agenda today?"

"I don't know. I have the whole day off." Her voice sounded closer to normal, but not quite.

"We need to take advantage of it. What do you want to do?"

"Something really relaxing."

"Like what?"

"Let's go to a bookstore." She wrinkled her nose, as if she expected him to reject the idea.

"Sounds like a plan to me."

She grinned, her face lighting up like a little girl whose pony arrived as promised. "You sure?"

"If that's what you want to do, that's what we'll do." He didn't know why she acted surprised every time he agreed to go to a bookstore or do anything equally routine, though he guessed by her responses he'd passed some kind of test.

She loved to spend a quiet night in and read, a personality trait he hadn't expected, contradictory to the sex-kitten air she naturally exuded. Spending time with her made him wonder about himself. He couldn't remember the last time the urge for speed or danger hit him.

Terri hopped up. "Okay, let's go take a shower. Last one in is a rotten egg!" She took off running.

Gavin rose from the bed but didn't follow right away. He took a long, hard look at the cucumber on the floor.

He liked to think his disposition was more like his mother's. He admired her even-tempered handling of problems over the years and thought the only characteristic he inherited from his father was the light color of his eyes. But the truth was, he had a bit of a temper, kicked in by a protective gene ten miles wide when a woman he cared about had been hurt—very much like his father. Years ago, Gavin used his fists to teach a lesson to a slimy young man by the name of Eric who'd shopped a video of Eric and Ivy having sex. His brothers had to pull him off the piece of shit.

So to think someone had hurt Terri infuriated him. If he had to guess, it was the man she didn't want to talk about on their date at SkyCity Restaurant.

Who was he and what exactly had he done to her?

Gavin clenched his teeth.

Whoever he was, he better hope Gavin never found out.

CHAPTER FOURTEEN

"Pull!" The target soared above the trees. Gavin followed it with his eyes and then pulled the trigger on the shotgun. The clay exploded and the pieces fell to the earth.

"Pull!" Xavier yelled to his left. He fired, but the target soared out of sight, like a bird. He swore and Gavin chuckled.

"Pull!" To Xavier's left, Ivy lined up the shot. Gavin couldn't see her eyes behind the shooting glasses, but she had excellent aim. When she pulled the trigger, fragments dusted the air.

They all removed their protective ear plugs and two attendants came running up to retrieve them, the guns, and Ivy's glasses.

"I beat you, little brother," she teased, resting an arm on his shoulder as they walked toward the back porch of the cabin. She loved rubbing in that she was five minutes older than him. "You've gotten rusty. You suck now."

"Xavier's the one who sucks," Gavin said, tossing a glance over his shoulder.

His brother scowled at him.

Ivy ran lightly up the steps ahead of them. "Either way, I just made ten thousand dollars." She held up all ten fingers.

"Check's in the mail," Gavin muttered as he climbed the stairs.

Ivy placed her hands on her hips. "Hey, don't you dare treat me like Trenton. He never pays his debts, but I expect my money."

He and Xavier should have known better than to take a bet with Ivy, but neither could back down from her trash talking. She was the best shot in the family and had even won a few skeet shooting championships over the years. Gavin's skills came in a close second, and he was the only one of his siblings to take his appreciation of firearms to another level. He owned a small collection of antique handguns from the early nineteenth century, including a set of dueling pistols purchased from a collector not too long ago. In his home, he kept guns stashed on every floor, just in case.

Xavier fell somewhere behind Gavin in shooting proficiency. Cyrus Jr., their oldest brother, had never taken to skeet shooting, but he was decent. Trenton never participated because of an aversion to guns.

Gavin and Ivy grabbed a seat in two of the Adirondack chairs on the rear porch of the cabin. Xavier stood facing them, with his back to the greenery. The "cabin" was really a luxurious eight-bedroom home they visited more often as children. Their mother used to love to take the drive in the fall when the leaves changed, and it was an easy way to pull their father away from work for a couple of days. They piled into five sports utility vehicles with nannies and servants, forming a little caravan to escape to the Cascade Mountains for the weekend.

Gavin breathed in the cool, fresh air of late February and let his gaze sweep over the triangular-shaped western hemlock and shrubs that covered the landscape for miles. He couldn't remember the last time he came up here. Now that the sound of gunfire had ceased, only the quiet of the woodlands could be heard.

An attendant came out and handed them each a mug of hot chocolate. Another one behind him set up a portable table and then they both removed themselves as quietly as they'd come.

"How are thing's going at the office?" Ivy asked. She took a sip of hot chocolate and then set the mug on the table.

"Good. Last week I was down in the mail room." Gavin dragged another chair in front of him and propped his feet on it.

"You haven't heard him whistling in the halls?" Xavier asked.

"I've been tied up in legal working on the franchise project the past few weeks. The numbers look good, but my biggest concern is maintaining the same quality in the restaurants once we don't own them all."

"It'll work out. There are lots of franchises out there," Xavier said.

"True. The consultants have been extremely helpful." She turned to Gavin. "So what's this about you whistling in the hallways?"

"There's nothing to tell," Gavin said. He shot Xavier a look.

"What was that?" Ivy demanded.

"That was a don't-tell-her-shit look."

"Why not?"

"Because you talk too much," Gavin and Xavier said in unison.

"I do not!"

"Actually, you do," Xavier said.

Ivy narrowed her eyes at him. "So this is a secret you guys have been keeping from me?"

"Not really a secret, but I figured you're on a need-to-know basis, otherwise you'll run and tell Mother everything," Gavin said.

Ivy crossed her arms and fell silent, but Gavin knew she wasn't finished. Sure enough, she asked, "What if I promise not to say anything?"

Gavin shot his older brother a look. "What do you think?"

Xavier shrugged. "It's up to you."

Gavin pointed at his sister. "Not a word."

"Not a word." Ivy made a motion with her hand to her mouth and turned, locking her lips with an imaginary key.

Gavin let out a heavy breath. "I'm seeing someone, and I really like her."

Ivy leaned closer. "Who?"

Gavin stared at her.

"My lips are sealed. I promise."

"Her name's Terri Slade. She's a friend of Alannah's."

"Why is that name so familiar? Do I know her? Who's her

family?"

"She's not from our circle of friends or the people we know, except for Alannah."

"Hmm…maybe that's how I know her. I must have met her before."

"Probably."

"Soooo, how long have you been seeing Terri?" Ivy placed an elbow on the arm of the chair and rested her chin in her hand, gearing up for the juicy details.

"Over a month."

"So you must like her a lot if you're seeing her exclusively."

"He never said he was seeing her exclusively," Xavier interjected.

"Well, that's implied." Ivy turned to Gavin. "Isn't it?"

"I like her, okay? We'll leave it at that." True enough, he hadn't been seeing anyone else. In fact, he'd even cut down the amount of time he spent with his entourage. When he wasn't with Terri, he spent time working and learning the ropes at the family business. Xavier had him on a rotating schedule to learn different areas. At the time, he thought it was ridiculous. He hadn't planned on staying for an extensive period in Seattle, but now, he wasn't so sure. Every time he thought of leaving, the excitement of going off on another adventure didn't hold the same appeal.

"Is she the reason you've stuck around in Seattle?" Ivy asked.

"The reason I'm still in Seattle is because I love being around my family."

Xavier snorted.

"Yeah, right," Ivy said. She crossed her legs. "So tell me about her. What's she like?"

"There's nothing to tell."

"Come on. Stop being so secretive." Ivy sipped the hot chocolate, waiting.

Gavin gazed out at the trees. "I don't know how to explain it. She's not like any woman I've ever known or been involved with. She's not an actress or socialite or any of those women. She's just real and honest and…Terri."

He thought about her when they weren't together, and
though they hadn't been together long, felt as if he'd known her
much longer. They were so compatible. Same sense of humor and a
desire to engage in the same activities. Nowadays, a fun night was
laying his head in her lap while she read to him from one of the
paperbacks on her shelf or the hundreds of books in her tablet. He
popped popcorn for their quiet evenings at her apartment and
searched out literary events they could attend together.

Their only bone of contention was her constant need to
assert her independence and keep their relationship in a kind of
nonexclusive limbo. She was very particular about the gifts she
accepted from him. The other day, he had dozens of Agent
Provocateur lingerie delivered to her apartment with a handwritten
note that said *Wear this for me* attached to a jade bra with matching
thong and suspenders.

When he arrived that night, she wore the pieces he had
selected, and posed seductively for him in the doorway to the
bedroom. The sight of the cool green against her warm caramel skin
almost caused him to rip the silk from her body.

Although she expressed no unease at the thousands of dollars
he spent on the Agent Provocateur garments, she stiffened when she
opened a jeweler's box and saw the gold necklace with double hearts
inlaid with rubies. She didn't let him fasten it around her neck, and he
hadn't seen it again since that night.

"You and Terri sound serious." Ivy watched him over the rim
of her cup.

Gavin shrugged. "Too soon for that. We're enjoying each
other for now."

"When was the last time you even had a serious girlfriend?"
Ivy asked. She frowned as she considered the answer to the question.

Xavier shifted his stance at the railing so he could lean back
on his elbows. "Not since…the daughter of the oil guy—the one in
Texas that Mother introduced you to, right?"

"We weren't that serious." They were together for a solid
year. She was serious, he wasn't. They parted ways because she
couldn't keep up with his schedule, being out of the country all the

time. It was a tough long-distance relationship, and one he hadn't been too interested in maintaining.

"What about Sharon?" Ivy asked.

"Wasn't interested in her."

"He wouldn't put a ring on her finger," Xavier supplied.

"Oh." Ivy rested her head against the back of the Adirondack chair. "You must really like Terri, then," she said quietly.

Gavin brushed dirt from his jeans. "Don't analyze me, Ivy."

"I'm not." She sighed heavily. "I'm glad for any reason you're staying home."

"Why is that so important to you?" He watched his sister closely. They used to be really close at one time, and he missed that. He needed to rectify the situation since he created the distance.

"Besides the fact that you worry us to death when you go on your dangerous adventures? I'm just glad that we're all here. If you come to work at the company—"

"Don't hold your breath. I'm not ready to do that yet. Going in to work just gives me something to do to kill time."

"Well, if you change your mind, it'll be nice, that's all." She wrapped her fingers around the mug.

"I guess it would be nice," Gavin admitted.

The minute he said that, Ivy turned her head…and smiled.

CHAPTER FIFTEEN

Terri followed Alannah from the building, yoga mats rolled under their arms.

"Good night," they called to the other members of the class.

The driver opened the door and Terri slid onto the seat beside her friend.

Alannah disliked having a driver drop them off and pick them up. Terri appreciated the convenience and agreed with Trenton that they were located in a sketchy area. Parking was in the back or down the street, which meant they had to walk to their cars in the near dark. Alannah thought the "whole driver mess," as she called it, made her look pretentious, but since most everyone knew she lived with a wealthy man, Terri didn't see why it was a big deal.

"What's going on? We haven't talked much lately." Alannah's eyes twinkled and her lips turned up in a knowing smile.

It was true. When Terri wasn't at work, she was with Gavin. Tonight was the first time in a long time that she'd even attended yoga.

"Get that look off your face," she said.

"Terri and Gavin, sitting in a tree—"

Terri shoved her friend. "Cut it out."

"K-i-s-s-i-n-g." Alannah giggled and dodged another blow by scooting into the corner. "Are you having fun?"

She and Gavin hung out together more than she anticipated

they would at the beginning of their affair. He spent time with her, even if they weren't having sex. "I am having fun."

Still, his latest request completely threw her off. He invited her to a retirement party for one of the top executives in Johnson Enterprises, someone who worked for the company for thirty years and had known his father well. His mother considered the man a dear friend and wanted to host a special event for him outside of the company, so she planned a formal dinner in her home, which would segue into a cocktail party with additional guests a couple of hours later.

Apparently, Ivy told their mother about her, and his mother invited Terri because she wanted to meet her. The invitation to attend came out of nowhere, during a late night run to Aldi's Market, a haven of gourmet foods Gavin introduced her to. Now she was addicted to the place.

Shocked by his invitation, she immediately turned him down.

"Why don't you want to come with me? There's got to be a reason." *They stood in the gourmet cheese section, trying to decide between the Camembert or the milder, creamier double cream Brie.*

She averted her eyes from his questioning gaze and perused the products on display. "I don't have a particular reason. I don't know why you want me there, that's all."

Gavin turned to face her fully. "Who else would I ask? Besides, my mother wants to meet you, and I didn't think it was a big deal."

Being with Gavin was starting to feel more like a real relationship and not the light-hearted fun she expected. Nothing was more real than meeting a man's family, and from the sound of it, they would all be there.

She shifted the basket to another hand. "I don't have anything to wear."

He came to stand directly in front of her, and she tipped her head back to look up at him. "Is that all? You're worried about what to wear? You have to know that I'd take care of that for you."

Gavin was generous to a fault, always trying to give her money or gifts. He hinted at leasing a bigger apartment for her, and though tempted, she flatly refused. Another time, he tried to pay her rent, but she refused that, too. Then the shoes arrived...just because she mentioned a love for Gianvito Rossi's beige crystal-embellished pumps, a pair showed up—in her exact size, no less—two days later. She still hadn't worn them and wasn't sure she would. She didn't want them scuffed or the bottoms worn out. She just wanted to look at them.

"You've done plenty already," Terri said.

"And I want to do much more. Let me, and stop arguing." He touched the tip of her chin with his finger. "I've never had to work so hard to give to a woman. Usually everyone's taking and taking. It's a nice change, but enough already."

He dropped a kiss onto her mouth, a fleeting brush of his warm lips that seared her to the bone and filled her heart with longing. She swallowed the pain that beat in her chest. She didn't want to pretend anymore. She didn't want to behave as if she didn't want to attend the party and meet his family, when her real fear was falling in love with him, falling in love with them, and then losing it all.

The cheeses were displayed on a two-toned board. Gavin lifted the glass, took one of the toothpicks, and popped the cheese into his mouth. "Have you decided which one you want?" he asked.

She shrugged. "I can't decide."

"Let's get both of them."

Gavin never hesitated. He knew what he wanted and went for it.

He added the cheeses to the basket and took it from her. "Come on."

Terri took his hand. "You really want me to go?"

"I wouldn't have asked if I didn't."

They walked along in silence, holding hands, on the way to the deli where a platter of antipasti Gavin had ordered waited.

"Okay, I'll come," Terri said.

"And you'll let me get you something to wear?"

She shoved down the twinge of anxiety by looping an arm through his and giving him her sauciest smile. This was Gavin. He was nothing like Talon. "If you insist."

"If you're having fun, why do you look so glum?" Alannah asked.

"Honestly? Because I'm *freaking* out."

"Why?"

"Because he wants me to attend a dinner party for some guy who's retiring from Johnson Enterprises."

"Oh, Walt Sternberg. He's the company comptroller and has worked at Johnson Enterprises for *years*. He's finally retiring, and he and his wife are going to, get this, drive a motorhome cross-country. Doesn't that sound like fun? But seriously, there's nothing to worry about."

"I'm sort of wishing I hadn't agreed to go. I want to get out of it." Attending the party worried Terri. She rolled her tense shoulders and popped her neck.

"You can't get out of it."

"Of course I can."

"Not if his mother invited you. And why would you want to?"

"Because..."

How to explain that she had never, not once, had a man introduce her to his parents, and mothers were notoriously *the worst* when it came to their sons. Add to the fact that Constance Johnson was cultured and part of the upper rung of elite society, she felt completely out of her depth.

The life she lived at one time in Atlanta was nothing compared to the life the Johnsons lived. They didn't own a plane. They owned a fleet of planes. Her ex had employed dozens of people to conduct his schemes. They employed tens of thousands across the globe. While she and Talon had enjoyed the spoils of new money, their old money riches went back generations.

So what in the world would she say when she met the matriarch of the family? A woman Gavin clearly adored and highly respected? How was she supposed to behave? Should she curtsy when introduced? She had no idea!

"I don't want to meet his mother or anyone else in his family." Terri gnawed a thumbnail, a bad habit that manifested whenever she was nervous.

"They're a cool family," Alannah said.

"Easy for you to say. You're practically one of them."

"You've met Trenton."

"That's different, and I met him through you. Now I'm expected to attend a formal dinner."

Alannah squeezed Terri's arm. "Relax. You're not going to meet the Queen of England."

"It sure feels like it," Terri muttered.

"All you have to do is be yourself," Alannah said.

"I doubt that will be a good idea." Terri nibbled on another nail.

"If you haven't figured it out already, they're not like typical rich people. They're very laid back and welcoming. Well…maybe not…"

"What? What do I need to know?" Terri demanded.

"One of the brothers is kind of…difficult. The oldest one, Cyrus. They call him Number Two because he's a lot like his father."

"I know him. He runs the company, right?"

"Yes."

Terri groaned. She'd seen photos of him, and he appeared to be a very serious person who seldom smiled.

"Don't worry. He's mellowed a little since he and his wife reconciled and they have a baby now."

"He's mellowed *a little*?"

Shrugging, Alannah said, "Well, he's still Cyrus, and he takes his role as head of the family very seriously. In all honesty, I wouldn't worry about winning him over. Get the women on your side—his wife, Daniella, and their mom, Constance. Ivy's nice, too. If you can win over the women, they'll buffer you from any negativity."

"You're going to be at the party, right?"

"I think so."

"Alannah!" Terri shrieked.

"Yes, yes, of course I'll be there. I'll make sure that I'm there."

Terri's head flopped against the back seat. At least, she'd have someone else there that she knew. Hopefully, that would keep her from screwing up.

CHAPTER SIXTEEN

Terri was a nervous wreck, her usual confidence having plummeted from a high of one hundred percent to a low of almost nil. A dark knot of worry hung overhead like a storm cloud. She couldn't remember ever having such a major case of nerves before, and all because she wanted to make a good impression.

For the umpteenth time, she checked her appearance in the mirror, smoothing sweaty palms over the sleeveless chiffon dress, a Balmain design which fell to her ankles in deep burgundy. The breezy lightweight charmeuse lining felt like silk against her skin, and the scooped neckline molded over her breasts but showed no cleavage. She examined the back. The dress dipped low, not enough to reveal the tattooed hearts strung together across her lower spine, but far enough that she used a foundation stick to hide the heart on her right shoulder blade.

She pulled her hair up and clipped a hair piece on top. Viewing the finished product, she exhibited elegance and style, even if she did say so herself. Diamond studs in her ears and a gold purse with matching gold Louboutin sandals completed the look. Since she always kept him waiting, Gavin would be shocked that she was ready on time for once.

He arrived punctually, in a dark suit and shiny black Bruno Magli shoes. He looked absolutely delectable, and she couldn't help giving him a quick peck on the lips, which he then turned into a long, thorough kiss, sweeping his tongue along the edge of her lips.

"You look great," he said, casting an appreciative glance over her body and letting his hand trail down to her hip.

"Thank you." Terri turned in a circle to give him the full view. "You sure it's not too much? I hid my tattoo."

"My family doesn't care about that, and neither do I. Have you seen all the tattoos on Trenton? And Xavier has some, too."

"But they're men. It's different. They won't get judged." She smoothed nonexistent wrinkles from the dress.

"And neither will you. If I thought for one minute my family would mind, I wouldn't put you in a situation that cast you in a negative light. Stop worrying."

Terri grinned. "Yes, sir."

"Besides, I wouldn't have picked out those dresses if I thought any of them would be problem," Gavin said, a wicked smile coming over his face. "I want to show you off."

She understood that sentiment. She knew how to be arm candy.

"Your neck is bare, though. Why don't you wear the necklace I bought you? The rubies would go well with this dress."

The suggestion came as a surprise and temporarily left Terri speechless, but she cleared her throat and quickly recovered. "I like what I have on. The necklace is too much. Let's go." She took Gavin's hand and pulled him toward the door, but he stood firm.

A curious expression entered his eyes. "You don't like it?"

She hadn't considered he'd take her comment that way. "I love it."

"I've never seen you wear the necklace."

"There aren't many occasions where I can wear jewelry like that, silly."

He didn't respond to her teasing in the way she expected. "All the more reason you should wear it tonight."

Terri licked her lips, anxious to end the conversation. "I'll wear it another time, okay?"

She tried again to pull him to the door, but this time his hand tightened on hers and his frown deepened. "Go get it."

Terri bristled. "Is that a command?"

Instead of answering the question, Gavin said, "Usually women want to show off the jewelry I give them."

"I told you from the beginning, I'm not like the women you're used to. I wish you would stop comparing me to them."

"Go get it, Terri." His tone definitely changed, from a curious inquiry to an outright command.

Terri snatched her hand from his and went on the defensive. "You don't tell me what to do."

Not one facial muscle moved. "This isn't about me telling you what to—"

"Isn't it? 'Go get it, Terri.' What is that? Who do you think you are? Because you buy me gifts, you think you own me?"

"Where the hell did that come from? I have never—"

"Maybe I shouldn't go with you to this party. I obviously don't know my place where you're concerned."

"That's ridiculous," Gavin said through tight lips.

"No, it's not. You're being a jerk. I'm not going." She stalked by him, but Gavin caught her arm and dragged her back.

He searched her face. Defiantly, Terri looked right back at him, not flinching, not backing down. But her insides quivered. She didn't want to fight with him, but she hated the tone of his voice— the commanding tone that brooked no argument.

"I'm not that guy." He spoke through rigid lips.

Her lower lip trembled. "You don't know what I've been through," Terri said, her voice hoarse.

"Because you won't tell me."

His eyes bored into hers and she looked away.

How could she explain the things she allowed? The threats and the verbal and physical beat downs crushed her spirit and kept her in line. He forced her to commit acts that even to this day filled her with shame.

"Forget it," Gavin said. "I don't want to fight. Let's just go."

Terri let out a quiet breath of relief and swallowed, watching his stiff back move across the room. He yanked open the door and waited for her to exit ahead of him. Still a gentleman, even when furious.

Neither said a word as they walked downstairs. The waiting driver opened the door as they approached.

"Hello." Her neighbor, Mr. Raymond, shuffled by with Max, eyeing them curiously.

"Hi," Terri returned, with a little wave.

Gavin stood aside so she could enter the vehicle first and seconds later they were off.

She gnawed the inside of her lip while Gavin stared out the window, jaw still set in taut lines. She had to fix this mess she created. She hated how his anger felt. It ate at her, burning like acid from the inside out.

"I love the necklace. Maybe I overreacted, but I'm nervous about meeting your family."

His gaze shifted to her. "There's nothing to be worried about."

"Well, I am worried. I've never…met a man's parents before. This is all new for me."

The first man she'd ever been involved with had kept her a secret—a dirty secret from his family and wife for six whole years. The man from the last serious relationship—Talon—treated her like a prop, used her, and savagely let her know she wasn't the kind of woman he could take home to family.

"The necklace isn't at my apartment. It's too valuable. I moved it to my safe deposit box."

"Why didn't you say that in the first place?"

She shrugged.

His darker hand covered hers. "What did he do to you?"

Tears filled her eyes and her lower lip trembled. "He hurt me. A lot."

He cupped the back of her neck and drew his face closer to hers. The warm clasp of his hand soothed her pain and calmed the tremors under her skin. In the silence of the back seat, his honey-colored eyes burned with a savage brilliance.

"Tell me his name." He said the words slowly, with deadly intent.

He wanted to be her hero and bring her justice, but Terri shook her head. "He's in jail."

He searched her face. "I will never hurt you the way that he did."

He'd said the same before, and she trusted him completely. "I know."

Gavin lifted his arm and she relaxed into the crook of his shoulder, breathing easier. Feeling safe and protected in a way she never had before.

CHAPTER SEVENTEEN

Upon arrival at Constance Johnson's estate, Terri leaned on Gavin, squeezing his arm as they walked to the entrance.

Lights poured from every window of the house on Lake Washington. According to Gavin, this home was smaller than the one that he grew up in, and Terri couldn't imagine what that mansion must look like when this place was so massive.

In the large formal foyer, a uniformed member of the household staff came forward with a friendly greeting and led them back to a sitting room with a grand piano in one corner. Standing near two of the windows was a man she recognized as Cyrus, the eldest son, nodding and talking with an older white male—whom she imagined might be the guest of honor—and another man with long dreadlocks.

Almost immediately, an older woman with dark brown skin and a pleasant smile broke away from a conversation with a white woman dressed in a formal gown and pearls. Terri was suddenly glad she'd chosen the more formal dress to wear based strictly on the women's attire.

Right away, she guessed the approaching woman was Gavin's mother. Constance Johnson reeked of elegance and charm as she glided across the carpet. The chiffon skirt of the floor-length evening dress she wore reinforced the image of her floating, and the light orange color, similar to a lobster bisque, complemented her dark features. The beading on the bodice and lace sequins that extended down to the three-quarter-length sleeves sparkled under the lights, much like her dark eyes when she first looked fondly at her son and then at Terri.

"Welcome," Constance said. She lifted her cheek, and Gavin dutifully planted a quick peck to his mother's skin.

"You must be Terri Slade." Constance took one of her hands in both of hers and smiled into her eyes. "My son was right. You're absolutely gorgeous."

Not one to be easily embarrassed, Terri's cheeks heated, but she appreciated the warm welcome.

"Thank you, ma'am."

Constance glanced at Gavin. "Such good manners." Her eyes returned to Terri. "Please, call me Constance. Or, as some people do, you may call me Miss Constance. I really don't have a preference. What would you like to be called?"

"Terri is fine."

"Terri it is, then." She smiled the entire time she talked. "Gavin, do you mind if I borrow your lady friend?"

Terri suspected the question was less of a request and more of a statement.

"Not at all." He smiled reassuringly at Terri.

"Good." She looped an arm around Terri's and patted her hand. "I want you to sit next to me at dinner so we can get to know each other better. All I know is that you're from Atlanta, where my future son-in-law is from, as well. He and my daughter will be arriving soon, so you'll meet him. I'm so happy you came tonight. My son never brings women home to meet me, so you must be very special."

"Mother."

"Well, she is, isn't she, dear?"

His eyes met Terri's. "She is."

Terri bit the inside of her lip, warmth seeping into her belly at the intense way he looked at her. He acknowledged her in front of his mother in such an open and frank way, without a hint of hesitation. Her heart strained against her ribs. This happened often—

a sensation like her heart was about to burst from her chest.

"And I will tell you all sorts of things he doesn't want you to know," Constance said in a conspiratorial voice.

"*Mother.*"

"I'm just kidding, dear," Constance said over her shoulder, as she led Terri away. She slid a wicked grin to Terri, and Terri looked over her shoulder at Gavin who winked and sent another reassuring smile her way. She grinned and winked back.

Constance introduced her to the few people already in attendance. The guest of honor and his wife were the first, then Cyrus, Jr.—who barely smiled when he shook her hand. She remembered Alannah's comments about him and didn't take the cool reception personally. His wife, Daniella, was much friendlier, but Terri was relieved when Alannah and Trenton finally showed up.

Not long after, Ivy and Lucas arrived.

Ivy was tall—nigh on six feet in heels—and greeted her with a quick hug. "It's nice to finally meet you. My little brother has told us all about you."

Gavin pursed his lips. "She's older by five minutes, but you'd think it was five years."

"I'm a twin, too, and I'm also older." Terri winked at Ivy and they both giggled.

"Oh, brother." Gavin sighed. "Before the two of you get together and start acting crazy, this is Lucas, Ivy's fiancé."

Lucas was an attractive man, tall and thick with a mustache and beard. "Nice to meet you," he said.

They shook hands.

Lucas stared at her as he released her hand. "Do I know you?"

The question took her by surprise. "I don't think so."

Her answer didn't satisfy him, and he continued to study her with a frown on his face. Terri's scalp prickled under his scrutiny. Shifting from one foot to the other, she searched her mind, concerned that Lucas did indeed know her from somewhere. If so, where?

"You look really, really familiar. I could almost swear we've met before."

"I have one of those faces," Terri said, waving a dismissive hand as true panic tossed the limited contents of her stomach.

"I don't think so," Lucas said slowly, rubbing his jaw. "It's something else. You're not an actress, are you?"

Terri laughed away the query. "No." She swallowed, brushing a hand along her clammy neck.

"Where are you from?" he asked suddenly.

"All over."

Gavin shot her a glance, and heat rose in her neck. She panicked at the question and delivered a not-so-truthful answer.

"All over Atlanta, I mean," she amended.

"Maybe that's where I know you from. I'm from Atlanta. We must have met at some point."

"That's probably what it is." Terri nodded.

"It'll come to me eventually, and then I'll kick myself because I didn't remember."

A gentle tinkling sound broke through the conversation. The butler stood in the doorway, tapping a fork against a glass goblet. "Dinner is served," he announced.

Terri clutched her abdomen, almost collapsing from relief.

The entire party left the sitting room and followed the butler toward the dining room. Bringing up the rear, Gavin turned to Terri with curiosity in his eyes.

"Are you sure you don't know Lucas? He seemed pretty certain he knows you."

"Never met him before in my life." Terri shrugged. "He probably met someone who looks like me before. You know they say everyone has a twin."

"Yeah, that must be it," he said thoughtfully, though he didn't sound convinced.

****

The evening went well.

Initially, Terri sat in the formal dining room with the rest of the group, overwhelmed by the number of elements in the formal table setting—seven utensils, not including the bread knife, several plates, and four glasses, one for water and the other three for wines. The first course of an amuse-bouche, a serving of pink shrimp with a drizzle of lime aioli, awakened her taste buds. Warm soup came next. Thank goodness for Alannah, seated beside her, who nudged her with an elbow and surreptitiously pointed out which spoon went with the soup course. For the subsequent dishes, she followed everyone's lead when each course arrived.

Gavin and Trenton provided much of the laughs during the light-hearted dinner conversation. Seated next to Constance Johnson, Terri reined her typical boisterous responses. Anxious to impress the older woman, she curtailed her lively laugh to a low volume titter and took care to moderate the tone of her voice.

Fascinating conversations swirled around her. Ivy mentioned she and Lucas found a house and would soon list her current property, a multi-million dollar condo, for sale. Cyrus and his wife shared that they planned to go house-hunting in Spain. Not because they were moving, but simply because his wife loved Costa del Sol and wanted a vacation home there.

Not once did Terri feel she wasn't wanted at the dinner—not even by the eldest brother, Cyrus. He appeared curious about her, asking questions about what she did and how many siblings she had—that kind of thing. Not overtly rude in any way.

At one point, she glanced across the table at Gavin and imagined being part of this family. Her heart ached when she considered a future with him, so overwhelmed she took a sip of water to hide the trembling of her lips.

Formal dinner parties and haute couture dresses were beyond her dreams. She never thought when she fled her life in Georgia she'd be a welcomed guest at a table with a family worth billions. But being with Gavin made her realize that anything was possible.

****

It was quiet in the back of the car on the way to Terri's apartment. Gavin checked his phone and saw a couple of messages from his friends, asking when he could hang out again. True, he hadn't really spent time with them lately. Work and Terri occupied all his time.

She sidled next to him and hugged his arm. "Well...?"

Gavin continued scrolling through the messages with his thumb. He paused at the text from his broker about a hot stock trade and a reminder from his assistant about a delivery arriving at the house tomorrow.

"Well, what?" he asked.

"What did she think?"

"Who?"

"Your mother."

He fired a quick response to his broker and then tucked the phone in his jacket pocket. "I don't know," he said, just to torture her.

"Gavin!" She beat his arm with her fists.

Laughing, he grabbed her wrists. "All right, all right. She liked you." His mother liked her a lot, in fact, having drawn him aside to mention that she hoped to see more of Terri and get to know her better.

"I passed the mommy test?"

"You passed the mommy test. And the sibling test, too."

She stared out the window at the passing scenery, deep in thought, seemingly unaware that he watched her. Finally, her gaze flitted up to him. "I'm not a good girl." She said the words quietly, as though revealing some deep dark secret.

"I'm not a good guy," Gavin murmured. He traced a finger along the line of her jaw. "We're two peas in a pod. Kindred spirits."

"I'm serious." Terri nudged him.

Gavin lifted her chin. "Me, too. Whatever you did in the past doesn't matter to me. Stop beating yourself up." His forefinger traced the line of her lower lip. "I hate to see that look on your face."

"What look?"

"Like you're hurting."

She tightened her grip on his arm and took a deep breath. Her upper lip twitched, and when she spoke, a faint tremor filled her voice. "Have you ever done something so stupid that it results in consequences so bad that other people suffer? And no matter how much you want to take it back, you can't?"

Pain spiked in his chest as guilt reared its ugly head. "Yeah." The emotionless response served to buffer the current reality and the memory of the night that changed the trajectory of his life.

Terri shifted to get a better look at him, her eyes questioning, but Gavin avoided her gaze and stared straight ahead. If he could avoid it, he never talked about the night a drunk driver hit the car he rode in with his father.

"If I had made some different choices, my father would still be alive today," he said quietly, barely squeezing the words pass his tight throat.

"I thought a drunk driver hit the car you and your father were in."

"Yeah," he answered. It wasn't a real answer.

Terri kissed his cheek. "Stop beating yourself up," she said, using the same words he said to her minutes before.

He almost laughed. Much easier said than done.

The car drifted along in silence for several miles.

Terri's hold tightened on him again, and she rested her cheek against his shoulder. "Stay tonight, okay?"

He kissed her forehead. "Okay."

She held on strong—as if holding on for dear life—and it took a little while for Gavin to realize, he was holding on just as tight.

CHAPTER EIGHTEEN

You were wearing the hell out of that dress.

Terri smiled at the text on her way back to the car after a lunch date with Gavin. They'd been practically inseparable since she attended the party at his mother's house over a week ago. A line had been crossed, bringing them even closer together, and allowing her to feel comfortable enough to make a surprise visit to his workplace. His enthusiastic smile and hug when he came down to the atrium to meet her eliminated the tiny doubt she experienced about the impromptu visit.

They ate on the first floor of the building, at The Brew Pub, the restaurant that made up the family's casual dining chain. Gavin ordered a meatball sandwich, and she indulged in a double cheeseburger with bacon and a fried egg on top. They also shared a plate of Wreck 'Em fries, a high calorie appetizer covered in a mountain of chili, cheese, and jalapeño peppers. Afterward, they went up to the executive floor for dessert, a quickie on the sofa in his office.

She texted back. *You didn't look so bad yourself, Pretty Lips.*

Gavin wore a charcoal designer suit and a horizontally striped navy and silver tie today. He always looked delicious in clothes or out of them.

If I didn't have to go out of town, I'd put these lips on you. He and his older brother Xavier were going to do an inspection at the Portland brewery and would be there for a few days, until the weekend.

She grinned, which had everything to do with him. Terri stopped beside her Jimmy. *I'll miss you*, she typed, and froze. She stared at the words, finger hovering over the send button. There was nothing wrong with telling him she'd miss him. After all, they spent a lot of time together.

She hit the button and flinched, immediately regretting the impulsive move. Her stomach a painful knot of nerves, she waited for his response. It arrived seconds later.

I'll miss you more.

Smiling again, she leaned against her vehicle, savoring the words. He made her want to do girly things like bat her eyelashes and twirl a strand of hair.

Gavin sent another message. *Gotta run. I'll call you tonight and bring you something back.*

She was about to tell him he didn't have to, but he hated when she put off his gift-buying. Instead, she typed, *Thank you.*

Terri climbed into the truck. First, a run to the post office to buy money orders for a few bills and mail the cutest little pink dress she bought on sale for her niece, make a quick stop to put gas in her vehicle, and then over to Aldi's Market for a box of gourmet cheese straws which, thanks to Gavin, she was now addicted to. All that before going home to change for yoga and then making sure she was relaxed and waiting by the phone in time to receive Gavin's call.

Before she drove off, her cell phone rang and she fished it out of her purse. Her heart leapt when she saw her brother's name and she quickly answered. "Hey, big head. How's my favorite brother?"

"I'm your only brother."

"That's why you're my favorite."

"You suck." Damian gave a short laugh. "Um, are you sitting down?"

The hesitancy in his voice caught Terri's attention and her hand tightened on the phone. "Yes," she answered cautiously. She watched a trio of women laughing on their way into the building, holding doggy bags from their recent lunch.

Her brother blew out a short breath. "He's out."

A jolt of alarm made her mute, and the world came crashing down around her.

"Leesh, you there?" Damian asked, using her nickname.

Terri gripped the steering wheel with her left hand to keep the world from spinning. "I'm here," she replied shakily. "How can he be out? They gave him five years."

"Good behavior or some nonsense, I don't know."

"He destroyed lives. He hurt a lot of people." *He hurt me.*

"I know, but the local news said he's been released. There was a write up in the paper about it, too."

"When?"

"Yesterday."

Terri rested her forehead on her arm. Nausea climbed her intestinal tract and threatened to spill from her lips.

Breathe. Breathe.

"Leesh, I can hear you breathing. You don't sound good. Talk to me."

She swallowed hard, fighting back the nausea and dizzying terror. "He can't find me. I covered my tracks and have a new name he doesn't know anything about. I'm far, far away. He *cannot* find me."

"He won't, as long as you're careful. No bank account. Nothing in the public eye."

She laughed bitterly. "As if I ever wanted to be in the public eye."

The media frenzy surrounding the trial caused her name and image to be plastered in newspapers, online, and on the local news channels.

During their relationship, Talon never saw her as a threat. He trusted that his intimidation tactics kept her securely under his thumb. But he was wrong. She was a key witness in the trial against him. She'd worn a wire and provided plenty of evidence, taking pictures of files and records, in exchange for immunity. So if Talon ever found her, she had no doubt he'd kill her. She collapsed his entire criminal enterprise and helped put him away.

"I didn't want to scare you, but I thought you should know," Damian said.

Terri lifted her head from her arm. "Thanks."

"Be careful."

"Don't worry about me. I'll be fine. He'll never think to look for me here. I pay cash for everything and there's almost no paper trail." Except for the safe deposit box at the bank that contained her birth certificate, change of name documentation, and the necklace from Gavin, she lived simply with no ties to the local community in case she had to leave under short notice.

"You need any money?" Damian asked, looking out for her in spite of everything that happened.

"I should be giving you money."

"Leesh, come on."

"You know it's true. You lost everything because of me." Damian invested his savings in the house flipping portion of Talon's "business," which turned out to revolve around inflated prices and easy closings fashioned by bribed appraisers and loan officers.

"Because of *him*," Damian said, voice hard. "You didn't know when you asked me to invest."

"But once I knew the truth, I didn't leave him."

She turned a blind eye to his questionable business practices because she appreciated being taken care of, having designer clothes, shoes, and handbags—possessions she could never afford on her own—and the peace of mind of having a place to lay her head. A vast change from the life she lived growing up and with her boyfriend of six years, with whom she lived simply in a two-bedroom apartment because he supported two households—theirs and the one for his wife and kids in Alabama.

When she finally did question Talon, he turned on her and made it clear she could never leave him. The threats and abuse became a regular occurrence.

"You paid for it by being his punching bag. If I'd known what he was doing to you..."

No one knew. Not until the trial, when all her dirty secrets came out. The physical abuse. The verbal abuse. The times he forced himself on her.

"Leesh, the past is the past. You paid your restitution when you went to the DA and helped them build a case against him. You risked your own safety to do that."

"So you forgive me, right?" she asked, quietly.

"There's nothing to forgive. You were a victim, too."

"Not everyone felt that way. A lot of people thought I got off easy."

"They're wrong," Damian said firmly. He sighed. "Listen, I have to get ready to go to my second job. You want me to call you later?"

"No, you go ahead. I'm fine."

"You sure?"

"Yes."

"Call me if you need anything. Anything at all."

"I will," Terri promised.

"I'll give you a call tomorrow, okay?"

"Okay. Bye."

Terri disconnected the call. She ran a hand over the soft fabric of her green dress, trying to remember the giddy joy she experienced during the hour and a half she spent with Gavin. The dress was new, purchased expressly because Gavin liked her in shades of this color. Lime green. Forest green. Jade green.

She crossed her arms over her stomach. The nausea was gone but now a dull ache filled her gut.

Rule number two, never fall in love. But she was falling for him. Hard. Breaking her own rule. She didn't do love. Love brought too much pain.

And what would Gavin think if he knew everything about her?

****

Trudging up the walkway after the driver dropped her off, Terri yawned. She arrived at the double doors that led to the lobby of her building but paused with her hand on the metal handle. A knot of unease settled in her shoulders, and she turned around to scan the parking lot.

She had the feeling she was being watched. No one sat in any of the parked cars, yet she couldn't shake the feeling. Her eyes scanned the shadows beside the bushes and trailed over the grass and trees outside the wire fence.

Her fingers tightened on the handle of the door. Nothing appeared out of place, but the uneasy feeling filtered into her stomach and sat—as large and heavy as a slab of stone. It kept her there, heart pounding, eyes darting to and fro. Still, nothing.

Probably her imagination, paranoia setting in after the conversation with her brother. Shaking off the disquiet, Terri entered the building and rushed up the stairs to her apartment and shut the door.

She slid across the chain. Flipped the first deadbolt. Turned the second deadbolt. Twisted the lock in the doorknob. She didn't turn on the lights but walked over to the window and peeped through the blinds, surveying the parking lot.

Still nothing. No movement, except for leaves rustling in the wind.

Breathing easier, she sat on the bed.

She was being paranoid. According to her brother, Talon was only released from jail yesterday.

No way could he be here already.

An hour later, she was sitting on the sofa when the phone rang. She snatched it up on the first ring. "Gavin," she breathed.

"Hey, there. I meant to call earlier, but I just wrapped up a meeting with my slave driver brother after we spent the night drinking with a bunch of executives." He laughed.

"They know how to party, I take it?"

"Do they ever." He yawned. "How was your day?"

"I wish you were here," she said softly, folding her feet beneath her.

"Me, too." He paused, quiet for a few seconds. "Are you okay? Your voice sounds funny."

"I'm fine. I just…" Her face crumbled. *Hold it together, Terri.* "Long day. Tired."

"I understand. I better go. I just wanted to call because I said

I would. We have an early day tomorrow. I'm turning into my worst nightmare, a corporate drone."

"Stop." Terri laid on her side with the phone pressed to her ear, the sound of his deep voice calming her fears and soothing her jittery nerves. "Pretty soon, you're going to ask to be put on payroll. I can tell you're starting to like it."

"Don't tell anybody," he said, lowering his voice.

Terri giggled. "I won't. It'll be our little secret."

"Good." He yawned again. "I'll see you on Friday. Good night, Sweet Ass."

"Good night, Pretty Lips."

****

Gavin stared at the phone.

"What's the matter?" Xavier snapped his briefcase shut and picked up his jacket, on the way to his own room after their quick strategy session in preparation for tomorrow.

"Don't know. Could be nothing." He tapped the phone on his palm. "She didn't sound like herself."

"Maybe she misses you."

"Maybe."

But he wondered if it could be something else.

CHAPTER NINETEEN

A bell was ringing. But why? And where?

Terri's sleep-drugged brain couldn't discern the details in the limbo state she hovered in between sleep and wakefulness. Rolling over, she rubbed her eyes as the scent of smoke drifted into her nose.

Her eyes snapped open and she glanced wildly around the room in an effort to get her bearings. The loud racket came from the hallway. The fire alarm!

Scrambling from the bed, wearing only a pair of short shorts and a cami, she rushed into the living room. It was warmer in there. Quickly, she released the top three locks, but when she reached for the doorknob, the metal scorched her fingers and she snatched away her hand. The fire must be right outside the door.

Wide awake now, she ran back into the bedroom and flicked up one of the blinds. The parking lot was crowded with her neighbors. Mr. Raymond stood out next to one of the other neighbors from the first floor, holding Max. Other people crowded around, some in pajamas, others wearing street clothes.

Terri swung away from the window and tugged on a pair of jeans. She grabbed her purse from the nightstand, pulled up the blinds, and yanked up the window.

"Help!" she screamed.

A man wearing blue pajamas swung his head in her direction. He pointed. "There's someone over there."

Terri stared at the grass three stories down, trying to gauge if she dared risk jumping. Better to have broken bones or a twisted ankle than be burned to a crisp.

She tossed her purse to the ground and then sat on the window and swung her legs out. Moving slowly, she twisted her body so that she faced the outer wall, using her feet to provide friction and her hands to hold her up. Arms trembling, heart beating at a rapid pace, she dropped onto a lip of wood, maintaining a grip on the windowsill above her head.

"Jump! We'll catch you," someone yelled. Four men stood below with their hands linked together.

Terri took two deep breaths and summoned the courage needed to let go.

"Come on!" one of the men called. "Don't be scared."

The money!

The thought dropped like an anvil into her thoughts.

No. No. In her haste to escape, she completely forgot the thousands of dollars hidden under the mattress.

Gripping the ledge, Terri tried to hoist herself up. Her right foot slipped and she scraped her arms in the struggle to stay on the ledge.

"Come on, sweetheart, we've got you," a man called from below.

Panting, Terri fought to pull herself up again. Dammit. Why wasn't she stronger? She couldn't see the fire from her vantage point, but it was obvious the flames had entered her apartment by the generated heat.

"Come on, honey, jump!"

One more time, Terri made an effort to lift her body higher, but she didn't have the strength. All the money she spent the last three years saving would be lost. But not just the money, all her books. Her clothes. The snow globes.

Tears of frustration filled her eyes. Shoulders slumped in resignation, she looked over her shoulder at the men below her, took a leap of faith, and jumped.

****

Terri sat with knees pulled up to her chest in the hotel room watching the news through puffy eyes that burned from a long bout of crying.

According to the reporter on the scene, the firefighters suspected arson at Stack Home Apartments. The flames spread quickly because the perpetrator used an accelerant. The fire started on her end of the hall, and her shaggy-haired neighbor died in the blaze because he didn't get out on time. A few people suffered from smoke inhalation, but other than the rock music lover, no other lives were lost.

Thanks to the American Red Cross, Terri had a place to stay for the next few days and food to eat, but she lost all her possessions, including the phone she left charging on the bureau in the panic to escape.

Wrapping her arms around her knees, she wondered if Talon could have started the fire. Would he risk killing others to get at her? Could he have found her already?

Terri burrowed under the covers and curled up on her side. She didn't want to think anymore.

Everything she'd accumulated on her own was lost. She'd have to start all over again.

CHAPTER TWENTY

Terri picked up her purse in the back room of the salon. She removed her keys, attached to a pink rhinestone-decorated tube of pepper spray, and then slung the bag over her shoulder. She didn't think Talon caused the fire, suspecting that when he came at her, he would use the direct approach. He'd want her to know it was him, but she purchased the spray anyway as a precaution.

"See you guys in a couple of days," she called on her way out. Her co-workers had brought in bags of clothes, all stored in the back of the Jimmy, until she could get on her feet again. She called Alannah from the salon and gave her an update and left a message for Gavin, too, letting him know where she was staying.

She exited the salon into the early evening. A light mist of rain dropped from the sky, and she pulled a mini-umbrella from her purse and popped it open. She paid close attention to the surrounding area, clutching the spray tight in one hand. Hurrying to her vehicle, she almost tripped when she saw Gavin get out of his black Spyder, parked right next to hers at the end of the aisle.

Her mouth went dry, and her knees weakened, almost buckling under the weight and intensity of his gaze. She took him in, from the top of his button down shirt and crossed arms, to the Bruno Magli loafers on his feet. She couldn't see his eyes, though. They were hidden behind a pair of sunglasses.

"You can always tell the people who aren't from Seattle. They carry umbrellas." He spread his arms wide and she tossed aside the umbrella to fling herself into him. His strong arms folded around her.

"I'm so glad you're here," she said softly into his shirt, so weak with relief she sagged against his hard torso.

"I got your message," he murmured in her ear.

Terri lifted her head from his chest. "The past day or so has been hectic. I don't have a phone. I don't have anything. I lost my clothes, my shoes, everything. I took off work tomorrow so I could just…think. I don't know what I'm going to do, where I'm going to stay. If—"

Gavin cupped her face and stemmed the rapid flow of words. He looked deeply into her eyes. "I'm here." The words had the desired effect, calming her beating pulse and letting her know she wasn't alone.

Swallowing against the lump swelling in her throat, Terri lifted her arms around his neck. Rain sprinkled dew on their skin and created a light haze around them. She pressed her lips to his, and his mouth moved gently over hers in a sweet and comforting kiss.

"Let me take you to dinner, but I want to show you something first."

"Gavin, I don't have anything to wear out. These jeans and T-shirt are the nicest clothes I own right now."

He smiled into her eyes with such tenderness, her heart melted and she forgot the fears of the past couple of days. "What you're wearing is fine. Come on."

Terri didn't argue, relieved that for now, she could stop thinking and let someone else take the lead. She walked around to the passenger side where he waited with the door open and slipped onto the seat.

When he was seated behind the wheel, she asked, "Where are we going?"

He started the car and glanced at her. "You'll see."

They drove into the heart of downtown Seattle and pulled up to the door of the Four Seasons Hotel. She frowned at him, but he didn't say a word. The valet opened her door and Gavin came around and handed the young man the keys to the car.

They rode the elevator in silence and then exited on a floor where there were only two doors, one to the left and the other to the right.

Gavin used a key card to open one of the doors and held it wide so she could pass through before him. She stepped onto the hardwood floors and gasped at the beauty of the place. "It's an apartment?"

"Condo. You can buy private residences here at the Four Seasons."

Terri's mouth fell open at the spectacular view before her. "Is that Elliott Bay?" She dropped her purse on the table beside one of the sofas and rushed over to the window but took a step back when a wave of dizziness hit her after she looked down. A place like this must cost millions.

"It is. Let me show you the rest of the place," Gavin said. He kept a reserved tone to his voice.

He walked ahead of her, opening doors and acting as tour guide as they went to the back. "Two bedrooms, a home office, and a media room between the two bedrooms."

The view in the master bedroom was just as breathtaking as the one in the living room. Plenty of glass with more views of the water, and a terrace with a view of the mountains in the distance. The ginormous walk-in closet was literally larger than her entire apartment, with shelves and racks waiting to be filled with the finest wardrobe.

They left the bedroom, and he showed her the well-equipped kitchen with top-of-the line appliances, and even a wine cooler and a huge pantry with a step stool inside the door.

"What do you think? You like it?" Gavin asked, leaning against the counter.

"Of course I like it!" Terri gushed, which prompted a smile on his face. "It's absolutely beautiful. You did good. Are you giving up the house and moving in here?"

"No," he replied.

Why show her all of this if he wasn't moving in? "This isn't your condo?"

He shook his head. "It's my sister's old place, and she was going to put it on the market since she and Lucas found a house, but I convinced her to hold off before selling it. I like the location and it's really nice. I leased it from her for a year, but I won't be staying here."

"That doesn't make any sense. Why would you…?" Comprehending what he'd done, she hesitated, an almost undetectable flutter of apprehension filtering through her bones. "I-I don't understand."

"You're going to stay here," Gavin said. "It's yours, for the next year at least, to help you get back on your feet. You have a concierge at your disposal, 24-hour staff to accommodate your needs. Fitness center, pool—all the amenities of the hotel and then some."

"You can't do this," Terri said quietly. "It's too much."

"Already done." He removed the sunglasses, stuck them in the pocket of his shirt, and locked eyes with her. Holding up the key card, he said, "This is yours and this is your home. It is absolutely and completely yours to do with as you wish. If you don't feel like cooking and want to have a meal brought up from the kitchen, that's fine. Come and go as you please."

"What you're doing doesn't make any sense."

"Of course it makes sense. I want you to stay here."

"*Why?* I can get another place. You don't have to—"

"Terri." Slowly, he came toward her and she looked up and saw the anger flickering in his eyes. "What kind of man do you think I am? How could I not take care of you when I have the means to do it?"

Terri glanced away, mind racing.

"I'm not going to impose on your space because I know how important it is to you to have your own place. I have a key, too, but I won't use it unless you tell me it's okay. Good enough?"

An affirmative answer should've tumbled easily from her mouth, but she worried about what this would mean. The control he'd have over her. A familiar fear squeezed her heart. "Gavin, I—"

He crowded her against the wall, forearms resting on either side of her head, not a single part of his body touching hers, but she felt his energy just the same. Their faces were less than six inches apart and his eyes burned into hers. "I was in Portland when I got your message and I couldn't reach you. I felt so damn helpless."

"You're not responsible for me, Gavin."

"Maybe I want to be." Neither of them blinked. They just stared into each other's eyes. "You'll have a car and a driver, an allowance and accounts at any store you want to rebuild your wardrobe."

The torture of being so close to him and not touching angled its way through her body.

"Thank you," she said quietly. "I'll pay you back." She didn't know how or when. If it meant working eighty hours a week, she intended to repay every cent.

"This isn't a loan, and no matter what happens between us over the next year, this place is yours, free and clear. What else do you need? Tell me."

"You're such a good man. What you've done is enough." She'd considered pawning the necklace he gave her as a gift, but didn't have to now.

"You're sure?"

"Yes, but I do have one question. Not just anyone can come up here, right? They must have a keycard?"

"If they don't have a card giving them access, they can't come up to the residence floors. Period."

"Then I don't need anything else."

Gavin pulled her into his arms and she went willingly, eagerly, grabbing onto him and pressing her body flush against his.

He pressed his lips against hers and she extended the tip of her tongue to trace the seam of his lips.

"You're mine," he murmured, grasping the back of her head in the palm of his hand.

Head tilted back, Terri fell into the sensation of his mouth on the underside of her jaw. His hands roamed down her sides and grabbed her ass and squeezed, forcing her to acknowledge the solid length stretched in his pants.

"I'm yours." The words came out of nowhere, simply

erupting from her throat in a trembling whisper. A forced truth, glaringly obvious for them both to see.

As if her words lit a fire in his blood, Gavin stripped off her clothes, starting with her pants, revealing a pair of panties in wine-colored lace, and pulling her top over her head without ceremony. When he'd stripped down to gray boxer briefs, he lifted her onto the counter and pressed his face to her bosom, clawing at the straps of her bra until they hung loosely down her arms.

She was shaking, and he was, too.

"I take care of what's mine."

He grasped the back of her head again and hauled her toward him, mouth devouring, demanding her consent. The kiss lasted an eternity, and she savored the taste of him.

Gavin, Gavin, Gavin. Hope for a future with him soared in her chest.

Legs closed around his hips, she smoothed her hands over the contour of his hard arms and shoulders. She pressed kisses onto his face, showering affection on his nose, his chin, and his delicious mouth.

"I thought we were going to get something to eat," she whispered, nipping at the lobe of his ear.

"We are." He kissed her neck and collarbone, tongue flicking into the hollow of her throat. He dragged the crotch of the panties aside and stared at her shaved mound. "But I want to eat you first. Then we'll order room service."

His tongue game was spectacular, enough to make her ache and long for his mouth at random times—at work, at the supermarket, in the library. The stuff legends were made of. She would write poetry about it if she were poetically inclined. Gavin lifted her knees, and she watched with breathless anticipation as he bent his head between her thighs.

CHAPTER TWENTY-ONE

Gavin dropped into the chair across from Trenton's desk. He always relaxed in this office. The dark furniture and dim lighting gave the room the air of a nightclub lounge rather than a corporate office.

He waited while Trenton's executive assistant, Diana, flipped pages on contracts and pointed to the places his brother needed to sign. Tall and plus-sized with a short natural, she had an air of efficiency and no-nonsense. In the short time he'd been at the office, Gavin recognized the extent of Trenton's dependence on her.

Diana eventually finished and left the brothers alone.

"Your social media department is mediocre," Gavin said.

"I'm fine today, and how are you?" Trenton asked, setting his pen on the desk.

"That wasn't the best greeting, but you know I'm right. All we do is talk about beer."

"We're a beer company."

"I know that, but we need to inject some personality into the interactions with the followers. Ivy's restaurant group has the same number of followers Johnson Brewing Company does on Twitter. Considering the size and position of JBC in the industry, we should have way more than seventy-five thousand."

Trenton narrowed his eyes and smiled. "You have some ideas."

"A few," Gavin admitted. He rubbed his jaw. "There are a lot more things we can do besides tweeting about beerfests and the latest brew."

"What did you have in mind?" Trenton asked, sitting forward.

"I'm not sure yet. Let me take a look at the marketing campaign and see if I can come up with some tie-ins."

He already had some ideas of how they could use videos. One idea was to partner with well-known chefs and have them create exclusive recipes using JBC's beer as a main ingredient.

A grin spread across Trenton's face. "Don't tell me you want to work in my department."

"And have you be my boss? Hell, no. Besides, I'm a science guy, not a marketer."

Although, he did see a potential marriage between marketing and science if they educated consumers on the basics, such as proper glassware for the different styles of beer. Size and shape of the glass affected foam retention, and foam helped maintain the product's volatiles, thereby affecting the aroma and ultimately the drinking experience, the same way the right stemware influenced the enjoyment of wine.

Gavin lifted from the chair. "When can I get the marketing materials?"

"By the end of the day. Sure you don't want to work in my department?"

"I'm not working anywhere." Gavin proceeded to the door.

"Oh, that's right. You're only here temporarily and learning what you can because Mother asked you to."

Gavin didn't miss the sarcastic tone in Trenton's voice, but he chose not to respond to it.

****

The pat-pat sound of rain hitting the windows filled the bedroom like woodpeckers relentlessly attacking the trunk of a tree. In the past week, they'd christened the kitchen counter, the dining room table, the shower, and now lay naked in the bed fooling around.

Terri pouted. "You hit me too hard. My butt is sore." She

rolled over to snuggle up beside Gavin in the big bed.

"I wouldn't have to hit you so hard if you'd behave."

"Rub it and make it feel better."

He let out an exaggerated sigh and sat up. Instead of rubbing, he pressed his lips into the fleshiness of each cheek and licked her bottom.

"Better?" he asked, bringing his face close to hers.

"Mhmm." Terri smiled.

He flopped onto his back again and she reached up to trace the line where his lips came together. "You know what I thought when I first met you?"

"What?" He sucked her finger into his mouth and she giggled and pulled it back out.

"I thought you had such delicious-looking lips, I wanted to sit on your face."

His head tilted toward her. "Is that why you did that the first time we had sex?"

Terri's head popped up from the pillow. "I did *not* sit on your face the first night."

"Damn near," Gavin muttered.

"You're so full of shit." She cut her eyes at him.

"That's why I have to keep spanking that ass. You curse like a sailor."

"You curse more than I do. Should I spank *your* ass?" She dropped her head to the pillow again, keeping an eye on his profile.

"That's not how ass spanking works," he said, dead serious.

"Oh, really?"

"The only asses getting spanked around here are of the female persuasion."

"Chauvinist pig."

He chuckled to himself and closed his eyes, settling down, ready to sleep.

"You think you're so funny."

"I'm hilarious."

"Take your act on the road, then."

"Maybe I will."

"Smart ass."

"Keep talking," he warned. He drew his bottom lip between his teeth and smacked one hand against the other, indicating what he'd do to her behind. She almost felt the sting of his hand against her soft bottom, and her nipples tightened.

She watched his chest move up and down in the dim room and dragged the tip of her finger along the scar running down his inner arm. "Are you still going to Hawaii for the free diving competition?"

"Yes."

Fear knotted in her chest. She thought he'd abandoned the idea since he hadn't mentioned it again. A few days ago, the committee contacted him to see if he was interested in participating. Having him there would attract great media attention to the event, and after some consideration, he agreed.

They didn't talk about the future, and his desire to participate made her wonder if he planned to go back to the life he lived before the fall in the Andes. The thought of him leaving hurt her heart.

"You haven't been training," she said.

"I've done it dozens of times before."

"You said you always train before you do any of your stunts, and you've been busy working," Terri pointed out.

"It'll be fine," Gavin said, speaking over a wide yawn. "A few days before the event, I'll head down to Maui and train."

He was so unconcerned, while she was terrified. She hated the thought of him risking his life. Just because he'd done it before didn't mean an accident couldn't happen. Not too long ago, a famed free diver—a record holder and someone with more experience than Gavin—died underwater.

"Why do you really do it?" she asked.

He turned to her. "Do what? Free dive?"

"Any of it. Free diving, free singling—"

"Free soloing," he corrected.

"I don't care what you call it!" Terri lifted onto an elbow and looked into his startled eyes. Her outburst had taken him by surprise. "Why do you do it?"

"I told you before, it's exciting. People like me—"

"I don't want to know about people like you. I want to know why *you* take these risks. You've been here for months and haven't done anything remotely dangerous. Why are you so keen to go out there and risk your life again?"

Gavin rubbed his forehead. "I don't know, Terri. I guess my family's right. I have a death wish." He laughed, but it was a hollow sound.

"Is that why?" she asked quietly.

He swallowed and his face became as expressionless as a paper sack. Staring across at the far wall, he said, "I don't know." Silence cloaked the room. "I think there are times when I...want to die."

His answer broke her heart and she blinked back tears. What burden did someone as carefree as him carry that made him say such a thing?

"Why?"

He didn't answer, only shook his head.

"I don't think you want to die. You just think you deserve to."

Abruptly, he closed his eyes and cut her off. "Go to sleep."

Terri stared at him for a while longer—the smooth brown skin, the short, wispy lashes, the strength in his arms and chest, and the power in his muscular thighs. If anything happened to him...

Heat exploded in her chest. What she felt for Gavin was much stronger than like and stronger than anything she'd felt for a man in a long time—perhaps ever. She didn't want to think about what that meant.

She lived by certain rules. Most important, rule number two, never fall in love. This couldn't be love. She was too smart to fall into that trap again. It never lasted and only brought pain.

Terri climbed on top of Gavin and nestled her head in the crook of his neck. Her breasts flattened against his hard chest, and she slid one leg between his hair-roughened thighs. She equated the rough sensation of his skin against hers with not only their differences as male and female, but with the word that always came to mind when she thought of him—*safe*.

"Good night." She closed her eyes, settling in for the night.

"So you're just going to lay on me like I'm a pillow or bed or something?" he asked, effecting a grumpy tone.

"You don't mind, do you?"

Lying on top of him was such a comfy position. Her body slowly succumbed to sleep. Gavin didn't answer right away, and she allowed herself to be tugged deeper into slumber.

"I don't mind." He placed a hand in the middle of her back. Big and warm, his hand was like a layer of security.

Her eyes fluttered open, and he traced a finger down the bridge of her nose. Their eyes met and held, and the moment felt as intimate as any sexual act they'd shared.

"Don't go," she whispered. She hadn't meant to say the words on her heart, but didn't regret them.

He didn't respond right away. He looked into her eyes, searching for something.

"Go to sleep, Sweet Ass," he whispered with a smile.

"Gavin…" she said, on the verge of begging. The thought of him going into the water and risking his life unsettled her so much her stomach felt queasy.

"I won't go," he said, solemnly.

The pain in her chest diminished somewhat.

Relieved, Terri touched his mouth. "Good night, Pretty Lips."

Then she closed her eyes and drifted off.

CHAPTER TWENTY-TWO

"So she's just a friend?" Terri said into the phone to Gavin.

The woman hanging on his arm in the photo at the Billboard Music Awards in Las Vegas didn't look like a friend. Plus, Twiggle O'Hara, the singer/actress/model was gorgeous, with bone-straight raven tresses cut in a blunt bob, ruby lips, and piercing brown eyes that challenged the cameras to find a bad side.

"That's what I said," Gavin confirmed, tiredly.

"If you say so."

"I invited you to come, remember?"

Terri had been tempted to accompany him but couldn't risk having her photo splashed all over social media, and to date, she hadn't told Gavin everything about her past. She preferred to keep their relationship low-key, but on the upside, the danger with Talon had safely passed. During the past six weeks, her online research indicated he remained in Atlanta, and according to her brother, local mumblings indicated he might start up another business—a legitimate one this time.

The fire at Stack Home Apartments turned out to be arson, started by her strange neighbor across the hall. After numerous letters about lease violations involving the condition of his apartment, and complaints about the noise level, the landlord had finally asked him to move out. In retaliation, her neighbor set fire to the place but miscalculated and lost his life in the blaze.

"I told you I'm not one for the lights and camera. And is that your excuse for being caught kissing another woman?" Terri demanded. The nerve. He was actually blaming her.

"I kissed her on the cheek because she's a good friend."

"That looked like more than a kiss on the cheek."

"It's the angle of the photo," Gavin said testily, sounding as if he spoke through clenched teeth. "I kissed her cheek."

"What about the other images? Your arm is around her, touching her hip. It looks like a very familiar touch, like you've done it dozens of times before." He touched Terri like that, resting his hand on her hip or just above her bottom. "I don't understand why the two of you have to be all up on each other if you're only friends—buddies, as you put it. And why did a headline say *Back Together Again*, as if you've reunited with a long lost love?"

She'd always been confident about her ability to hold a man's interest and wasn't the jealous type. Yet there was no doubt the burning sensation in her belly was ugly, putrid jealousy.

"To sell magazines. To get clicks on their website. I have to deal with this nonsense all the time." Frustration poured through the lines.

"I thought you liked attention."

"I like when I can control what the media says about me. Frankly, the stories never mattered before."

"So it's me?"

"Yeah, it's you."

That stung. "Fine. I'll pretend I didn't see you with another woman. I'll pretend a famous floozy pawing all over you doesn't bother me."

"That's not what I said. I just..." He sighed. "I'm coming back tonight."

"You're at an important event and have parties to go to. You can't do that. We're good. Have fun with your *friend*. Not like we both can't have friends."

"You know when you say shit like that, it drives me crazy." Quiet rested on the line. "I'll see you when I get back."

"Don't worry. I'm over it."

"Are you sure? I don't want to hear about Twiggle and our supposed kiss when I get back."

"I said it's fine!" Terri snapped.

He muttered something unintelligible, and she strained to hear but couldn't distinguish any of the words.

"Fine," he said. Then he hung up.

Hung up. Without saying goodbye.

Terri lifted a hand above her head to fling the phone across the room, but changed her mind and simply tossed it onto the sofa.

"Fine," she spat to the empty room.

Terri bounced up from the chair and went into the kitchen. Minutes later, a pint of chocolate chip ice cream in hand and a two-liter Pepsi wedged under her arm, she dragged herself over to the sofa and plopped down. Flipping on the television, she stared at the screen, cursing herself for nosing around Gavin's social media account. Now she wished she hadn't been so curious.

Screw him, she thought, and settled in for the night.

****

Loud pounding startled Terri from sleep. She bolted upright, frowning and searching the dim room for the source of the racket. Melted ice cream pooled in the container on the coffee table, and an infomercial extolling the virtues of a new and improved diet pill played on the oversized flat screen TV.

The pounding came again, and she wondered who in the hell had the audacity to pound on her door this time of night. There better be a bomb scare in the hotel.

She scampered to the door and peered out the peephole. *Gavin.* His intense stare focused on the door, as if he could see her. A shiver shimmied up her spine.

"Open the door," he said.

"Maybe I have company," she called out snidely to annoy him.

"Maybe you want me to break this goddamn door down."

Terri unhooked the latch and opened the door, and he lanced her with an icy glare.

"You think it's funny to make me wait out here?"

"I was asleep. I didn't know you were out here." In black pants and shirtsleeves rolled up on his muscular forearms, he looked delectable. "Why didn't you just come in?"

"I don't have the key on me, and besides, I told you this is your space. You have to invite me in."

He stated those conditions in the beginning, and not once had he ever broken his promise.

Terri stepped back and widened the door. "Come in."

Gavin marched in, tension rippling off the rigid set of his spine. She followed him to the middle of the living room, where he cast a glance at the half-empty bottle of Pepsi and melted ice cream.

She folded her arms over her yellow cami. "What are you doing here? You aren't due back until day after tomorrow."

"That was the plan, but my woman called me a few hours ago, acting like a damn fool."

My woman. When exactly the change took place, Terri couldn't be sure, but he was hers and she was his.

"If I'm such a fool, what are you doing here?"

"To talk to you in person and prove to you there's nothing going on between me and Twiggle."

"How do you plan to do that?"

"I have a message for you." Gavin showed her the phone, Twiggle freeze-framed on the screen.

"What—"

He turned on the video and the actress spoke in her lilting Irish brogue.

"Hello Terri, please don't be mad at Gavin-pooh. He's a dear, dear friend of mine and was only doing me a *huge* favor. Helping me save face, actually, after my dreadful ex humiliated me." Her lips turned downward into an exaggerated sad face. "You don't need the sordid details. Please don't be mad at him. For him to ask me to record this message means he must be crazy about you. I would feel terrible if doing me a favor caused him any trouble at all. You have nothing to worry about, love. He adores you, and there is absolutely nothing going on between us. There never was."

Terri's face burned from embarrassment, but she was very

pleased, too. "You came all the way here to show that to me?"

Gavin tucked the phone in his pocket. "Are you satisfied now?"

She nodded. He made her so weak. Unstable. "You could have just sent me the video."

"We both know that wouldn't have been enough."

"So you're upset with me?"

Gavin hardly ever expressed anger toward her, but she tested his patience with her tardiness. Last week she rushed out of the bedroom, full of apologies. He waited with crossed arms and mouth pressed together.

"Next time, I'm leaving your ass," he warned.

She sidled up to him and pressed kisses to his lips. He was unmoved, so she grabbed his junk. "You sure about that?" she asked, as he grew in her hand.

He bit his lip to keep from smiling, but amusement sparked in his eyes.

"That's what I thought," she said and cockily dragged her lips across his mouth. This time, he succumbed to the kiss. Then she took his hand and led the way out.

"Of course I'm upset. I can't do this every time," he said, handsome face hard and unyielding. "You'll have to trust me. Can you trust me?"

"Yes," Terri answered. She licked her lips, imagining sucking on his full bottom lip.

"You sure?"

"Mhmm." The heat of arousal crawled up her thighs. Unable to bear the separation anymore, she pressed against him. "I can't believe you came all the way back here." She looked up at him from beneath her lashes. "That's so hot."

His eyes narrowed on her upturned face. "Hot, huh?"

"Mhmm." Terri trailed her fingers down his shirt, pressing the tips into the hard muscle. "You have no idea how hot."

Gavin's lids lowered over his eyes. "You drive me out of my mind, you know that?"

"Mhmm." She fit a hand over the massive bulge in his pants. As a result, his body stiffened, and his nostrils flared.

"You don't even know how to behave, do you?" he asked,

voice low and hoarse.

"Nope."

He pulled her in until their bodies rested flush against each other. Gazing up at him, lost in his eyes, the helplessness she often experienced flooded her body.

With him, she was liquid. Putty.

He kissed her, his mouth gentle and moist as it moved over hers.

"So you're not mad anymore?" he murmured against her lips, the light brown of his eyes barely visible through the thin slits his eyes had become.

"How could I stay mad when you flew all the way back here just to deliver this message?" Terri flicked her tongue against his mouth and nipped his bottom lip. "You knew I was upset and came to fix it."

"So how jealous were you?" he asked, sounding smug.

Pursing her lips, Terri wound her arms around his neck.

"Hmm?" he dropped a kiss to her pouting mouth.

"Only a little."

"I have to admit, it's kind of sexy. Women usually let me do whatever I want."

"That's the problem. You're spoiled."

Tightening her arms around his strong neck, Terri raised up on the tips of her toes and opened her mouth. She gave him a deep, thorough kiss—one that made her moan and her breath catch when he cupped her bottom, possessive and rough, and hauled her tighter to his groin.

Her fingers ran over his closely shorn hair, the faux hawk completely abandoned now, and ventured below his collar to caress the back of his neck. The kiss deepened as their lips tangled together, both of them moaning and tasting. He plucked at her bottom lip with his teeth and she teased his top lip, sucking it into her mouth.

Their movements became more frantic as Terri smoothed her hands over his hard chest. The muscles underneath the expensive shirt flexed beneath her palms. When he hastily shoved her shorts down around her ankles, she tugged his shirt free of his waistband

and slid her arms along the warm flesh of his narrow waist.

"I want to make love to you bad, baby, but I don't have anything." He breathed the words into her neck, urgency in his hands as he massaged the smooth globes of her bottom and ran his hands over her hips and down her thighs.

"It's okay," Terri said. She yanked the two sides of his shirt apart and three of the buttons popped off. Undoing the last button as she pressed her lips to the expanse of brown flesh revealed, she flicked her tongue and dragged her teeth along his firm pecs.

Gavin groaned, placed a restraining hand on her shoulder, and eased back. "Give me five minutes and I'll run—"

"No," Terri whined, shaking her head vehemently. She dragged the tank top over her head and tossed it to the floor to stand naked in front of him. "Just pull out. I want you. Now."

His breath came faster and irises darkened to vivid copper. He bit down on his bottom lip—simultaneously cute and sexy— wrestling with his decision.

"I'll pull out," he said, sounding like he was trying to convince himself that he could.

They moved over to the sofa and he disposed of his shirt. Terri arched her back, wrapping her legs around his waist. He pressed his face between her plump breasts and gathered them together, sucking the tips and laving the nipples with moisture from his tongue. She urged him on, moaning until he raised up on his elbows and their gazes met.

When he eased into her warmth, his eyes closed, the pleasure of entering her raw so unbearably sweet he could hardly stand it. He filled her, thrusting into her wet sex, and she met each forward drive of his hips by lifting hers up to greet him.

"You're so sexy, baby. You feel so good." Terri moaned, rotating her hips against his.

Gavin stilled, looking deeply into her eyes, in such a way it appeared as if he was seeing her for the first time. "You know why I came back?" he asked.

Terri's heart pounded. She couldn't look away. He'd ensnared her with his gaze.

"Because I hated that you were upset, and I *did* want to fix it." A slow smile crossed his face. "I love you."

Terri gasped. Her heart now racing out of control. "Gavin…"

"I just wanted you to know how I feel. You don't have to say it back. There's no doubt in my mind that you care about me."

"Gavin…"

"I love you, baby." He touched a finger to her cheek, the tenderness in his gaze pulling at her heart. Emotion seized her vocal chords. "I didn't expect this to happen, but it did. You're beautiful on the outside and on the inside. You have no idea how rare that is."

Terri loved him, too, but the words lay wedged in her throat. She'd fought the emotion tooth, nail, and dagger, determined not to break the most important rule of the new life she created in Seattle. To never fall in love. But he charmed his way into her heart, and how could she not love a man like Gavin? He was a series of lovely, exquisite contradictions. Strong but tender, firm but affectionate, arrogant yet humble. From the first night they met and he decided to pursue her, she never stood a chance against his advances.

He kissed her neck, gently biting the skin on her collarbone, and Terri closed her arms around his neck and hugged him tight. "Gavin," she whispered again.

"I love you, baby," he said again, offering the words freely, even though she didn't reciprocate.

His hips started moving again. His thick length slid in out of the slickness between her thighs.

"I love you," Gavin panted, keeping an eye on their joined bodies.

"Gavin," she gasped, pressing her cheek against his. Her legs clenched tight around his waist, loathe to allow even the merest distance between them.

Gripping her bottom, he thrust with greater speed, pressing her deeper into the sofa, his breaths rough and heavy. He bit into her nipple, and she arched her back at the searing pain. He made her wetter, made her hotter.

Harder and faster, he drove into her, her cries growing louder with each solid pump of his hips.

"Oh god," Terri breathed. She bit his shoulder and gripped his broad back, sinking her nails into his flesh as he rotated his hips and used long deep strokes to drive her out of her mind. His tongue dipped into her mouth, stirring a passionate response that made her hips move faster. He matched her pace and released her mouth to drop kisses along her jaw and down to her neck.

She gasped his name again, and he swore viciously as their bodies became a tight bundle of thrusting hips and panting breaths.

Terri came first with a loud cry. Limbs contracting, rough tremors shaking her body as she pulsed around him.

Gavin placed his hands on her hips and yanked her even closer, digging deeper, knocking his hips against hers fast but with such precision that another orgasm broke from her loins. She shivered, burying her face in his neck, fingers and toes constricting against the tremendous force of ecstasy that hijacked her nerves, her cells, her muscles.

Above her, Gavin gasped as his body shuddered and emptied, his hand tightening on her hips, his forehead resting on the cushioned pillow beneath her head.

In the afterglow, spent, his sweat-damp body collapsed atop hers. That's when Terri realized the mistake they made.

He hadn't pulled out.

CHAPTER TWENTY-THREE

"I've been thinking about opening a mechanic shop. Been working on a business plan." Damian's voice on the phone sounded timid, as though embarrassed or afraid to get his hopes up. "Found a couple of books at the library that were helpful."

He loved cars and went to tech school to work on them. He'd done well, too, and apprenticed under another mechanic at one time.

"I believe in you. I know you can do it," Terri said.

"Yeah well, we'll see." Damian cleared his throat. "Hey, the money you sent the other day—"

"Was a gift." Since she didn't have to pay rent or utilities anymore thanks to Gavin, Terri took the extra money and put away half for herself and sent the other half to her brother. "You have a wedding to plan, and it's the least I could do."

"You don't owe me anything. When are you going to forgive yourself for what happened?"

"It was only a few hundred dollars," Terri said, but planned to send more next month.

"Leesh, if you're—"

"Don't worry," Terri said, recognizing the warning in his voice. "I'm not doing anything stupid. I learned my lesson."

"I hope so, because I'm beginning to wonder how a nail tech can afford to send her brother that kind of cash when she has bills of her own."

Terri didn't respond.

"Are you seeing someone?"

She remained silent, wavering on how much to share with her brother.

"You gonna answer me or not?"

She sighed. "I'm seeing someone, and...I like him."

"A lot?"

"A lot," she confirmed. "Actually, he told me he loves me, and I love him, too."

Damian let out a heavy breath. "Damn, you and this love thing."

"He's different," Terri assured him.

"How does he treat you?" her brother asked, skepticism lacing the question.

"The way you treat Shanae, like I'm special. He opens doors, and he likes taking care of me." In fact, he asked her to move in with him a couple of days ago. The question surprised but thrilled her, and she told him she'd think about it. She worried about repeating the same mistakes, but Gavin was different. No doubt about it.

"What about his family?"

"I met them. I like them, and they like me, too."

Boating season started in May, and she'd joined the Johnson clan on their yacht during the Seattle Yacht Club's Opening Day Parade. The boat was crowded with the entire immediate family, a few cousins, and friends, standing out on the deck and waving to people on the shoreline during the parade of boats. Gavin participated in the sailboat race, and he and his crew had won first place. She looked forward to the Fourth of July party where they went out on the boat again, ate, drank, and enjoyed the fireworks.

She'd participated in several outings to restaurants where the extended family, including spouses and girlfriends, dined in private rooms. Friends sometimes joined them, but for the most part, they seemed more inclined to spend time with each other.

She'd even had an occasion to wear the ruby necklace Gavin gave her, during a charity event she attended as his date. When she saw the satisfaction on his face, she was happy she hadn't done something foolish like pawn it to get money when she lost everything in the fire. She apologized profusely for not wearing it before. He seemed to get such pleasure from taking care of her, and what woman in her right mind didn't like getting spoiled by her man— even a little bit.

There always seemed to be some local engagement the Johnsons, or at least a representative from the family, must attend. Terri had become lax about being seen at public events with Gavin, but she restricted the appearances to local ones, managed to stay out of most publicity shots, and insisted Gavin not share her image on social media.

During evenings out with the family, she noticed the eldest brother, Cyrus, had warmed to her, and was much more polite than the first time she met him. Last time they all went out, his wife shared pictures of the new house they bought in Spain. While Cyrus smiled indulgently at her, Daniella complained about the task of having to decorate their new home long-distance, at which point Constance recommended a decorator in France she had worked with.

It was very interesting to watch them have these conversations, talking as casually as someone like her would mention needing to find a pair of shoes to match a new outfit. Charity events, interior decorators, and vacation homes was their normal, and she had an insider's view into that lifestyle.

"Does your new guy know everything?" Damian asked.

Terri hung her head and stared at her sandaled feet propped on the coffee table, toenails painted in a creamy beige this week. "No."

Her brother grunted. "When are you going to tell him?"

"I don't know," Terri snapped. "Why are you badgering me?"

"Because I don't want to see you get hurt. Is this great, wonderful man who's so in love with you going to understand everything about you and your past?"

"I'll tell him when I'm ready."

"I heard the smile in your voice when you talked about him. If you're serious about him, you have to be honest. Now, before he finds out on his own and everything blows up in your face."

Terri was fairly certain that wouldn't happen, but she did have doubts, and those doubts reined in her natural inclination to declare her love for Gavin—shouting it from the rooftops—even as she basked in the warmth of his love.

"Tell me again that you love me," she said.

His hand moved to her belly, pulling her tighter against his body. "I love you." He kissed the top of her spine. "Did you kill someone?" he asked, amusement in his voice.

"No." But she had a sordid past.

"I bet whatever you did isn't even as bad as you think it is."

"What if it is? What if it's really bad?"

"It can't be that bad," he said with confidence.

Terri twisted around and threw a leg over his hip, seeking his heat. She wanted more of this. Every single day, she wanted to wake up next to him or roll over in the middle of the night and feel his warm body.

"You always smell good," she said to his chest.

"You smell better. Every time I see you, I want to eat you."

She giggled, running her fingers through the sprinkling of curly hairs on his chest. "Stop."

"I'm serious." His arms tightened around her. "I'm not going to stop loving you because you did something bad. That's not the way love works."

"I'll handle it, Damian. Stop worrying about me all the time and worry about yourself and your family."

"You're my family, and I can't stop worrying about you." His voice sounded resigned and defeated.

Terri gnawed a nail. "I'll tell him about my past. Soon."

"Will you let me know how the conversation goes?"

"Yes."

They hung up a few minutes later, and Terri sat with her knees pulled up to her chest, the heels of her feet on the edge of the sofa.

Over the years, she'd grown adept at answering questions about what she wanted to do with her life and where she saw herself in five years. She gave the same answer each time, extolling the virtues of being an entrepreneur and how much she wanted to run her own salon one day. Because those were the politically correct answers.

The truth was, she didn't want any of that. It was strange in this day and age to be ashamed or embarrassed about her real desires, but being a business woman sounded much better than admitting she wanted nothing more than to be a wife and mother. To have the security and protection of a man who really loved her. Each time she tried to go down that path, she had failed miserably, playing house with men she shouldn't have.

Her arms tightened around her legs, and she closed her eyes. She felt in her heart that Gavin was different, but he only knew one side of her. What would happen when he found out everything?

Would he walk away? And take away this feeling that she enjoyed so much more than ever before. For once in her life, she felt…loved.

CHAPTER TWENTY-FOUR

Gavin didn't have any idea whether or not his ideas were good. The team Trenton assigned to work with him acted nervous in his presence. He was pretty sure they'd agree with any crappy idea he came up with simply because he was one of the owners.

At a soft knock on the door, his head tilted up. He welcomed the interruption after staring at the designs on the easels for a long time without the spark of a better idea.

"Come in," he called. Ivy poked her head in the door. "What's up?"

The tentative smile on her face made him aware that something was wrong, and right away, he stood up from the desk.

She came in all the way and clasped her hands behind her back. "How's it going?"

"Could be better. Not sure marketing and promotions is my thing. I can't get an honest answer out of the team."

She smiled, a genuine smile this time. "It's because they're not used to you. They're very candid with Trenton."

"I'll talk to him about the situation because this isn't working." He waited.

Ivy inhaled deeply and her eyes skirted away from his.

Shoving a hand in his pocket, Gavin asked, "What's going on, Ivy? You look like you have something to say."

"I didn't want to do this, but…it's about Terri."

Worry sliced through his stomach. "What about her?"

His sister took another breath, her expression pained. "Remember Lucas thought that he recognized her from somewhere?"

Recalling the night of Walt's retirement dinner, Gavin nodded.

"The reason he knows her is because she has a record."

"A what? You mean a police record?"

"Yes. There was a big scandal in Atlanta over three years ago, and Terri was at the center of it." Ivy pulled sheets of paper from behind her back. The name Candi Rayne appeared at the top of one page. "I printed this from the Internet."

"Who the hell is Candi Rayne? Whatever she's said about Terri is probably bullshit. You know how it is—people try to take you down when you're on top. She's dating a rich man, so now folks are going to come out of the woodwork and do everything they can to hurt her. I don't want to see that shit."

"You need to read this, Gavin."

"Get it out of my face, Ivy. Seriously."

"Gavin, Candi Rayne is Terri Slade." Ivy slid the papers across the desk to him, but he refused to look down.

"Did Cyrus put you up to this? Because this is exactly the kind of crap he'd do."

"He doesn't have anything to do with this," Ivy said softly. She bit her bottom lip, an expression of pity filling her eyes.

"You're judging people now? That's what you do? Because she made a few mistakes in the past, she's not good enough for me? I thought you were better than that considering your fiancé barely passed the background test his damn self."

Ivy's face went stony. "I'm going to let that slide," she said, her voice as frigid as an Antarctic winter, "because I realize you're having a hard time digesting this information." She inhaled. "But I had to share this with you before someone else puts you, and the family, on blast. It's only a matter of time, and frankly, you need to decide whether or not you can handle Terri's past. Candi Rayne is only one of several aliases she's had over the years."

"How do you know that?" Gavin demanded.

"The photos."

Ivy lifted the top sheet but Gavin still didn't look down. He stared into his sister's eyes, feeling as if the walls were closing in and he was about to be crushed under the weight. He'd known he should do a background check. For the Johnsons, it was as normal as conducting an introduction, sharing your occupation, or where you were born.

But he'd stalled and eventually given up on the idea completely, even as doubts ate at him. Even when he listened to Terri's hints about her past, he simply hadn't wanted to see or hear anything negative. Now Ivy stood over his desk armed with a truth he didn't want to face, backing him into a corner.

The silence extended to an uncomfortable length, but Ivy didn't move or speak, and neither did he. Dammit, he didn't want to know the truth. He wanted to remain in the euphoric bubble he'd made for himself and Terri.

He'd risked his life doing daring stunts over the years, but nothing scared him as much as looking down at the papers that sat on his desk.

Finally, Gavin lowered his eyes and the walls that threatened to close in on him tumbled down and knocked him back into the chair. The muscles in his neck and shoulders tightened unbearably. That picture was her. The hair was different—cut short and brown with dark blonde highlights—but there was no mistaking the long lashes and saucy grin.

****

Tonight was the night.

Terri took her time rubbing all parts of her body in the scented bathwater. She stretched her legs, scrubbing the loofah over her toes, ankles, and legs. She wanted to be good and tasty when her man came over.

He didn't sound at all like himself when he called earlier, but the good news she planned to share with him should change his mood. She hummed to herself as she stepped out of the tub onto the plush white rug and wrapped her body in the oversized white towel.

She had an answer to his question, and her answer was yes. Yes, she would move in with him. She was ready and tonight she would tell him what was on her heart. That she loved him, too.

She listened to the water empty down the tub drain in a loud gurgle and let down her pinned-up hair, assessing her face critically before she started putting on lotion. Even in the bathroom she smelled tonight's dinner, a feast of his favorites ordered from the hotel restaurant. Their meal was warming in the oven, ready for Gavin's arrival. She checked the time on the nightstand clock, noting he should be there soon. She donned a strapless cream dress and a pair of wedge heel sandals in a darker cream tone. Parting her hair in the middle, she let it fall into loose waves around her face and applied lipstick before going down the hall to the kitchen.

She removed the food from the oven and set the table. She giggled, excited about her future with Gavin. As she finished pouring red wine in a decanter to breathe, she heard him at the door.

Terri hurried into the hallway and admired Gavin when he walked in wearing a custom suit and carrying a briefcase. How her life had changed! She had a man who carried a briefcase.

"Hi!" Terri hurried over and gave him a big hug, pressing the length of her body against his. But he stiffened, became downright rigid. Holding on to his strong upper arms, she pulled back and searched his face. "Rough day?"

"Pretty rough."

He brushed past her and dropped his briefcase beside the sofa. After tugging off his tie and jacket, he tossed them on an armchair. That wasn't like him at all. Poor baby. He must have had a really bad day.

He poured himself a huge helping of wine and gulped it. "You have anything stronger than this?" he asked.

"No." Terri eased closer and watched him pour another healthy serving. "Babe, are you okay?"

Gavin tossed back the second drink and then slammed the glass on the table. Terri jumped at the loud bang, surprised it didn't shatter.

"Honey, what's wrong?"

He watched her silently, his upper lip curling into a sneer. Then he laughed a sinister, humorless laugh. "It's true what they say, isn't it? If something's too good to be true, it probably is."

An uneasy feeling took root inside of her. "Not always."

"Always." He looked dead at her, and the unease found its way into her chest cavity. His comments were obviously directed at her. But why?

"I thought you were too good to be true, but you're not," she said cautiously. "I'm lucky we found each other."

"Lucky?" he repeated, a definite edge to his voice. "I don't think so."

"*Okay*," she said, struggling to better gauge his mood.

"I hate fake people."

Terri swallowed. "Everybody does." She fell silent, waiting to see what would be revealed.

"You're a fake."

Terri shook her head slowly. "I-I don't know what you mean."

"You're going to hold on to the end, aren't you? I guess that's what hustlers and con artists do. Deny, deny, even when you're caught."

Terri's heart raced. "No."

"That's right. I know exactly who you are, *Candi*."

The realization that he knew about her past landed like a fist to the gut. The breath left her lungs in a rush. "My name is Terri. Terri Slade."

His nostrils flared, anger flashing in his eyes. Anger directed at her. "You're not Terri Slade. You're Felicia Linscott, from 16013 Washington Avenue. Born and raised in Hopewell, Georgia."

"No, no, *no*." She shook her head. "Felicia is the past. Now I'm Terri."

"One brother, Damian Linscott."

"No." She kept shaking her head, trying to make him stop. This couldn't be happening. This was *not* happening.

Gavin picked up the briefcase and ran his thumbs over the combination locks. They flipped open and he dragged out a bunch of sheets and tossed them onto the table—beautifully set for dinner. The documents fanned out on the dishes and covered the silverware. He continued, without even looking down at the papers—clearly having memorized every detail. "Let's see, theft by taking, money laundering—" His mouth tightened, unable to go on. He snatched up one of the pages then dropped it, as if touching the evidence of her misdeeds sullied his fingers.

Her eyes gravitated to the mugshots of the life she left behind.

"What should I call you?" he asked. "Is it Lac-i, or is it Cand-i, or is it Trac-i?" Each name landed with the force of a sledgehammer. "You get a gold star for consistency. Traci, Candi, Laci, Terri. *Argh!*" It was a cry of anger, pain, and disappointment. "You damn liar!"

"I never lied to you." Terri hung her head and wrapped her arms around her body. Fifteen minutes ago she'd been euphoric, and now the perfect life she planned to live was falling apart.

He grabbed her by the wrists and forced her to look up at him. She trembled at the fury in his eyes, heart beating so hard it hurt.

"Did you use me?"

"No." Terri shook her head vehemently.

"Why should I believe you?"

"Because...because I love you."

He chuckled, his entire body shaking as if she'd said the funniest thing ever. The mocking laugh hurt, wounding her pride and reinforcing his utmost disdain for her. "Oh, you love me now? Now that you're busted and I know the truth about who and what you are?" His grip tightened and she winced.

"Gavin, you're hurting me." Her pleading voice penetrated the haze of anger and he immediately released her. Backing away, he crashed into the wall, staring as if he couldn't really see her.

"I was going to tell you," Terri said, voice quivering.

"When?" He fired in a tight, clipped tone.

"I was waiting for the right time," she mumbled. "You're so angry. Let me explain. Please."

"Explain how you could be involved with a man who headed up a criminal enterprise. You participated in his activities. *Explain*."

"I never wanted to do those things. He made me do it," Terri said in a small voice.

"You're a grown woman. Why didn't you go to the police or tell someone in your family?"

Clearly, no explanation would be good enough in light of the damning evidence. Her reasons sounded weak, even to her. Looking back on past actions, she felt nothing but disgust, but at the time, she'd been trapped, with no way out of her predicament.

"I asked you to move in with me. I introduced you to my family." Gavin sucked in a harsh breath. "You know who I am. You know my position. You know who my family is." The disgust on his face twisted like a jagged knife in her heart.

"You don't know the whole story." She reached for him and he recoiled.

"You did good. Look at this place." He swept a hand in the air, encompassing the room. "All that practice you had running scams and pilfering money from unsuspecting idiots paid off, didn't it?"

The cold churn of despair filled her heart. "I was going to tell you everything."

"Sure you were. You really think I'm an idiot, don't you?"

"I didn't ask for any of this."

"That's part of the con, isn't it? Make me think I came up with the idea on my own?" He wagged a finger at her. "You're good. You're damn good."

Terri shook her head, trembling, but refused to cry. "I'm not a bad person. You're wrong about me. What we have—"

"What we have? Let me guess, I'm different, right?" He laughed again, such an ugly, bitter sound. He advanced across the room, a menacing expression in his eyes. She felt the dining room wall against her back. When he clutched the back of her neck, she shivered from the memories of past abuse.

"I will give you this…" His gaze ran down her attire—the sexy dress and heels she put on for him, and then waved his hand around the room. "All this…you earned it."

Her face burned. "Don't."

"Matter of fact, I'm going to let you stay in the condo, just like I promised. See how generous I am? It's already paid for, so what the hell. But the accounts, done." His hand sliced through the air. "All the extras, done. You and me, *done*."

Terri wanted to yell and scream and tell him he couldn't take back those things and he couldn't treat her like this. Hurting from the pain of his rejection, she fisted her hands at her sides. Lifting her chin, she glared at him and managed to keep her voice steady. "Don't do me any goddamn favors. I don't need shit from you. I took care of myself before you, and I'll do it again."

His honey-colored eyes flashed in annoyance. "Perfect. The sooner you get the hell out, the better." He grabbed the briefcase and stormed off without the jacket and tie.

Terri watched him march with long strides to the door. She grabbed onto the wall, forcing her feet to remain in place and not run after him. But when the door slammed shut, the finality of it sent her into a panic.

"Wait!"

She hurried down the entryway and grabbed the doorknob. Her breaths came in short, panicked huffs. Her fingers tightened around the steel but she held back from turning the knob.

"Gavin." The sob broke from her chest and tears doused her eyes, running over onto her cheeks. "You said—" The finality of his words slammed into her.

Done.

"You said you wouldn't stop loving me," she said in a broken whisper. She crumbled to her knees and dropped her forehead against the door. "I love you. And I'm ready." He left her. She wrapped an arm around her hurting stomach, the pain of losing him wringing a deluge of tears onto her cheeks. "I'm ready."

CHAPTER TWENTY-FIVE

Under the cold spray of water, Gavin cursed his body for being hard, for wanting her, for missing her. Nothing had changed in the week since they split.

He scrubbed his skin and swished water through his mouth. He wanted to forget her taste, her smell, her everything.

For so long he'd felt wrong and out of place. The family screw-up. With Terri, he'd felt right and needed in a way he hadn't before. He even started to think he could contribute to the family business and she made sticking around in Seattle much more palatable. But he should have been gone. Needed to be high. Needed to not feel. And there was only one way to do that. Danger. Speed. Flying. Anything but remain in Seattle so the pain could fester and pollute his soul.

He left the shower and dressed quickly, his mind focused on the next trip, an escape to a nightclub in Mozambique. A secret hideaway where the rich and famous liked to party and the mainstream media hadn't yet discovered. A swim-up bar, three dance floors, partygoers that were a mix of celebs from the continent of Africa and international superstars, and sick beats blasted all night long on one of the most beautiful beaches in the world until the sun came up. The perfect escape.

He sank onto the side of the bed and buried his head in his hands.

His head hurt. He let her get way too close to his family without doing a background check. The press would have a field day if they caught wind of her criminal past and the connection to his family. He should have been more careful but let his penis lead him astray.

Why am I such a fuck up? Always had been and always would be. Nothing had changed. *I'm sick of fucking up.* Fucking up took a lot more energy than people realized.

A general heaviness rested about his neck, shoulders, and in his body. His entire soul felt empty yet full at the same time. It didn't even make sense, yet that's how he felt. Full of emptiness.

Gavin pushed up from the bed and picked up the phone. He instructed the valet to take his bags to the car, and minutes later was on his way to his mother's house. He'd already kissed his niece Katie and said goodbye to his siblings. The conversation with Ivy had been the worst. She didn't want him to go and blamed herself for him leaving.

Gavin walked down the stone steps into the back yard of his mother's house. Shielding his eyes from the sun, he caught sight of Constance near the roses. Somehow, she managed to make garden gloves and a floppy hat look chic. He smiled a little. She loved her roses, and since gardening was the only exercise he knew she indulged in, he recognized how much she enjoyed herself when outside.

He trudged down the tiered slope to her side. A female member of the staff stood nearby holding a shallow Nantucket basket filled with red roses, while Alicia waited quietly with a large round silver platter held flat against her thighs.

He nodded at each of the women.

"Mother, I'm leaving," he announced. He couldn't quite look her in the eye. Something he'd become good at—avoiding eye contact with her whenever he left home. He hated saying goodbye because he didn't want to see the look on her face—the disappointment that always accompanied each time he said goodbye. He imagined her reaction would be even worse this time because he'd stayed at home for so long.

"Before you leave, we should take a moment to have a cup of tea together." Snip. Snip. She placed two more stems in the basket.

"I'm not really—"

"Or would you rather coffee?"

He would rather fly out of there, quickly, but apparently, that wasn't going to happen. "Tea is fine," Gavin said with resignation, staring off over the landscape to the tranquil waters beyond the green grass.

The sun reflecting off the surface of the water reminded him of the time he and Terri took the boat out with his friends and he tried to entice her to water ski. After some resistance, he figured out she couldn't swim. He hired a private coach for her, and after a few lessons, she grew brave enough to enter the water with a vest. They never did get a chance to go back out on the skis.

"Good." Constance removed her gloves and Alicia came forward, holding up the silver platter. His mother deposited the gloves and pruning shears on it. "Please have Adelina prepare my afternoon tea, and let her know Gavin will be joining me."

"Yes, ma'am." The young woman walked away.

His mother smiled at him. "I don't know when I'll see you again, so I want to have a chat with you before you go. I'll meet you in the sunroom after I freshen up a bit."

She took off back to the house with the basket-holding assistant following her.

Whatever his mother wanted to talk about, he had a funny feeling he wouldn't want to discuss it.

****

"Your father would have loved this room, don't you think?" Constance held the delicate china cup and saucer in her hand and looked around the room, as if seeing it for the first time. She downsized to this house several years after his father died.

"Probably," Gavin said.

"Have some tea. It's a Caribbean herbal blend and really quite good." She sipped from her cup and then placed it on the table in front of her.

Gavin sipped the warm brew and conceded she was right. He

tasted mango and a hint of passion fruit.

He knew she had something else to say. He just didn't know what, so he waited, like a criminal awaiting full disclosure of the prosecution's evidence.

"Ivy told me you and your young lady friend, Terri, aren't seeing each other anymore." She crossed her legs, and that's when he knew she was going into interrogation mode. "Why is that?"

"Didn't work out."

"She was wonderful company when she joined us for dinner and quite nice when we went out on the boat. She obviously has a fondness for children. During that outing, I think she spent more time with Michael and Katie than the babysitters."

That was one of the special things about Terri. She obviously loved kids and didn't mind getting down on the floor and playing with his nephew Michael or entertaining his niece, Katie.

"She seemed pleasant enough," his mother added.

"Looks can be deceiving."

"Are you saying she deceived you?"

"Yes," Gavin bit out.

"About...?"

He didn't want to have this conversation, but he knew better than to fight. "Who she is. Everything. She would have embarrassed the family."

"I see." Constance clasped her hands on her lap. "You've been working at the company and both Cyrus and Xavier reported that you're doing a fine job. Why are you leaving?"

Outside the window, Lake Washington stretched beneath the sun. "It's time to go."

"So I suppose you're going back to your race car driving and space jumping activities?"

"It's called B.A.S.E. jumping, Mother." He smiled a little.

"Whatever it is, I know it's dangerous." She examined her fingers. "I don't approve of your activities, Gavin. I never have, but I've let you live your life because I understood. Even though every single day I said a prayer that you stayed safe no matter where you were or what you were doing."

"You don't have to worry about me."

Her gaze met his. "I will always worry about you. You're my son."

He saw the sadness in the depths of her eyes, and gut-wrenching guilt filled him that he was the cause of her pain, again. A never-ending misery created by his selfish behavior.

The air stilled between them.

"What do you think you're doing when you risk your life like that?" Constance asked.

"Having fun. It's an adrenalin rush."

"Makes you feel high?"

He shrugged. "A little. Better than drugs."

"Is it?"

"Nothing's happened to me yet."

"Just some broken bones and scarred flesh."

He swallowed. He took another drink of the tea and then set the cup on the table, the dishes rattling a little as he did.

"You know what I worry about?" she asked, staring down at her fingers. She still wore her engagement and wedding ring, as if she weren't a widow and had a husband who came home to her every night. The sight pained him and he looked down into the dark tea.

She continued. "I worry that one day, I'll get a call and they'll tell me that you fell off a mountain or drowned or..." Fear vibrated in her trembling voice. "I worry that I'll get a call that I've lost you. That my son is dead."

He remained silent.

"I don't want you to go, Gavin."

"Mother, what you're asking me—"

"I don't want you to go." She said the sentence firmly, with the authority and confidence of someone who knew their every wish would be acceded to. "You're a grown man, and you don't have to listen to what I say, but I'm asking you not to leave. Your father wouldn't want you to go. He would want you to stay, because he would never condone you putting yourself in danger the way you do."

Gavin stood up. "Mother, I have never disrespected you."

"And you won't start today. Have a seat and let me finish."

He didn't move, but then just as she instructed, he lowered onto the chair.

"Look at me. Look me in the eyes."

He did as she asked.

"Stay." She spoke softly, head tilted to the side. "I don't blame you. No one blames you. You've punished yourself enough."

Tears blurred his vision. "I don't know what you're—"

"I lost your father. I don't want to lose you, too."

His throat closed up, an invisible band tightening around his neck, making it hard to breathe. His head dipped and his breathing became ragged. The memory of the accident came back with the force of a cannonball shot from a cannon, almost knocking him sideways.

He gripped the edge of the sofa.

That last night, he and his father should have left the party at ten, but he dallied in the kitchen, flirting with one of the servers until she gave him her number. When his father found him, he gave him a good tongue lashing. They argued in the limo, with his father insisting he was throwing his life away on women and having a good time. Demanding yet again to know why someone so smart had dropped out of college.

He'd yelled and cursed at his father, wanting to be left alone to live his own life. In fact, he'd said those very words. *"Leave me alone. Let me live my own life!"* Then he'd turned away to stare out the window of the limo, fuming, arms folded across his chest.

He didn't remember much after that. A crash. Glass breaking. Metal crunching. His father's body on top of his.

"He covered me," Gavin said hoarsely.

"I know, dear."

He lifted tear-filled eyes to his mother's face. "Then why don't you…h-hate me?"

"Because he did exactly what I would have done. He saved the most precious thing in that vehicle. My son."

Gavin's nostrils flared as he tried to fight back emotion and swiped the tears that spilled from his eyes. When his vision cleared, he noticed his mother's wet cheeks.

"I miss him," he said thickly.

"Me, too," she said softly. "Not a day goes by that I don't miss that loud, obnoxious, controlling husband of mine. I think about what he'd be doing. How proud he would be to see what wonderful adults you all turned out to be. To see his grandchildren and the growth of the company his family founded. I know he's smiling and he's proud. Of all of us. That includes you, too." She opened her arms. "Come."

Gavin walked over to her and fell to his knees and dropped his head in her lap. She stroked his head. "My baby, my poor baby. It's okay. It's okay, son."

More tears squeezed from his eyes. After the funeral, he'd deprived himself of tears. He didn't deserve to grieve because his father would be alive if not for him. If he hadn't lingered in the kitchen, they would have missed the drunk driver.

If, if, *if*...

"He gave his life for me."

He choked out the words, squeezing his eyes tight against the memory of being pinned under Cyrus Senior's limp, damaged body. Covering him. Protecting him.

The tears continued to fall. Years of pent-up grief. Regret. Guilt. His head remained buried in his mother's lap and his arms tightened around her.

"It's okay, son," she whispered. She rubbed his back, mouth close to his ear. "You don't have to run anymore."

CHAPTER TWENTY-SIX

Gavin jolted upright in bed.

Temporarily disoriented in the dark room, he swiped the dampness from his sweat-slick face and groaned in disgust. It was the same dream as always. It started with he and Terri enjoying dinner, then dancing, then running along the pier, her laughter drifting back to him on the wind. Then all of a sudden, they were in the condo on the sofa. They locked eyes as he thrust into her, reveling in the raw sensation of her vibrating around him. The curve of her lush behind rested in his hands, and he thrust hard, going as deep as humanly possible to gain the fulfillment only she could give.

He rubbed sleep from his eyes, shoulders bent under the weight of his inability to forget. The fortified master suite doubled as a safe room and could damn near resist a nuclear explosion, but couldn't protect him from thoughts of Terri Slade.

Almost four months had already passed since he last saw her, yet she continued to invade his thoughts. It should be easy enough not to think about her since he spent over thirty years of his life not knowing her, hence not thinking about her. If only he could go back to that time and empty his mind of every moment they spent together, every sexy smile she sent his way, every touch of her soft hands.

Sometimes, he could block her out—at least during the day—when he stayed busy learning about Johnson Brewing Company. At promotional and networking events he attended with the sales team, she occasionally left his mind. But nighttime was nearly impossible to avoid thoughts of Terri. At night his subconscious wrested away control and placed her prominently in the foreground of his head.

He rubbed a hand over his semi-erect penis and groaned.

Since he'd decided to stay in Seattle, he bought the house he'd been renting and expelled his entourage from the premises with one way tickets to their destination of choice. Now that he had a permanent residence, he needed a woman in his life. Until then, he should get ready for work. A few months ago, he officially went on payroll and became a productive member of the team, and today was a big day.

He rolled off the bed, thinking about the morning meeting, nervous but excited about the possible outcome. Nine months ago he'd known practically nothing about Johnson Enterprises, but now, he better understood the ins and outs of the beer making and restaurant industries and the role the family business played in those markets. Recently, he pitched an idea to Trenton first and then approached Xavier and Ivy. The last person to convince was Cyrus.

Gavin dressed quickly and grabbed a travel mug of coffee on his way out the door, calling a goodbye to his housekeeper, Edie.

Soon, he was at the company headquarters and seated in a meeting with his siblings. The nervous excitement tightened in his gut, but knowing his siblings backed the idea made him confident. He sat up straight, seated across from Ivy. To his left sat Cyrus, and across from him Xavier.

Trenton took the floor to go through his presentation, a very basic one using an easel and bright graphics on sturdy paper. Each time he came to a new point, he lifted off a sheet to reveal the details.

Gavin's eyes made the rounds of the table, and he couldn't help but smile. His mother was right. Father would be proud if he saw them today, and he wanted to honor his father's memory and make him proud.

"In conclusion," Trenton said, "customers want to do business with a person. Talk to a person. Social media has allowed them insight into the lives of people they do business with." He lifted off one of the sheets and pointed to the numbers on the graph. "Gavin has millions of followers on Instagram and Twitter, and we need to take advantage of the opportunity those 'fans' represent. What we need to do is create a brand strategy around him by playing up the action and adventure angles of his life. We make *him* representative of our beer and incorporate *him* as part of our advertising campaign."

Cyrus rubbed his jaw. "The idea worked for Jim Koch at Samuel Adams. Doesn't mean it'll work for us."

"Not only Jim Koch. When you think about The Most Interesting Man in the World, what immediately comes to mind?" Trenton looked around the table, but didn't wait for the answer. "Dos Equis. Dos Equis increased sales by more than twenty percent when they launched that campaign."

Ivy leaned forward and directed her comment to Cyrus. "It's not just beer. Consumers like being able to identify with a specific figure that represents a brand. The Marlboro Man and the Energizer Bunny, all figures who, the minute you see them, bring the brand to life."

Trenton rested his palms on the table. "What we plan to do, is use the same strategy to launch a brand for Full Moon beer. Gavin's social media accounts will become less personal and more business and we'll merge them with our corporate accounts. By including the personal component, we offer customers that feeling of familiarity that's so important to establishing a solid connection and separating us from the other beer companies out there."

Unconvinced, Cyrus shook his head. "What makes you think this is going to work for us? We've managed to do very well so far by simply producing good beer—without a mascot."

"We knew you'd say that, so we ran some tests. Ivy." Trenton nodded at their sister.

"Trenton prepared a few ads for Twitter and had Gavin tweet them, using geographic targeting to send customers to our restaurants in Baton Rouge. The lines were out the door and one of the restaurants ran out of beer."

Cyrus's eyebrows raised. "Ran out of beer?"

"Yes," Ivy confirmed, her eyes bright with excitement. "Food sales at both locations went through the roof. They had to call in extra wait staff."

"Xavier," Trenton said, obviously enjoying the moment by the smug smile on his face.

Xavier slid a few stapled pages across the table to Cyrus. "Over the course of a week, we asked Gavin to tweet about the new vanilla flavored brew that's popular in California—again, using geographic pinpointing. We had to temporarily increase production at the Portland plant because of the rise in demand."

Cyrus stroked his jaw, staring down at the numbers. "That's a notable spike."

"Exactly."

"Social media is the new word-of-mouth," Gavin interjected. "It's not the only way to spread the word about a product, but it's a very effective way to do it. We could offer coupons, let customers know about new beer flavors, share videos—the options are limitless."

Cyrus frowned. "We already have social media accounts to handle those things."

Trenton sat down. "But the personal touch isn't there. That's the difference."

Xavier folded his hands on the table and went in for the kill. "We're not suggesting Gavin become our main focus. We're suggesting he be added to the list of things we're already doing. If we can effectively use his image, we could end up becoming the number one beer company in the country within the next few years."

Such a lofty goal caught Cyrus's attention. He looked around the table at all of them. "Number one," he repeated in a low voice.

If they became number one in the country, they would achieve the goal their father dreamed of one day accomplishing.

"How much money are we talking about to launch this campaign?" Cyrus asked.

Trenton placed a bound report in front of Cyrus. The eldest flipped the booklet open, scanned the text, and then flipped several pages over to the financial projections.

Time dragged as he punched numbers into the calculator on his phone. Gavin, Trenton, Xavier, and Ivy knew that if anyone could find holes in their idea, Cyrus could. They glanced at each other, waiting for the final verdict.

Ivy pulled her thumb between her teeth. Trenton and Xavier leaned across the table, eyeing Cyrus's calculations. Gavin tapped his foot.

At last, Cyrus looked up, a competitive gleam in his dark eyes and a slow smile sliding across his face. "Let's do it." He leaned forward, and Gavin was struck by how much he looked like their father right then. "Let's take the number one spot. Let's show them what Full Moon beer and the Johnson family are made of."

"Yes!" Trenton pumped his fist.

Ivy clapped her hands and broke into a big grin, and Xavier gave Gavin the thumbs-up sign.

Cyrus turned to Gavin, and for the first time in years, he saw respect in his brother's eyes.

"Welcome to the family business," Cyrus said.

****

Today turned out to be the best day Gavin experienced in a long time, but he no longer wore a smile when he caught up with Cyrus outside his office at the end of the day. His wife Daniella, as elegant as ever in a chocolate pantsuit with her long hair cascading over her shoulders, was holding the diaper bag. Cyrus held his son, Michael, in his arms, playfully tweaking the almost-one-year-old's nose. The little boy wrinkled his nose and laughed happily at the game.

"Hi, Gavin," Daniella said.

"Hello, Daniella." He gave his sister-in-law a brief hug.

Cyrus's questioning eyes met his. "You need something?"

"Do you have a sec? I need to talk to you privately for a moment."

"Here, let me take him. We'll meet you down in the car." Daniella lifted Michael from Cyrus's arms.

With a pitiful pout, the little boy stretched out his hands to his father and babbled incoherently.

"Don't be so cranky. Daddy will join us soon," Daniella cooed, nuzzling her son's neck.

Both Gavin and Cyrus watched them leave the suite of offices before entering Cyrus's domain and shutting the door.

"What did you need to talk to me about?" Cyrus studied Gavin with intense, perceptive eyes, a complete one-eighty from the soft, affectionate gaze he'd bestowed on his son.

"I need your guy to look into something for me."

"What?" Cyrus asked, folding his arms.

"A case that involved Terri."

Cyrus's eyebrows lifted in surprise. "You've been done with her for months."

Gavin ran a hand down the back of his head. "Yeah, I know, but I haven't been able to forget something she said."

"What did she say?"

"'You don't know the whole story,'" he answered.

Unable to help himself, Gavin had done some preliminary digging on his own, but the bits and pieces he managed to put together didn't give him the entire picture. On the one hand, it seemed as if Terri was a willing participant in her boyfriend's criminal activities and turned on him solely for the opportunity to get immunity. On the other, he recalled her panic the night they played with the cucumber and the pained expression in her eyes when she admitted, *He hurt me. A lot.*

"I need him to pull together anything he can find about the Talon Cyrenci case in Georgia. Court transcripts, government files, photos, and anything else he can get his hands on."

Maybe there was more to the story. Maybe he was looking for excuses to accept her. Whatever the case, he had to know the whole truth.

Cyrus went around the desk and unlocked the top drawer. He removed a card, locked the desk, and handed the card to Gavin. "I'll let you handle it," he said.

There was only a first name and number on the card.

"I hope you find what you're looking for," Cyrus said.

Gavin swallowed, worried he may find more than he wanted

to know but ready to take the plunge. "Thanks."

****

The driver pulled up outside Aldi's Market, and Gavin left his
tie and jacket in the car and strolled into the specialty store. In the
deli section, a platter of antipasti awaited with his name on it. Aldi, a
French Moroccan and the owner, was working behind the counter.

"Bonsoir, Aldi. How's it going?"

"Bonsoir, Gavin, how are you?"

"Never been better, and looking forward to the platter you
have prepared for me."

"Ah, yes. I'll be right back." Aldi hurried to the back and
returned with a platter that made Gavin's mouth water. It contained
artichoke hearts, olives, thinly sliced salami, marinated tomatoes,
pickles, and two different types of cheeses.

"This looks great. I've got a date with this late night snack
and a movie tonight."

"No pretty lady for you?"

"Not tonight, my friend." He'd thought about going out but
changed his mind at the last minute. Gavin handed over the cash and
Aldi gave him his change. "Later."

Aldi wished him a good night, and Gavin headed toward the
front of the store. Walking down the aisle, he side-stepped a woman
and her small brood of three as they pushed a cart filled with
groceries. He smiled at the little girl, who looked up at him and
grinned, and was so distracted that he took three more steps before
he saw a very familiar back. One that he could never possibly
forget—clothed or unclothed—and his traitorous heart jolted with
unexpected joy.

Gavin stopped in the middle of the aisle and watched her.
The bright red top she wore was unusually large, with big sleeves that
came down to her elbows and reminded him of trumpets. It fell to
the middle of her thighs so he couldn't see her beautiful behind, but
he knew it was Terri. She had her hair up in a ponytail that exposed
her neck, which he'd know anywhere, even with a blindfold on. He'd
kissed it often and listened to the accompanying breathless laughs too
many times to count.

Reason returned and consumed the happiness he instinctively felt, replacing it with sadness. Her testimony of what Talon Cyrenci had done to her gutted him. The pain she must have suffered at the hands of such a monster, all because he wanted to keep her in line and made sure she did what he demanded. But Cyrenci underestimated her. She plotted with the Georgia Bureau of Investigations and the local police to bring him down. Almost single-handedly, she toppled his multi-million-dollar criminal enterprise while enduring unspeakable abuse in the process.

He wanted to at least apologize and let her know that he did know the whole story. He was proud of her. She was not only the bravest woman he'd ever met, she was strong enough to have recovered from years of abuse and live a healthy and productive life.

The next thing he knew, he was standing a few feet behind her. "Terri."

He said her name softly, but she swung around as if he'd yelled it. Eyes wide, she clutched a box of gourmet cheese straws and stared at him.

Her reaction seemed completely out of whack to the situation at hand, except when Gavin's gaze descended below her breasts, he realized why she had such a strong response.

His eyes shifted back to hers. "You're pregnant."

CHAPTER TWENTY-SEVEN

All Terri could do was stare. His mouth was slightly ajar, and his light brown eyes had widened to the size of quarters.

"It's mine, isn't it?"

Not knowing what to expect, Terri placed an arm across her stomach, and her fingers tightened around the handle of the small red basket she carried. "Leave me alone."

"That answers my question." His mouth tightened and nostrils flared. "More *fucking* secrets, Terri? How long did you think you could keep something like this from me?" he demanded, his voice raw.

"Indefinitely," she shot back, defiant.

Dammit. Why did she have to have to come here tonight, craving expensive items like gourmet cheese straws dipped in creamy gelato?

"You never planned to tell me?"

"You told me we were done, and I accepted your decision."

His eyes narrowed. "What game are you playing?"

"I'm not playing a game."

They both kept their eyes on a woman who passed by them, her gaze lingering on Gavin. She looked about to speak—perhaps because she recognized him—then thought better of it and hurried past.

Gavin waited until the woman walked out of earshot before

he spoke again. "That child you're carrying is a goldmine. You know it and I know."

"I don't want your damn money or anything else from you. Is that really so hard for you to believe?"

"You expect me to believe you're different from everyone else in this world?"

"I don't give a damn what you think. You can go fuck yourself."

Fire flared in his eyes, and for tense seconds, they simply stared at each other.

"You have some explaining to do," Gavin said.

"I don't owe you any explanation," Terri snapped back. What right did he have to be angry at her? She hadn't approached him. He approached her.

"We need to talk." He tugged the basket from her hand. "What else are you getting?"

She wanted to yell and scream. Kick him. She wanted to be left alone, but instead angled her chin higher and faced him squarely. "I'm done shopping. This was the last item on my list." She tossed the box of cheese straws on top of the other groceries.

Without another word, Gavin stalked away, fully expecting her to follow him. Arrogant ass.

Beautiful ass, she thought, albeit reluctantly, her gaze lowering to his tight behind.

She trailed after him and at the cashier's stand, he shot her a dark look when she pulled out her purse to pay for the items. Immediately, she tucked the wallet back into her bag and stood silently fuming beside him.

At the end of the transaction, he paid for the groceries and in his hand carried the two paper sacks by the handles, his platter of antipasti, and marched out of the market.

Sulking, Terri shot daggers at the back of his head. Who did he think he was? They were done. She wasn't good enough for him or his precious family. Her past would embarrass him. His words still stung.

You know who I am. You know who my family is.

He'd dumped her without giving her a chance to work things out. His so-called love had been frail and conditional, and she was disgusted with herself for the moments of weakness when she'd groveled and even worse—admitted she loved him.

"Are you going to talk to me?" she asked.

His long strides led them to a black sedan parked near the beginning of a row of cars. As they approached, a driver hopped out of the front seat and opened the back door.

Terri stopped a few feet away. "I'm not leaving with you."

"Yes, you are." Gavin didn't even turn in her direction.

"No, I'm not."

He swung around. "Get in the car. This isn't up for debate."

"Where are you taking me?"

"To your apartment. Wherever the hell that is," he said derisively.

"My apartment is perfectly fine. It's not a condo at the Four Seasons, but it's all I could afford after I pawned a lovely ruby necklace that some asshole gave me."

His head jerked back as if she'd slapped him. She'd wanted to hurt him, and clearly did, but immediately regretted her petty revenge. The necklace had been a glaring reminder of their relationship and she'd not only wanted to get rid of it, she'd needed the cash while she figured out what to do. Then she found out she was pregnant.

Terri glanced at the driver, who carefully kept his eyes averted during their argument, staring at an object in the distance.

"I don't want anything, Gavin."

"Everybody wants something."

"Not me." The only thing she'd wanted, dared to reach for, was his love. But he had callously withdrawn it.

With extra care, Gavin set the platter on top of the car. He took a deep breath and then walked over to where she stood, looking down at her with such fury in his eyes, her insides quaked. When he spoke, his tone was low enough that the driver couldn't hear, but the perfect pitch for Terri to pick up every word. "There's something you need to understand right now. That baby is half mine, a Johnson, and will have all the privileges that come with that name. I'm worth billions. There's no way I'm going to have my child out in the world, struggling while I'm driving around in chauffeured cars and eating the finest cuts of meat money can buy. I told you before I don't take no for an answer, and I meant it. Get in the goddamn car. Now. Or I'll drag you in."

He turned again and disappeared inside the dark interior of the sedan with all the foodstuffs. Terri stood there a few more seconds, partly to annoy him, but partly because she didn't want to go with him.

His face had been stony during their entire interaction. The Gavin she used to know smiled and laughed and teased. She wanted him to make an appearance, because she missed that Gavin. To her shame, she needed him.

Cheeks burning, she glanced at the chauffeur, whose erect posture and politely averted eyes must come from years of practice. She was angry, too. Angry that Gavin thought he could railroad her and take over her life after such a long time apart.

But she was no fool. She gathered up the courage necessary to handle him and what was to come and joined him in the back seat.

****

Terri stared at Gavin as his eyes scanned the new efficiency she rented in the same complex she lived in before.

"How far along are you?" He spoke in tight, clipped tones.

"A little over four months," Terri answered.

"You can't raise a baby here. Certainly not my child."

Terri crossed her arms over her swollen stomach. "I'm not staying here much longer. A cousin of mine in Tampa is going to let me stay with her for a while." Since she couldn't risk returning to Atlanta, she called her closest cousin, Tracy, who offered her guest bedroom to Terri without judgment or reservation.

"You're moving to Florida?" Gavin asked, a peculiar note to his voice.

Her eyes sought his, but she couldn't read anything in his expression. His face remained stoic and emotionless.

"That's the plan. I can't afford to stay in Seattle and raise…" She took a deep breath. "Raise two children. I'm not pregnant with one baby." Her fingers spread protectively over the lives in her womb. "I'm having twins."

His nostrils flared. "Like me and Ivy."

"And me and Damian."

Gavin paced the floor. "There's only one solution." He stopped pacing and faced her. "We have to get married."

Laughing, Terri shuffled back a step and watched his eyes darken. "Is that your idea of a proposal?"

"Under the circumstances, that's the best you're going to get," Gavin snapped.

"Well, I don't want to marry you, and I'm sure your precious family wouldn't want me to be a part of it. So forgive me, but I'll have to pass on the enticing offer. You want to take care of your kids, fine. But I'm moving to Florida to get what little support I can from my cousin, and I'm not marrying you."

After the callous way he dismissed her, it never crossed her mind that he'd want to have anything to do with children made up of half her DNA. For her part, she never thought she would refuse a wedding proposal from the man she loved. With Gavin, she could have everything she ever wanted—a home, a husband, a family. But it would all be a lie, a front. Because he didn't love her anymore. And the pain of it, to live through that, would be unbearable.

Instead of ranting and raving, Gavin spoke in a suspiciously calm voice. "Understand that you cannot keep my kids from me."

"I have no intention of keeping you apart, but this isn't a package deal."

"I'm afraid it is. Johnson men don't have baby mamas. Our children will be born within the confines of marriage. That's the way it's always been and that won't change with me."

"You can strut around beating your chest all you want, but we're not doing this. You can't make me."

"I have no intention of making you." He continued to speak in the same deceptively calm voice.

Terri eyed him suspiciously. "You don't?"

"Absolutely not. You'll make the right decision all on your own."

Terri swallowed. The hard look in Gavin's eyes worried her. Instinctively, trembling fingers covered her burgeoning belly while she waited for him to expound on his statement.

"You have three choices. I shouldn't even mention the first one because it'll never happen. You try to take my kids from me—emphasis on try—and I hire the best legal team money can buy to not only obtain full custody, I'll have you stripped of your parental rights."

Shocked, Terri took a few steps back and reached for the counter to hold her up.

"Or you could marry me and we raise the children together."

"And the third choice?" Terri asked in a trembling whisper.

"After you give birth to my children you walk away, a free woman. I'll raise my kids with the help of family and nannies."

My children. My kids. He was already cutting her out.

"I'll never give up my babies."

His face remained cold and emotionless. "Then all you have to do is marry me."

CHAPTER TWENTY-EIGHT

"I thought we were friends," Alannah said, disappointment in her face and tone.

"We are, but I needed time alone. And I couldn't tell you about my pregnancy and risk you telling Trenton or Gavin." Terri had effectively disappeared after she and Gavin broke up. She left her job and didn't return Alannah's calls. But she'd missed her friend.

Now they sat at their favorite brunch spot. The fall weather was nice enough that they could sit out on the porch and enjoy the meal.

"I understand, I guess."

Terri sipped her orange juice but continued to ignore her strawberry French toast. The meals here were delicious, but neither of them had much of an appetite and hadn't touched the food on their plates.

"I don't care about your past. I hope you know that," Alannah said earnestly.

Terri blinked away the tears. She should have placed more trust in their friendship. "I do. Thank you."

"You were very brave. I don't think I could have done what you did."

They both reached across the table and held hands.

"What are you going to do about Gavin's marriage proposal?" Alannah asked.

"I haven't made up my mind. I don't like the idea of getting married for the sake of a child—or children, in our case." She placed a hand on her belly. Their conversation last week rested heavy on her mind.

"He was upset you didn't tell him you were pregnant."

"Why would I tell him anything? We were done. I...I couldn't, Alannah. After the way we split, I didn't have the strength." Terri shook her head. "If I told him and he rejected us, I don't know what I would've done." The thought of him dismissing her and their children had been a possibility too hard to face.

"I've known this family for years. They're loving and kind and work really hard. Your children will be part of that family. And..." Alannah fidgeted in the chair and looked uncomfortable.

"What?" Terri prompted, releasing her friend's hand.

"They're very powerful."

"I know."

"They're going to do everything in their power to make sure your children want for nothing." Alannah spoke with a heaviness in her voice, the words weighted with hidden meaning.

"We don't have to get married for that to happen."

"Don't you want to get married?"

"Not like this. I want to get married for love. I want..." Clenching her teeth, she stared at her plate. *I want the fairytale.*

"You won't have a choice." The words were spoken quietly, but were no less of a warning.

"Are you saying you think I should marry Gavin?"

"I don't want to tell you what to do. The decision is yours. But I know the Johnsons, and they'll only accept one answer. If you don't give them the answer they want..." Alannah shrugged as her voice trailed off.

The gravity of her suggestion weighed heavy on Terri's mind. "He threatened to take my babies if I don't marry him."

Pity filled Alannah's eyes. "That wasn't an idle threat."

Terri fisted her hand on the table. "He can't do that. *They* can't do that. I won't let them."

Alannah's mouth downturned into a sad, sympathetic

expression. They both knew Terri didn't have the financial resources to fight a family so powerful and wealthy.

"I'm not walking away from my children," Terri said firmly.

"Then you know what you have to do."

"We don't even love each other," Terri whispered. Sighing, she added, "I want what you have with Trenton."

"It doesn't have to be all bad. Gavin's always sort of been the black sheep of the family. The bad egg. He's trying to do the right thing for once, and you and your children won't want for anything."

Except she wouldn't have his love. Terri lowered her gaze to her lap.

"The two of you were good together once. Maybe when you spend some time together again, you'll rekindle the relationship you had before."

A couple walked by, laughing and holding hands, and a spike of jealousy entered Terri's heart. "Yeah. Maybe."

****

On the last day of her one-week stay at her future mother-in-law's estate, Terri stared out the window of the guest room, overlooking the grounds where she would be married in less than a month.

Married to a billionaire.

She let out a short, dry laugh. Her life sounded like the plot to a romance novel, but it was happening, and happening to her.

After accepting Gavin's proposal—if one could call it that—right away, the Johnson family wheels started turning. She hadn't truly understood the extent of their wealth and what she was getting herself into until she said yes.

Constance insisted she come stay with her as they ironed out the details of the wedding. While Gavin worked and traveled for the company, she and her future mother-in-law handled the arrangements. A myriad of professionals came in and out of the house during those days. Terri let Constance run the show, and every now and again said yes and no where appropriate. Although they planned for an intimate gathering on the property, three wedding planners were employed to coordinate the activities. They covered everything from food, to the types of tents that would be erected on the property, to the guest list that mainly consisted of Johnson family members and close friends.

Terri's brother and his fiancée were being flown in. Her favorite cousin, a friend from the salon, and Alannah agreed to be bridesmaids, while Gavin's three brothers would stand at the altar at his side.

On the second day of her stay, a representative from the house of Carolina Herrera arrived to take her measurements for the one-of-a-kind dresses that she would wear to the wedding ceremony and the reception afterward. After listening to her preferences for the gowns and discussing the best ways to complement her growing belly, the rep flew out the same day, with a promise to have sketches to them within the week.

The Johnsons knew the full story about her past and took great pains to protect her reputation by having the family publicist craft the right tone for the rushed wedding and get in front of the bad publicity that would result when Terri's background was revealed. The blogs had already blown up when the engagement was announced, and she was called everything but her name—whore and gold digger being the most bandied about names—and accused of trapping Gavin. The fact that she'd managed to stay out of the spotlight while they dated made the news even more shocking for the gossipmongers.

Ivy advised her to ignore the press and not read the nasty articles, and after feeling depressed about the ugly comments that accompanied each piece, she finally agreed it was best to avoid them for her own peace of mind.

A security expert went through the house and walked the grounds, taking copious notes. He and his staff were responsible for keeping out uninvited guests and the press. They were also charged with working closely with the wedding planners to ensure that the caterers and other vendors didn't have moles planted in their midst.

Everything moved forward, and on the surface, she gave the impression of being somewhat happily resigned to her fate. She was marrying into a family whose legacy spanned generations. She and her children would have every need met and every want satisfied.

Deep down, however, her heart ached for the relationship she and Gavin used to have. The sexy conversations. The playfulness. The quiet evenings at home.

The few times she saw Gavin, he never smiled, she hadn't heard him laugh, and not once had he touched her.

CHAPTER TWENTY-NINE

Cyrus pointed across the room to Gavin. "Talk to your brother," he bit out. "He thinks he's Paul McCartney and doesn't need a prenup."

Gavin glowered at him, Xavier standing in the middle of Gavin's office, and Ivy, to whom the mandate was directed. She'd walked in after being summoned by their eldest sibling.

His twin shot a dark look at Cyrus, but when she turned her gaze to Gavin, her face softened. "Gavin, you can't seriously be thinking about marrying Terri without getting a signed prenup. That just isn't done."

He knew that. He knew it was a foolish decision, and yet, he hesitated to get the papers drawn up. Maybe he wasn't thinking straight, but who could blame him. Everything was happening so fast. He was getting married and going to be a father soon.

Amazing how he'd risked his life on too many occasions to count over the years, but the thought of a prenup terrified him so much he couldn't even initiate the paperwork.

"It's my decision. I know what I'm doing."

"Obviously, you don't," Cyrus interjected.

Xavier approached. "You're worth billions. If this woman—"

"*This woman* is going to be my wife and the mother of my children." Gavin shot his brother a warning look. "Watch your mouth."

Xavier rubbed a hand down his face and let out an exasperated puff of breath. "I wasn't going to say anything negative about her. I know what she went through. But if you think it's a good idea to get married without a prenup, you've fallen off too many mountains, or maybe you've finally been affected by the lack of oxygen to your brain from the dangerous diving trips you take."

"I'm not going to take advice from a man who I haven't seen date the entire year I've been back in Seattle."

"What does my dating history have to do with you getting a prenup?" Xavier growled.

"Out. Both of you." Arms akimbo, Ivy glared at Cyrus and Xavier. Their older brothers shook their heads in disgust but marched toward the door.

Cyrus, the last one out, couldn't resist getting in one more comment. "Talk some sense into him."

"Let me handle it," Ivy snapped. She waited until Cyrus and Xavier left before she turned on Gavin. "What are you thinking?"

"Et tu?"

"Don't give me that. I'm not against you, but you have to admit this is ridiculous. Cyrus and Xavier are right."

Gavin folded his arms over his chest and rested his butt against the heavy credenza.

"What's going on?" Ivy asked.

"They won't mind their own business. They've been badgering me about drawing up the papers ever since we announced the engagement."

Ivy came to stand beside him, also resting her butt against the credenza. "You're making a mistake, and I need to understand why you're doing this. You're not stupid. You know the risks. Mother and father had a prenup. Cyrus and Daniella have one. Lucas and I are going to have one. It's common sense."

Silence. Not even their breaths could be heard.

Gavin swallowed hard. "What if she doesn't sign it?"

"If she doesn't sign it, then we get a team of lawyers to…" Ivy covered her mouth with one hand, eyes wide. "Oh my goodness, you're worried she won't sign it, and then she won't marry you. You love her, don't you?"

Gavin scrubbed a hand across his forehead. "Yeah. Which makes me the biggest chump in the world."

"Oh, Gavin. It doesn't make you a chump."

He slanted a glance at his sister. "No? I want to marry a woman who I'm not sure ever cared about me and has more aliases than a CIA operative." Gavin pounded his hand on top of the credenza. "She wasn't even going to tell me she was pregnant. How could she do that?"

Ivy winced. She had kept her child a secret from her fiancé for years.

"Damn. Sorry, Ivy."

"Don't apologize. I had my reasons, and I'm sure Terri had her own. Fear. Hurt. It could have been for any or both of those reasons."

"Whatever her reason, she had no intention of telling me. Which means she doesn't want my money. Which means she could walk away." Gavin grasped the edge of the furniture behind him.

Ivy studied him. "You never had any intention of taking the kids from her, did you?"

"She loves kids. You saw how she was with Michael and Katie. That's how she is with all children. What kind of monster would I be to take the twins away from her?"

They both fell silent.

"You could continue to let her think that's what you're going to do," Ivy suggested.

"But that's not what I want." Gavin slid his gaze to his sister. "I want *her* and our kids. But I feel like I'm stuck between a rock and a hard place." He swore.

"All you have to do is make the offer attractive."

"What if she doesn't sign it, Ivy?"

"She'll sign it." Ivy sighed. "A prenup should be mutually beneficial, and that's how you get her to sign. Make her an offer she can't refuse. But you cannot marry her without one. I don't care how much you love her. If you even consider doing it without the contract, I'll have you declared mentally incompetent." Ivy grinned.

Laughing, Gavin shook his head. "I know you're right."

"Of course your big sister is right."

"Here we go," Gavin grumbled.

Ivy grinned up at him with sympathy in her eyes. "Make the right decision, Gavin. If you don't, if you end up divorced, you've basically written her a blank check."

"Does it sound crazy that I don't even care?" He searched her face but didn't see any trace of judgment.

"It does sound crazy." She smiled slightly. "But believe me, I understand."

****

Gavin paced the boardroom floor, nervous energy growing in his stomach as the minutes ticked by. Twenty minutes past the hour and Terri still hadn't shown up. What if she didn't come? It was a crazy thought, but one that had haunted him all morning.

To date, they hadn't received any response from her attorney. He didn't even know who she had hired, but surely they recognized his generosity in the package. He'd tried to be fair, but his idea of fair and hers may not coincide. Terri and his children would be well provided for in the event they divorced, and the prenup included six-figure financial incentives for every year they remained married.

The phone on the table rang and Gavin snatched it up. "Yes?"

"Your fiancée is here."

His gut twisted. It happened every time someone referred to her as his fiancée. Before, she'd been referred to as Terri or Ms. Slade. But hearing the receptionist call her his fiancée was as sobering as it was...thrilling.

"Send her in."

Gavin walked over to the table where his attorney, Jesup Hardwick, was already seated with the documents spread out in triplicate before him. Gavin rubbed his hands together and waited for Terri to enter. When he saw her, he stopped breathing for a few seconds. She appeared almost angelic in a cream maternity dress and small earrings shaped like hearts. She wore her hair loose today, and it was longer, thicker, and shinier.

Realizing he was staring, he briefly looked away and cleared his throat.

Terri smiled hesitantly, closed the door behind her, and walked over to the table. "Sorry I'm late."

Gavin waited for her to sit before joining them at the table. "Where's your attorney? Is he running late, too?"

"I don't have one." She spoke calmly.

"What do you mean, you don't have one?"

"I can't afford to hire a lawyer." She said it simply, as if it was common knowledge.

Gavin stared at her. "You're being ridiculous, Terri. You can't sit down and sign these documents without legal counsel."

"That's what I intend to do."

"Quit the martyr act."

"I'm not trying to be a martyr. I couldn't afford an attorney." Her dark eyes blazed at him.

Attorney Jesup cleared his throat. "Perhaps we should leave this as is, Mr. Johnson."

Gavin turned angrily toward the man. "What are you thinking about? Why would we leave this as is?"

"You're about to get everything you want," his lawyer said.

"The prenup should be a mutually beneficial arrangement," Gavin said, annoyed the lawyer wanted him to take advantage of her.

"Where do you need me to sign?" She was serene, while he was the one losing his mind.

The attorney shifted the papers a few inches away from her. "You should have an attorney present to protect your interests, Ms. Slade."

"I don't need one."

"What do you mean, you don't need one?" Gavin interjected.

The attorney placed a restraining hand on his arm. "Mr. Johnson—"

"I could take advantage of you. There could be anything written on those pages. What are you thinking?"

"I'm not worried." Her hand went to her stomach. It was as if she were always checking to make sure their children were there, or protecting them. "All I care about is our babies. I know you'll do everything in your power to take good care of them. No matter how you feel about me, that won't change." Silence fell over the table, and then she looked at the attorney. "Where do you need me to sign?"

Gavin jumped up from the table with such force, the chair rolled back and slammed into the wall. "I want to talk to her alone. Get out."

Terri didn't move. She didn't flinch. She held his gaze.

"Mr. Johnson, I think that you should—"

"Get out!" Gavin glared at the man, whose face turned fire engine red. Gavin didn't care what he thought. He was paying the bills and his attorney needed to get the hell out of there.

Jesup straightened his tie and quickly exited the room.

Silence reigned between them. He stared down at her. She looked up at him.

Gavin leaned on his hands toward Terri. "What are you doing?"

"I'm here to sign a prenuptial agreement."

"You trying to make me look bad?"

"I don't know what you want me to say, Gavin."

"You don't want anything. You don't need a lawyer."

"Correct," she said quietly. "I just want you to provide for our children. That's it. Whatever you do is fine with me."

"How can you say that? How can you be so sure?"

She didn't answer right away, but then she said, in a very quiet tone, "You're angry, but I know you would never harm me, and I know you want to provide for our children. You couldn't do anything less. You're too honorable for that." Her eyes softened. "Just tell me where to sign."

CHAPTER THIRTY

Terri might as well be living alone for all she saw of Gavin. She spent more time with the housekeeper, Edie, and the chef, than with him. Since the wedding, he kept his distance, and the few times he actually touched her, she almost cried from relief of the physical contact. But as much as she enjoyed their moments together, she hated them, too. Stalled conversations started and ended with weighty silence and awkward hand gestures.

Most nights, he came home late and slept in a guest bedroom, stating he didn't want to disturb her, but he kept some clothes in the master suite for appearance's sake. And why wouldn't he avoid her? She wasn't the same woman. Before, she'd been confident and never insecure about her body. Not anymore.

Her nose had spread wider, and her signature sexy walk with swinging hips had been reduced to a penguin waddle. At six months into the pregnancy, her waistline had stretched to the size of ten basketballs, and if her butt got any bigger, they'd be able to serve dinner for eight on it.

Terri sighed, dragging the loofah over her chest and relishing the rose-scented water. Running her hands over her large belly, she imagined the moment when she met her son and daughter. Gavin may not care to pay her any attention, but she would have her new babies to shower with love and affection.

Time for her to get out of the water before she turned into a prune. She'd stayed in there long enough and the water was getting cooler. She released the water. As it swirled into the drain, Terri pressed her hands on one side of the Jacuzzi tub and pushed up. But she barely budged.

She tried again, repositioning her hand to push herself from the bottom. Still nothing. Panic set in. She may not be able to get out of the tub.

Terri laughed to herself. How ridiculous. Surely, she could get out. But the more effort she exerted, the more she realized she was stuck.

"Edie." Her voice bounced off the tile in a mocking echo.

Had the housekeeper left already, and if not, could she hear Terri all the way in the bathroom?

"Edie!" she called again, louder this time. Anyone listening could hear the panic in her voice, and she wasn't even sure when Gavin would be back.

"Edie!" she screamed. Tears of frustration filled her eyes.

I'm stuck.

****

Gavin dropped his briefcase in the bedroom he slept in most nights. The quiet house meant Edie had already left. He came home early because he didn't want Terri to be in the house alone. Even if they barely talked, he could still be there in case she needed him.

They should get the house fully staffed soon. She needed a driver for sure, and they should start interviewing nannies—one for the weekdays and the other for the weekend.

He tossed his tie onto the bed and walked down the hall to the master bedroom suite. Outside the door, he took a deep breath and then knocked. He hated himself for forcing Terri into a marriage she obviously didn't want. The vivacious, energetic Terri he fell in love with was nowhere to be found, because of him. He was so ashamed of his behavior, he could hardly face her.

He knocked on the door and heard a muffled voice from the inside but couldn't distinguish the words.

"Terri?" He waited.

Again, muffled sounds that he barely heard. He pushed open

the door and heard the tail end of Terri's cry.

"...in here! In the bathroom."

Gavin rushed toward her panic-stricken voice and found Terri in the giant tub, one arm resting on the side and her eyes wide and pink from tears.

She reached a hand to him. "Help me."

"What's the matter?" He hurried to her side.

"I'm stuck. I can't get out."

He pulled up short. "Wh—stuck?"

"Yes."

She looked so pitiful, and the circumstances sounded so comical, he couldn't help it. He started laughing.

Her eyes widened. "It's not funny!"

"I'm sorry, sweetheart," Gavin said. Still, his shoulders shook from the humor in the hilarious situation. "Let me help you."

Placing a hand under each arm, Gavin lifted her from the floor of the tub and got the full view of her gloriously naked caramel-toned skin, damp from the bath she'd taken and smelling as divine as a rose garden filled with fresh blooms. His body reacted immediately, and he ground his teeth to fight the instinctive response.

She looked huge, immensely uncomfortable, yet never more beautiful. Her skin glowed and her hair, piled on top of her head, held a glossy sheen.

Terri's arm came across her breasts, which were even larger now that she was pregnant. The other hand covered her privates.

"Could you hand me a towel, please?"

He hardly breathed. He hadn't seen her naked body in months. "No. Move your hand. I want to look at you."

She didn't budge. Only stared at him.

"Please, Terri. I want to see you."

He pulled her hand away from her breasts, and the other eased away from her pelvis. She stood there and let him examine her, looking like a goddess with her belly stretched taut with his children, and her fuller, heavier breasts capped by darker, plumper nipples. Damn, he wanted desperately to take one of the sensitive buds into his mouth.

"Are you in any pain?" he asked, touching the firm skin of her stomach.

A black line stretched down the middle of her belly. The changes in her body fascinated him.

I did that.

"No. This is supposed to be the easy part." She smiled, appearing a bit hesitant about him and his intentions.

Gavin palmed her belly. "Damn, you look beautiful."

He lowered to his knees and kissed the top of her stomach, the sides, and below her belly button. His touch was soft and affectionate—toward her as well as the children she carried.

"Beautiful," he said again, amazed that this woman was carrying life inside of her—life that they'd created.

"I thought you would think I was ugly," she whispered.

He looked up at her. "No way. This is amazing." He closed his eyes and rested his head against her belly.

Her fingers slid over his hair, a soothing massage that relaxed him. He missed her touch. He missed his woman.

He kissed the underside of her belly and molded his hands over her hips. On her sharp intake of breath, his mouth moved more boldly, kissing her hips and then moving horizontally until he brushed his mouth across the dark cloud between her legs. His tongue flicked the clit nestled among the curls, and she moaned out loud, gripping the back of his head.

Gavin's heart rate picked up speed. He wanted more. He kissed her lower lips, easing his tongue along the slit, and she gasped his name.

The sound of his name on her tongue catapulted him into action. Rising quickly from the floor, his eyes met hers and he kissed her soundly, clasping her face in his hands, delving into her mouth with his tongue. When he released her, he led her into the bedroom and laid her on top of the sheets, head nestled against the pillows.

"I just want you to feel good," he said, tossing off his shirt. He undressed quickly, removing every item of clothing except his boxer briefs, and then joined her on the bed.

"Just lay back and enjoy yourself," he said.

He stroked his hand over her naked skin, over her thighs and up to her hips where the results of her pregnancy marked her skin.

"Stretch marks," she whispered, as if he didn't know what they were.

He grumbled low in his chest and maneuvered so he could kiss the roundness of her belly. One hand cupped one of her fuller breasts as his lips traveled along her hips. He nudged her thighs apart with his hand, and his lips pressed to the goal, lifting one leg over his shoulder.

She melted as his tongue eased over her slick flesh, swirling against the tight bud at her center. Terri opened her legs wider and let him press openmouthed kisses to her throbbing flesh. She gasped, tension coiling in her core. He licked and tugged the knot of nerves with his pretty lips and lapped at the moist dew with a groan.

The tension finally snapped, sending waves of pleasure crashing through her. Terri cried out, a broken, ragged sound torn from her lips as he feverishly licked at her skin, moaning into her flesh as he took every drop and dragged every spasm from between her trembling thighs.

He made his way back up to her mouth and kissed her thoroughly again. Still reeling from the onslaught of bliss, Terri managed to kiss him back, whimpering, clinging to his wide shoulders.

When he released her mouth, she rolled onto her side and into his arms. Using his shoulder as a pillow, Terri nestled tightly against him. His arms folded around her, drawing her against his warm skin. One hand rested around her back and the other on her stretched belly where their babies rested.

Breathing finally back to normal, Terri traced the groove of his top abdominal muscle. "Gavin?"

"Yes."

"Will you stay in here tonight?"

He pressed his lips to her forehead, and although she couldn't see it, she felt the smile his mouth made against her skin. "I'll stay in here every night."

She relaxed and breathed easier, and before long, they both

fell asleep.

CHAPTER THIRTY-ONE

Terri rubbed her belly. Too much Oreo pie. Lucky for her, she could eat as much as she wanted and blame it on eating for three. Being pregnant definitely had its advantages.

Turning sideways in the bathroom mirror, she admired her newly done hair, long blonde braids reaching down the middle of her back. Even though her delivery date was still two months away, she knew that the likelihood of having a preterm birth increased with multiples and wanted to be ready.

Aside from having a hard time getting up sometimes, she loved being pregnant. She loved shopping for baby clothes—finding little matching outfits for her son and daughter—in blue and pink. Over the weekend, she and Alannah flew to Los Angeles for a meeting with the owners of Petit Trésor. They left the luxury baby store with thousands of dollars in clothes, accessories, and a designer diaper bag made of tan cow leather.

The first time Terri visited the store, she met with the owners alone for a consultation on designing the babies' room in a décor fitting for a boy and a girl. The nursery was on the third floor with the master bedroom and she chose soothing colors in tans, creams, and beiges.

Their daughter's crib was decorated in the palest rose with a mattress made of natural latex and organic lambswool and bunnies etched into the wood. Long silk bows were attached to the side, and handstitched bedding in luxurious fabrics waited for her little angel to arrive and lay her head. Their son's crib was similarly designed, except they kept the colors a neutral white. Above each bed, a Blabla sheep mobile rotated, knitted by Peruvian artisans and made of only the finest natural fibers.

Terri rubbed her belly again, imagining what her little boy and girl would look like and their personalities.

"Mrs. Johnson?" The housekeeper called at the door.

"Yes?"

"I'm leaving. Would you like me to set the alarm before I go?"

"No, I'm going to pick up a few things at the store." She tugged on a robe and padded out to the bedroom. She opened the door.

The housekeeper frowned, her brown face showing wrinkles around the corners and a spattering of tiny moles down her left cheek. "Ma'am, if you need me to get something…"

"Not necessary." Terri waved away the concern. As the woman of the house, the employees were expected to tend to her every need, especially since she was pregnant, but it was nice to run her own errands sometimes. "You go on. I'll be fine."

"Well, if you're sure…" Edie hesitated.

Terri figured the woman was probably worried about word getting back to Gavin, but he was still in Missouri, where he and Xavier had gone to examine the operations of a small craft brewer that they were considering buying out.

"I'm sure. And this will be between the two of us."

"Yes, ma'am." Edie folded her hands in front of her. "The chef prepared a fried chicken meal using your grandmother's recipe, as you requested. I hope you'll find it to your liking."

She had the strangest cravings since getting pregnant. Gourmet cheese straws and gelato were only the beginning. She also craved baloney sandwiches and her grandmother's fried chicken.

"I'm sure I will."

"Good night."

After Edie left, Terri put on an oversized shirt that stretched across her belly and breasts and a pair of elastic waistband jeans.

Chuckling at the vision she made, she flung her Gucci purse over her shoulder and took the elevator down to the first floor. As she neared the kitchen, the aroma of fried chicken, mashed potatoes with cheese, and sautéed corn filled the air.

She went into the kitchen and lifted the cover from the pot and pinched off a piece of meat. Crunchy skin and moist insides danced in her mouth. "Mmmm. He did good, Nana Elisabeth," she said to the empty kitchen.

Terri re-covered the dish and picked up the tablet resting on the counter, scrolling through the images to ensure all the doors and windows were securely closed before setting the alarm. She stopped when she saw the sensor on a door at the back of the house glowed with a red warning light. Someone must have left it open. Again. It could have been one of the gardeners or one of the workmen Gavin had knocking down a wall to build a library for her.

Sighing, Terri set down the tablet. She'd have to shut it properly before she could set the alarm.

At a soft sound behind her, the hairs on the back of her neck immediately went vertical and she swung around.

She almost fainted when she saw Talon Cyrenci standing in the doorway. Grabbing onto the counter, her eyes darted around the room. Was she hallucinating?

Those cold green eyes were no hallucination.

Talon was of average height with a long body—the best way to describe him. He had a narrow, elongated face and arms and legs that seemed to extend to three times the length of his torso. But he had the body of a long distance runner, with lean muscles and a hidden strength not easily discerned at first glance. The kind of strength used to subdue a woman and keep her in her place.

Sharp as ever, he projected an image of refined wealth in a long-sleeved shirt with gold cuff links, dark slacks, and gleaming wingtips. But the fine covering hid his true personality—that of a common street thug who dragged her into his life of crime.

"Hello, Felicia." The familiar slick smile turned her stomach. "Pardon me. It's Terri now, isn't it?"

A chill scurried down her spine. "H-how did you get in

here?"

"Don't look so afraid, sweetheart." The evil grin stretched further across his face. "I just came for what you owe me."

"I-I don't owe you anything."

He wagged a finger at her. "Don't be coy. You know what you did. I lost everything because of you." He looked around the Poggenpohl-designed kitchen—sophisticated simplicity with its sharp lines and flat surfaces of white and metallic gray. "Now look at you. Pregnant. Married. To a fucking billionaire, at that. Best damn scam you ever pulled, and I didn't even have to put a gun to your head to make you carry it out."

He came around the island and Terri edged away, sliding along the counter. The knives were in the drawer in the corner. If she could get to them, she should be able to stab him and make an escape.

"What do you want?" she asked, trying to distract him with conversation.

"I want money."

"I don't have any money. My husband—"

"Your husband. Isn't that sweet?"

Terri's hand tightened on the counter at his sarcastic tone. "I don't keep much cash, but I have—have some jewelry upstairs."

"There's a safe here somewhere. These rich types always have safes."

"There is, but I don't know the combination. He's never given it to me."

"The jewelry's a start. Then you and I are going to the bank tomorrow to withdraw some funds."

Terri's legs became unstable, and she gripped the counter even harder for support. Did he plan to stay here all night? "Tomorrow?" she brokenly whispered.

"That's right. We're going to be spending a little time together. You owe me money, and you owe me the time I spent behind bars." His face turned into a vicious snarl.

"You can't stay here. Gavin will be home any minute."

"Tsk, tsk. You think I'm stupid, don't you? I already know

your husband is in Missouri." He nodded when her eyes widened, his eyes filled with triumph. "Yeah, that's right. I've been keeping an eye on you for a minute, and lucky for me, the newspaper, magazines, and Internet let me know everything he's up to. Hell, even his Twitter account announced where he is." The sly grin died on his face. "Show me the jewelry. Now."

"Okay. I have to go upstairs." She started moving again, keeping an eye on him from the corner of her eye as he followed. Then she dashed for the drawer and had her hand on a carving knife before Talon's hand slammed onto her wrist.

Agonizing pain shot up her arm. Terri screamed and almost crumbled to the floor. She staggered out of his reach, tears filling her eyes as she clutched the counter for support. Her breathing came fast and heavy.

"That was dumb," Talon said.

He picked up the knife and hooked the blade in one of her hoop earrings. "What if I did to you what you were planning to do to me? Hmm? Tell me you're sorry."

"I'm sorry." Her hand protectively covered her bulging midsection.

"Louder."

"I'm sorry."

"Less attitude," he said through gritted teeth, fingers tightening around the handle of the weapon.

Terri took a breath. "I'm sorry."

He glanced at the hand covering her belly. "You always wanted to get married and start a family. Everything was about you, what you wanted, and what you didn't want. We had a good thing going, but you—you turned on me. Thought you were better than me, didn't you?" The fact that she didn't answer didn't stop him at all. He nodded his head. "Yeah, you thought you were too good for me."

He rubbed his jaw, and a wicked smile crossed his face. Terri's heart bottomed out at the evil intent in his eyes.

"You owe me."

"I'll get you the jewelry and any money you want."

"No, something else. Something I was deprived of for four years during the trial and my incarceration." He caught her by the chin and hard fingers burned into her flesh. "I want you on your knees."

Her eyes opened in horror. "I'm pregnant."

"That's going to make it even sweeter. On. Your. Knees."

Worried that if she didn't immediately comply he would hurt her, Terri held onto the counter and clumsily lowered to the floor, landing sideways onto her hip. Pain shot through her side when she hit the tile. She grimaced, but Talon gave no indication that he noticed or intended to aid her. He slammed the knife on the counter and unbuttoned his pants.

"You know what to do." He grabbed her chin and forced her eyes up to him.

She saw nothing but evil there. Hate. Anger that she'd dared to turn on him and succeed in having a better life than the one they had shared.

"I want you to look at me when you suck me off."

"You don't have to do this. I can get you money," Terri said, trying to reason with him.

"I'll get the money, too. This first."

His actions weren't just about revenge. They were about feeling superior to the man she married. His fragile ego made him want to take her, own her, and force her to submit.

Terri unzipped his pants, fingers trembling. Her eyes shifted to the knife on the counter.

"Don't even think about it," Talon warned.

She pulled out his limp penis and held it in one hand.

"That's right," he rasped. "Handle your business."

His penis grew firmer, and she fought back the nausea, lifted her other hand, and punched him hard and swift in the balls.

Talon yelped and doubled over, and that's when Terri took off. She couldn't get to her feet, so she crawled as quickly as she could on her hands and knees toward the door.

"Bitch. Bitch. *Bitch*," Talon panted behind her.

Terri grasped the doorjamb with both hands and struggled to

her feet. Not an easy task with all the weight at her center, but she succeeded. Glancing back for a split second, she saw Talon staggering to his feet, face contorted and one hand on his crotch. He sent a venomous glare her way. In no uncertain terms, she would be dead if he caught her.

Terri raced down the hall, clutching her belly.

The elevator. She had to get to the elevator. Upstairs, she could lock herself behind the sanctuary of the bedroom door.

She ran around the corner and stood anxiously in front of the lift, jabbing her thumb constantly into the button. The doors slowly opened and she hurried inside. Punching the button for the third floor, she was almost home free when Talon's pale hands forced their way between the closing doors.

Terri screamed and backed into the corner. She watched in horror as he pried apart the two sides. Her knees collapsed and she slid along the wall to the floor. This couldn't be happening.

"You thought you had me, didn't you?" His face was red and angry. His long hands held the doors wide. "There's no getting away from me tonight."

"Please."

"Get out here!"

"No." She rapidly shook her head.

Talon rushed forward and without thinking, without any premeditation, Terri lifted her foot and kicked him in stomach.

"Oof." His eyes crossed and he doubled over. Terri slammed the heel of her shoe into his forehead, kicking him so hard he fell sideways. Moaning and clutching his face, Talon rolled on the floor.

Breathing hard, Terri stepped over him and raced toward the stairs. Talon was strong, and now enraged, which meant he could probably break down the door of any room she entered with one solid kick. Which was why she had to get to the top floor. He couldn't get her in the bedroom, which doubled as a panic room. She could call for help from there.

She rushed up the stairs, stumbling on the third step and quickly putting out her hand to brace against the impact on her belly. She recovered quickly and pressed onward. She climbed as fast as she could to the second floor and then bolted toward the second staircase. She paused, winded. With so much weight at her center, she was struggling. Almost there.

"Felicia!" Talon bellowed behind her.

His voice catapulted her into action.

Oh god, oh god.

Halfway there. Tears blurred her vision as she clutched the railing for support, heaving her bulky body up to safety.

Her right foot landed on the top step, but when she lifted the left to join it, Talon's hand closed around the ankle. Terri kicked with all her might and his weak hold released her.

"*Fel-i-cia!*"

She didn't stop. She didn't pause. She flew down the hallway as fast as she could go, but he grabbed her around the neck from behind and knocked her to the floor. Searing pain cut across her back and side.

"You stupid bitch. Now I have to kill—"

The words were cut short by a strangled sound coming from his throat. Terri looked up to see another body in shirtsleeves—dark, tall, and athletic.

Gavin. He came back early. She almost sobbed with relief.

His fist landed with a crack across Talon's jaw, knocking the other man into the wall.

Gavin turned to her, fists at his side, eyes filled with murderous rage.

"Get in the bedroom. *Now.*"

He didn't have to tell her twice. Terri scrambled to her feet and ran the rest of the way to their bedroom. She closed the easy-swing door, fifteen hundred pounds slamming into place and metal bolts sliding home to lock out the danger.

She walked backward and sank onto the bed. She couldn't stop shaking. Her entire body, her breath, her insides—everything quaked. The fortified room was impenetrable, but she kept her eyes on the door.

Tears running down her face, she waited.

CHAPTER THIRTY-TWO

The pain in her hip throbbed, and Terri gingerly rubbed the sore spot. She would be badly bruised. Just like all the times in the past when Talon hurt her.

She couldn't hear anything in the hallway. Then there was a loud thump and she froze. Listening.

"Terri, are you all right in there? Talk to me." Gavin's voice came through the wall.

"Yes, I'm fine." She rushed to the door but pulled up short halfway across the floor. Searing pain cut across her abdomen. She took a few deep breaths and the pain subsided. Then she resumed her trek to the door.

Too excited and relieved to think straight, she fumbled with the lock. Then she swung open the door and gasped at the sight before her. Gavin held Talon against the wall, one hand gripping his neck, the other gripping a gun with the barrel lodged in Talon's mouth. Her ex's face was battered and bruised, and blood oozed from a cut at the corner of his mouth.

"Are you all right?" Gavin asked, keeping his eyes on the other man.

"Yes, I'm fine." Still, he didn't move. He seemed to be frozen.

She rushed to his side and placed a hand on his arm. "Gavin, I'm fine."

He didn't respond.

"Baby, he's not worth it. Think about what you're doing."

Gavin turned to her, and the only way to describe the look in his eyes was murderous. "Are you sure you're okay?"

"Yes," Terri answered quickly, petrified he might pull the trigger if she hesitated one iota. She didn't care about her ex. She just didn't want Gavin locked up for murder.

He shifted his gaze back to Talon, jaw tight with tension. The rank odor of urine filled the air, and Terri looked down to see a wet spot at the front of Talon's pants.

"Baby, please. I'm fine. We're fine."

This time she seemed to get through to him.

"Call the police." Gavin spoke in an even, controlled voice, but she sensed the violence simmering near the surface, demanding to come out. "Tell them to hurry."

****

Gavin looked around the living room as he spoke privately with his attorney in one corner. The property was a flurry of activity. Officers were going through the entire house and grounds to make sure no one else had arrived with Cyrenci. They also collected fingerprints and took photos of the places where he scuffled with Terri and Gavin.

A detective questioned Terri, seated on the sofa with another family attorney next to her interjecting every so often. The family publicist was present with a member of his staff, already working on a statement to be released first thing in the morning.

Gavin kept his eyes on Terri. She nodded and answered questions but looked wan and frail, and every so often, she rubbed her stomach as if in pain.

He walked over to the trio. "How much longer?" he asked.

The detective looked up from his notebook. "Just a few more questions, Mr. Johnson."

Terri suddenly cried out and gripped the underside of her belly. Gavin dropped to his knees and put a protective arm around her shoulder. "What's wrong, baby?"

She turned wide eyes to him. "My water just broke. I'm going into labor."

****

Gavin sat on the side of the bed, watching Terri's eyes twitch as she dreamed. She jumped in her sleep, and he placed a calming hand on her shoulder. After a moment, the twitching stopped and tension eased from her body. He combed his fingers through the long braids splayed out on the pillow before pulling the duvet higher around her shoulders and standing from the bed.

She had been through too much. When he saw the bruises on her body at the hospital three weeks ago, the fury that erupted inside of him had almost sent him to the jail to remove Talon Cyrenci from this earth, limb by limb, with his bare hands.

The only thing that had kept him from firing a bullet inside Talon's open mouth were her pleading words.

Baby, he's not worth it.

Although it could be argued that he was defending his family, he couldn't take the chance. He wanted to wake up next to his wife every day. He wanted to hold his children, play with them, and watch them grow. By acting rashly, he risked letting Talon Cyrenci take all of that away.

Since that night, he'd hired an architect who'd drawn up plans to install panic rooms on each floor of the house. One in the library behind a bookcase on the first floor, and the hall bathroom on the second floor would become the other safe room. A home security expert was working around the clock to have a keyless entry system installed by the end of the week using biometric recognition software. The cutting edge technology transformed each occupant of the house into a key, able to open doors through facial and voice recognition.

He waited a few more minutes to make sure she was all right before quietly leaving the room.

In the nursery, he found the nanny, Esther, placing Elisabeth in her crib. Terri had been very instrumental in choosing the nannies. She once said to him, "There's no way a hot young thing is coming here to watch my kids and try to take my place. Not gonna happen."

While he didn't like to comment on anyone's appearance, Esther was a boxy woman who looked like more man than woman with her tall height and long-fingered hands.

Greedy little Gavin, Jr.—who ate about a third more than his sister, was being fed from a bottle by Gavin's mother as she rocked back and forth in the tan wingback glider chair. His drowsy eyes followed Gavin as he moved to stand in front of the matching glider beside his mother. Elisabeth and Junior had Gavin's light-colored eyes, but they both had Terri's nose and honey-brown complexion.

"Good night, Esther. We'll see you in the morning."

The nanny nodded and left to go to her room on the second floor. Gavin sank into the chair and, sighing, buried his head in his hands.

"Are you all right?" Constance asked.

He looked up and nodded. "Been a rough few weeks." His shoulders ached and he was operating on very little sleep.

Delivering the twins lasted almost fifteen hours. Then the doctors kept the babies in the hospital until their tiny bodies could function well enough to sustain them in the world outside the incubators. They'd only been home one full day so far.

"How's Terri?"

"Could be better but she's strong." The doctor had offered to prescribe a sedative to help her sleep, but she turned down the offer, reluctant to take any medication while breast-feeding.

"You really love her, don't you?"

Gavin nodded. "Yes."

His mother rocked his son quietly in the chair. "Have you told her how much you love her?"

"Not recently," he admitted. He rested his head on the back of the chair and looked at his mother, awaiting her sage advice.

"Tell her again. Sometimes, we need to hear it, especially when things aren't going very well." A little smile came on her face. "Your father was a master at that. No matter how upset I'd get, he knew that was the one thing that calmed me down."

Gavin used to avoid conversations about his father, but in recent months he'd grown more comfortable talking about him, even though it hurt.

"You had Father wrapped around your finger," he said.

217

"Oh, I don't know about that. Although he did seem smitten with me from the first time we met. Did you know our parents set us up?"

Gavin nodded. "I've heard the story."

She pursed her lips and shook her head. "They tried to be sneaky about it, pretending they'd gotten together because of a business deal, but they were so obvious. Cyrus and I figured it out right away."

In her arms, Gavin, Jr. dozed, and she removed the bottle's nipple from his little mouth and rested her hand on the cushioned armrest of the chair. Gavin sensed the sadness in her and reached over to squeeze her arm.

His mother turned to him with a wan smile. "Tell her again how much you love her." She spoke in a quiet voice, a sheen of tears coating her eyes. "A woman can never hear that too much."

****

"What are you doing?"

Terri spun around from the stove to see Gavin standing at the island in the middle of the kitchen. She'd been so preoccupied with fixing a late night snack, she hadn't heard him enter.

"You're supposed to be resting," he said. "If you need something, you should let me get it or one of the servants."

"I'm not an invalid," Terri said, though she probably looked like one. She wore an oversized cotton nightgown because she still had some of her baby stomach, ankle socks, and a satin bonnet on her head to protect the blonde braids.

Gavin had been coddling her ever since the incident, but she'd been through worse, and all she really cared about was that her children were fine, and they were. Both healthy and beautiful and a greater blessing than she could have ever imagined. She woke up with a smile on her face every day thinking about them—even when her sleep was disturbed by nightmares. Her children made all of that go away.

"What are you making?"

"A fried baloney sandwich."

The craving for them hadn't subsided. Terri enjoyed the food they ate when they went out or the meals the chef prepared, but a fried baloney sandwich could not be found on the menu of any fine dining establishment, and she didn't intend to ask the chef to prepare one for her. They had to be done just right.

"A what?"

"Fried baloney sandwich." Terri placed the second piece of bread over the other. "Don't tell me you've never had one."

"I'm not sure what that is."

"You're going to love it. Want to try?"

"No, thanks. I'm not hungry."

Terri walked around the island and stuck the sandwich against his pressed-together lips. "Open."

He resisted and she shoved harder until he finally parted his lips and took a bite. He chewed slowly, frowning. Eventually, the lines in his knitted brow disappeared.

"Mmm. Not bad."

"Told you."

She turned away but he grabbed the plate.

"Hey! You said you weren't hungry."

"I wasn't, but this is good." He ate a third of the sandwich with another bite. "Fried baloney," he said in wonderment.

"I can't believe you've never had a fried baloney sandwich before. You're so privileged."

She shook her head and set about making another sandwich for herself. This time, she added cheese, and Gavin had to try that, too, which meant he also ate part of that sandwich, and she settled for the rest and pieces of a tangerine, which he insisted she share.

Terri muttered, "You're so spoiled, I swear."

He ignored her, taking a sip from her glass of ice water.

They sat beside each other, quietly eating and drinking, and when they finished the late night snack, Gavin cleaned up the counters and put everything in the dishwasher. Her gaze lingered on his broad back as he bent over the dish rack. It was too soon for them to make love again, and she missed that level of intimacy with him. She missed…something. She didn't even know what it was, except it wasn't there. Just a hole that needed to be plugged. A void that needed filling.

He straightened and closed the dishwasher. Turning around, he rubbed his hands together. "Let's go…"

She hadn't been fast enough in fixing her face. She'd gotten good at it, but he saw the truth, and her face burned. "Let's go."

She hopped off the stool and rushed toward the door, but he was too fast. He blocked her path and placed his hands on her arms.

"Baby."

Such a simple word, a common endearment, but one that made her feel weak and achy. She pulled her lips in and hung her head to hide the welling tears.

"Baby," he whispered again. He kissed the bonnet, then her forehead, then her eyelids.

Terri rested her head against his chest and his strong arms closed around her.

"I'm sorry," he whispered. He rubbed her back. "I abandoned you. Please forgive me."

Sniffling, Terri rubbed the tears from her cheeks.

"I wanted to tell you everything, but I was scared," she said softly.

"I know."

"You said you wouldn't…" She sniffed. "You said you wouldn't stop loving me."

"I didn't. I didn't stop loving you. Not for a minute, but I hurt you. I regret how much I hurt you." He bent his head to her neck and rubbed a hand over her bottom, over her hips, and back up to her waist. "I love you, and I'll always take care of you."

There it was. The words she needed to hear. What was missing.

He pressed soft kisses into her neck and up the line of her jaw to the corner of her eye where salty tears leaked onto her cheek.

"There's something I need to tell you," Terri said.

"What is it?"

She sniffed and lifted her eyes to look at him. "I love you, too. You believe me?" She smiled shakily.

Gavin grinned at her and thumbed the tears from her cheeks.

"Yeah, I believe you."

Then he gave her the longest, sweetest kiss he'd ever bestowed on her.

CHAPTER THIRTY-THREE

The party was in full swing, with toasts being made and lots of cheering. Gavin looked out at the sea of people and saw Terri surrounded by several of the corporate business types. He watched her for a moment. She laughed easily, her face bright and beautiful. Engaging.

It was always like this whenever they went out or attended a function. Men naturally gravitated to her, circled her like sharks that smelled fresh blood in the water. The three men hanging onto her every word didn't even see Gavin watching, but Terri looked up and when she saw him, her face lit up even more, and his insides burned with pride and love.

She excused herself and sashayed over in a cloud of perfume. "You finished with your meeting?"

"All done."

He placed a hand at the base of her spine, touching the bare skin along her back where the tattoo of four hearts rested right above her bottom. As they headed to the other room, he glanced back and caught the three men still gazing after Terri, and he slipped his hand lower on her spine, right onto her butt.

Yeah, she's mine, he thought as they went into the other ballroom.

They spent the rest of the evening chatting with guests and getting to know everyone who attended the formal gala.

By the end of the evening, the main event was about to take place—something very few people knew about. He and Terri stood on the outskirts of the crowd as Trenton went down on one knee, holding a red velvet box, in front of Alannah. Gasps filled the room and silence reigned as he asked her to marry him.

Alannah started crying and nodding her head vigorously, at which point Trenton placed the diamond on her finger. Even from where he stood, Gavin could clearly see the stone. Cheering went up from the crowd.

Trenton jumped up with a huge grin on his face that threatened the brightness of the expensive chandeliers overhead.

"She said yes!" he bellowed.

As the group whooped and cheered, he lifted his new fiancée off the ground and kissed her soundly on the mouth, resulting in more cheers and more whooping. Alannah looked at him with such adoration in her eyes, her love was almost a tangible entity in the room.

A year ago, Gavin had his doubts about the two of them, but they made a cute couple and Alannah was such a sweetheart. He couldn't imagine a better woman for his brother.

Later, after the excitement died down, Gavin and Terri stood out on the balcony with a few other couples. He stared out at the Space Needle, thinking about the first night they went out and wondered if she regretted not having a public declaration of their love, the way Trenton and Alannah did.

"You miss any of that?" he asked.

"What? The production of an engagement?"

"Yeah." He leaned casually against the stone terrace, his eyes resting squarely on her face as he waited for the answer.

"No."

"What about a big wedding? We could—"

"No," Terri said quietly. She slipped a hand around his waist and leaned against him, lifting her face to his.

"No, huh?" he said, smiling down at her.

"Definitely no," Terri confirmed. "It's nice but not the most important thing." She ran her hand up and down his back under the jacket. "I already have what's most important. We skipped to the best part."

Gavin bent his head and touched his nose to hers. "That's one of the reasons I love you, you know that? You find the positive in everything."

"There's nothing for me to be negative about. I have all I need and more. My cup is overflowing."

"In that case, you ready to go home and see our babies?"

"I like that idea."

"Thought you would. Let's say good night to Mother and then go home."

****

Terri kicked off her shoes and changed clothes before dismissing the nanny and bringing the kids into the bedroom. She and Gavin had made a habit of this lately—feeding the babies in the bedroom while they read or watched TV.

She loved it, of course, having her little family all together. They wanted to have more children right away and discussed having three more. A big family, just like she had always wanted.

Gavin walked in as she was changing Elisabeth and Junior lay on his back, talking to himself, with his little hands and feet punctuating each nonsensical word.

"Dane Stewart has another book out," Terri said, snapping Elisabeth's diaper into place.

"What's it called?" Gavin lay down on the bed and lifted his son onto his bare chest.

"Colder Blood," she replied.

She walked with her squirming daughter in one arm, entered the sitting room, and picked up the tablet from the bookshelf where it had been charging. Then she walked back over to the bed and lay down beside Gavin. Little Elisabeth settled onto her breasts.

Gavin's eyes followed her and he smiled lasciviously. "Mm, mm, mm, Junior. Look at what you and your sister did to Mommy's body. Her butt is bigger and her hips are wider."

"Gavin, quit," Terri warned. She slapped his bicep.

"And look at those big, pretty thighs." He leered at her.

"Seriously, that's not funny."

Gavin gently patted his son's back. "Son, I have so much to teach you about women and the difficulty they have accepting compliments."

Terri turned on the device and pulled up the book. "Don't fall asleep tonight."

"I'll try not to, but your voice is so soothing, baby."

The last book they read together had been a few days ago. "That book was boring, I guess. It was hard to get through."

"True," Gavin agreed. He leaned over and kissed her neck, then her ear, then her cheek.

Tingles of pleasure sprinkled across her skin.

"What was that for?"

"For being you. For this." He waved a hand at their children laying on their chests.

"I should be thanking you." Her voice quivered.

"No way." He smiled into her eyes. "Do you have any idea how much I love you?"

"I do."

It was true. In so many ways, he let her know of his love—in words, in deeds. There were little things he did, like surprising her with a rare, mint-condition copy of *Charlotte's Web* at Christmas, inscribed by E.B. White himself. The book must have cost upwards of twenty-five thousand dollars. All he'd said was, "It's time for you to start rebuilding your library."

"I'm going to keep telling you that I love you," Gavin promised.

Terri brushed the back of her fingers across his cheek and thought of how much she'd fought to stick to her own rules to preserve her heart. Rule number one, maintain control. Rule number two, never fall in love. Luckily, she'd broken them and found the happiness and security she'd searched for all her life.

She pressed her lips to Gavin's and smiled.

"Please keep telling me. I'll never get tired of hearing it."

MORE STORIES BY DELANEY DIAMOND

Hot Latin Men series
The Arrangement
Fight for Love
Private Acts
The Ultimate Merger
Second Chances
Hot Latin Men series (a limited edition boxed set)
More Than a Mistress (coming soon)
Hot Latin Men: Vol. I (print anthology)
Hot Latin Men: Vol. II (print anthology)

Hawthorne Family series
The Temptation of a Good Man
A Hard Man to Love
Here Comes Trouble
For Better or Worse
Hawthorne Family Series: Vol. I (print anthology)
Hawthorne Family Series: Vol. II (print anthology)

Love Unexpected series
The Blind Date
The Wrong Man
An Unexpected Attraction
The Right Time (coming soon)

Johnson Family series
Unforgettable
Perfect
Just Friends
The Rules

Bailar series (sweet/clean romance)
Worth Waiting For

Stand Alones

Still in Love

Subordinate Position

Heartbreak in Rio (part of the Endless Summer Nights anthology)

Free Stories

www.delaneydiamond.com

ABOUT THE AUTHOR

Delaney Diamond is the USA Today Bestselling Author of sweet, sensual, passionate romance novels. Originally from the U.S. Virgin Islands, she now lives in Atlanta, Georgia. She reads romance novels, mysteries, thrillers, and a fair amount of nonfiction. When she's not busy reading or writing, she's in the kitchen trying out new recipes, dining at one of her favorite restaurants, or traveling to an interesting locale. She speaks fluent conversational French and can get by in Spanish.

Enjoy free reads and the first chapter of all her novels on her website. Join her e-mail mailing list to get sneak peeks, notices of sale prices, and find out about new releases.

www.delaneydiamond.com